U0136647

English Public Speaking and Presentation

英語簡報演說技巧

國立台灣科技大學應用外語系專任助理教授

黃玟君 博士

眾文圖書股份有限公司

內容與技巧兼重

　　一般人每天都在說話，但許多調查發現，大部分的人都害怕公眾演說 (public speaking)，甚至將其列為人生最恐懼的事物之一！然而在現今社會中，不管求學或就業，常會遇到需要做公眾演說的場合，因此想要與之絕緣，幾乎是不可能的事；尤其在這個國際化的社會，能夠專業且有效地做好英語簡報或演說可說是現代人必備的技能之一，例如大學生在課堂上用英語演說、研究生在國際研討會上用英語發表論文、上班族用英語向國外客戶做公司簡介，甚至是自行創業者用英語向國外買家做產品介紹等。

　　或許你會說，我是工程師、我是電腦專家，只要面對機械與電腦就好，不需要在眾人面前演說，但是世事難料，或許有一天你會臨危授命，必須在國外客戶面前做公司產品的簡報。又或者某一天主管要晉升員工，在一群都具備高度專業的下屬中，英語佳且能在眾人面前口若懸河的人，便能獲得最大的晉升機會。所以說，身為現代人，你應具備英語公眾演說的能力！不過這個能力很少與生俱來，通常必須接受特別訓練或刻意培養。本書的目的便是訓練與培養你用英語進行公眾演說的能力！*

　　這本書是我在大學教授英語演說課程十多年經驗的集結，內容除了涵蓋西方世界教授公眾演說的各項技巧外，還包含許多根據亞洲國情所修正的資料，同時也彙整了我長期觀察我的學生實際做英語簡報的優缺點。也

---

*「公眾演說」(public speaking) 涵蓋演說 (speech)、簡報 (presentation) 等類型，為求簡潔，本書以「簡報」一詞取代公眾演說、演說、簡報等說法。

因此，本書的資料十分完備，除了可以作爲高等學院英語演說與簡報等相關科目的授課教材外，還可供需要時常做簡報的專業人士來使用。此外，對於想自修或增進自己公眾演說能力的讀者來說，本書也是一個相當好的選擇。

雖然公眾演說是一門複雜且高深的學問，但究其重點不外乎兩個——內容 (content) 與技巧 (delivery)。這兩者是讓公眾演說成功的兩大要素，缺一不可。爲什麼這麼說？因爲講者就算本身再有知名度、職位再高、外表再吸引人，若簡報內容乏善可陳，聽眾很快地便會失去興趣，甚至失去耐心，因此公眾演說的第一步便是要有好的內容，這點無庸置疑。不過光是有好的內容還不夠，因爲如果講者的演說技巧或風格不夠吸引人，那麼再好的內容也會讓聽眾夢周公！這也是爲什麼進行公眾演說時，有時「如何說」(how to say it) 甚至比「說什麼」(what to say) 還重要。關於這兩大演說必備要素，本書將會做詳細且深入的介紹及解說。

本書總共分成九章，每章包含數個單元，內容循序漸進、由淺入深，從演說前的準備工作到演說結束時必備的英文用語、從演說所需具備的內容到演說技巧的演練等，都會進行完整的解說及介紹。除了詳細解說公眾演說的理論和策略，本書還包含題材多元、簡練實用的英文演說用語，讀者可以根據自己的實際需要套用或變化，以便在演說時暢所欲言。此外，書中也提供許多練習題 (Exercise) 及「延伸學習」專欄，讓你在學完一項概念或技巧後便能夠立即演練，學以致用。

值得一提的是，本書為了幫助讀者了解英語簡報實際「執行」的成效，除了 MP3 音檔外，還特別錄製多段影音示範影片，只要你掃描書中隨處所附的 QR Code，或到 YouTube 搜尋作者和書名關鍵字，便可以看到由我的學生根據書籍內容所演示的簡報影片。這些學生在台灣土生土長、沒有留過學，然而在修過我的簡報演說課並多次實際上臺做簡報後，都可以毫不費力地成為專業簡報的高手。如果你願意按照本書內容學習精進，相信有一天也會成為令人刮目相看的簡報專家！

使用本書時，如果你的時間充裕，我會建議從 Chapter 1 開始循序漸進地閱讀，將整套技巧完整地學起來；不過若你的時間緊迫，則建議你直接先參考 Chapter 3～6 的英語簡報用語，從每個單元中挑出幾句背下並活用，待日後有時間時再回頭學習本書其他單元。擁有了良好的公眾演說能力後，你除了可以更有效地將資訊與他人分享外，也從此握有求學、就業、升遷的一大利器，相信你的人生道路會更加順遂、寬廣。讓我們一起努力！

國立台灣科技大學應用外語系專任助理教授

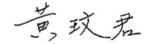

Contents

Contents

Contents

Contents

Chapter 1
簡報前的準備工作

Unit 1 了解聽眾

Unit 2 確定簡報形式

Unit 3 建立簡報目標

Unit 4 熟悉簡報流程

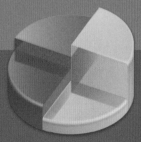

English Public Speaking
and Presentation

If I am to speak ten minutes, I need a week for preparation; if fifteen minutes, three days; if half an hour, two days; if an hour, I am ready now.

—Woodrow Wilson

我需要一星期的時間來準備一個十分鐘的演說；三天來準備 15 分鐘的演說；兩天來準備 30 分鐘的演說；但若要講一個鐘頭，我現在就可以開始。

——伍德羅·威爾遜（美國第 28 任總統）

　　由上面威爾遜總統的名言可以得知，一個成功的簡報需要許多練習和準備；尤其愈短的簡報，愈需要長時間周延的準備。為什麼呢？這是因為短的簡報所需的內容必須更精簡，語言也必須更簡練，因此難度更高，正所謂「臺上一分鐘，臺下十年功」。不管如何，一個成功的簡報絕對需要許多前製作業。本章將分四個單元詳述這些準備工作，請你在準備時確實做到，以確保簡報的順利與成功！

在你接到做簡報的任務或邀約時，首要之務便是了解你的聽眾，因為你的簡報內容、方式、語言等，都可能隨著聽眾屬性的不同而有所改變，因此事前了解聽眾的背景十分重要。了解聽眾的面向包含了解聽眾的專業、教育、語言、性別、教育程度、年紀等；此外，事先知道聽眾對你簡報的期望也很重要，例如，他們最想聽到什麼內容？最想學到什麼東西？還有，他們期望你是直接告知 (inform) 資訊，還是需要你說服 (convince)，甚至挑戰 (challenge) 他們？

因此在你一知道要做簡報時，便可開始對簡報對象的產業或公司進行研究。你可在簡報前幾天透過電子郵件或電話，了解聽眾的背景。若這些方式不可行，那你可以先大約設定聽眾的背景，並據此演練講稿，然後在簡報當天提早抵達會場，把握機會先從主辦單位的人員那裡得到相關資訊。若這個方式也不可行，你還可以在簡報一開始時直接詢問聽眾，了解他們的需求以及期望，據此快速調整簡報內容，並在簡報中途不時向聽眾確認他們的需求及期望。若你想要更謹慎些，還可以在簡報後請聽眾做一份意見調查表，以確實知道自己是否圓滿完成任務，並作為改進下次簡報的參考。

1 聽眾背景調查表

為了幫助你了解聽眾的背景，你可以在每次簡報前先完成以下調查表。這個調查表是要藉由勾選幫助你了解這次簡報的聽眾背景。

- ☐ 聽眾人數是多少？
- ☐ 聽眾的性別、年紀、母語爲何？
- ☐ 聽眾的教育程度爲何？
- ☐ 聽眾是你同領域的專家，還是普羅大眾？
- ☐ 聽眾是學生，還是教師？是新進員工，還是資深員工？是舊客戶，還是新客戶？
- ☐ 聽眾的職業及位階爲何？聽眾是否曾在其他公司任職？聽眾中是否有決策者？
- ☐ 聽眾對你或你所屬的單位了解多少？
- ☐ 聽眾對簡報的主題了解多少？
- ☐ 聽眾期望你是告知、說服或挑戰他們？
- ☐ 聽眾最想獲得什麼資訊？希望聽到重點摘要，還是詳細說明？
- ☐ 根據聽眾屬性，簡報是否有必須特別提出或避免提及的內容？
- ☐ 根據聽眾屬性，簡報時是否可以表現幽默？如果可以，應採行何種方式？
- ☐ 聽眾對你或簡報內容是支持、懷疑或反對？
- ☐ 聽眾爲自願或被強迫參加這次簡報？

2 跨文化溝通

　　另一個與聽眾息息相關的議題是「跨文化溝通」(cross-cultural communication)。雖然你做的是英語簡報，但並不代表聽眾都是歐美人士，或者其母語都是英語。也就是說，在地球村的今天，你做簡報的對象有可能是美國人，也有可能是日本人，或者是來自不同國家的人，其母語

有可能是英語，也有可能是日語，或者是其他語言。而針對不同國家、地區、文化的聽眾，溝通的方式也會有所不同。以下是針對歐美及亞洲聽眾的簡報方式。

A. 聽眾是歐美人士時

- ❑ 簡報內容應力求簡單明瞭，儘早進入主要重點 (main point)，須附上最新資訊或統計資料，並將焦點放在數據及圖表上。

- ❑ 簡報內容不宜過長，必須講究事實，並提出具體可行的解決方案；如果你有任何想法，就必須明確向聽眾提出，對於聽眾的問題也必須明確回答。

- ❑ 問答時段 (Q&A session) 可預留長一點的時間，並事先準備聽眾可能提問的問題與答案。回答時必須清楚明確，溝通方式可較為直接，對談中若有語言交鋒也不要意外，應該將重點放在問題及議題本身，而不要視為是對自己的人身攻擊。

- ❑ 現場氣氛可以較為輕鬆，因此若能適時展現幽默感最好，但這並不代表簡報內容或你的態度可以輕忽或隨便。

B. 聽眾是亞洲人士時

- ❑ 簡報前應先向在場人士（尤其是重要人士）致意、交換名片，並弄清楚聽眾中不同人員的階層關係，確保滿足最高位階者的需求。

- ❑ 簡報內容必須豐富且扎實，問答時段通常無須預留太長時間。

- ❑ 若為商業簡報，進入簡報內容前最好先說明自己所屬公司或單位的歷史背景及績效等，並將重點放在雙方的長期利益上。最好不要當場要求對方做承諾或下決定，並且要能聽出對方的言下之意。

- ❑ 簡報現場宜營造和諧的氣氛，不要強迫聽眾互動或回答問題。對於沉默且沒有回應的聽眾也無須感到氣餒。

要特別注意的是，這些只是概括性資訊，只能作為你做簡報時的參考；建議你還是盡量避免刻板印象，同時也必須考量族群中的個別差異。

　　最後，跨文化溝通是一項複雜的課題，對你來說，最重要的是了解不同聽眾的不同需求，並體認彼此間存在著差異性。例如義大利人雖為歐美人士，但他們多注重家庭及人與人之間的關係，因此義大利人開會或做簡報的方式可能更類似於亞洲，因此不能將所有歐美人士一概而論。

在現今多元且高度發展的地球村時代，幾乎任何行業及場合都可能有簡報需求。簡報需求雖多，但通常可歸納為「資訊型」(informative) 與「說服型」(persuasive) 兩種類型。

1 資訊型簡報

顧名思義，這類簡報的目的是傳達資訊，常見的主題形式包括在（國際）會議上發表研究成果、在公司向上司報告業績、在產品發表會上說明產品資訊，以及各類計畫／政策／流程的說明、公司介紹及員工訓練、各類議題說明等，內容包羅萬象，算是最常見的簡報類型。

在資訊型簡報中，主要重點的安排常因內容而有不同，一般按照以下五種順序。

A. 時間順序 (chronological order)

由時間推進的遠到近、近到遠等依序陳述議題。

B. 空間順序 (spatial order)

由空間及方位的前到後、左到右、上到下、遠到近、裡到外等依序陳述議題。

C. 主題順序 (topical order)

依據議題的不同主題 (topic) 進行陳述。

D. 因果邏輯順序 (causal order)

首先說明議題的起因 (cause)，接著再陳述結果 (effect)。

E. 問題與解答 (problem/solution order)

首先說明議題所存在或所遇到的問題 (problem)，接著再提出相關的解決方法 (solution)。

2　說服型簡報

顧名思義，這類簡報的目的是說服聽眾，因此講者會將自身意見充分傳達給聽眾，並希望獲得聽眾認同、改變原有想法，甚至有所行動；而所謂的「行動」可以是下訂單、上街頭抗議、寫信給議員、開始做資源回收等。這類簡報常見的主題形式包括政策或政令宣導、闡述具爭議性議題 (controversial issue)、商品推銷及行銷計畫發表會、集資大會、營運方針改變說明等。

說服型簡報的內容結構常因主題及聽眾屬性的不同而有所改變，常見的結構有以下兩種。

結構 1

講者提出一個議題 ➡ 告知聽眾自身的立場 ➡ 告知聽眾選擇此立場的理由 ➡ 鼓勵聽眾採取行動

結構 2

　　講者告知聽眾一個議題的背景資訊和現況 ➡ 提供聽眾幾個選擇方案
➡ 告知聽眾自己的提案及理由 ➡ 鼓勵聽眾採取行動

　　當然，資訊型及說服型簡報的類型並非涇渭分明，有些簡報甚至會結
合上述兩種類型，例如有些國際會議的學術報告屬於資訊型，但也稍微帶
有說服型的性質。

Memo

建立簡報目標

　　你在準備簡報時，除了必須了解聽眾、確定簡報形式，還必須建立明確的簡報目標 (goal)。何謂簡報目標？簡單來說，就是你對自己的期許，以及對聽眾的期望。例如你會希望聽眾「可以理解我的簡報內容」、「可以記住我所說的重點」，甚至「聽完我的簡報後可以積極採取行動」等，這些都可能是簡報目標。

1 建立主要目標

　　由此可知，講者基於對自己的期許，以及對聽眾的期望，必須替自己的簡報建立一個最主要的目標。如果你不知道該如何設定此目標，可以試著完成下面這個句型（畫底線處為簡報目標）。

建立主要目標句型（資訊型） MP3 **01**

The purpose of my presentation is to let the audience understand...
我簡報的目標是讓聽眾了解……

The purpose of my presentation is to let the audience understand the importance of energy conservation.
我簡報的目標是讓聽眾了解節約能源的重要性。

. . . .

The purpose of my presentation is to let the audience understand the K-Pop trend.
我簡報的目標是讓聽眾了解韓國流行音樂的趨勢。

. . . .

The purpose of my presentation is to let the audience fully understand <u>all the key sales features of the new product.</u>
我簡報的目標是讓聽眾完全了解新產品的賣點。

The purpose of my presentation is to let my colleagues understand <u>the new computer system and how to use it for checking inventory.</u>
我簡報的目標是讓我同事了解新的電腦系統，以及如何用此系統檢查存貨。

The purpose of my presentation is to let the higher-ups understand <u>the importance of my proposal to develop a new marketing campaign for our customer.</u>
我簡報的目標是讓高層了解我的提案很重要，即為顧客做一個新的行銷活動。

● higher-up (n.) 高層人物，要員

　　上面句型及例句中 understand（了解）的後面接的就是你想要達到的簡報目標。有了這個句子，你便可以在製作簡報檔案時常常據此檢視，確保簡報真的符合你所設定的目標，沒有離題。

　　要特別注意的是，上面的句子多為針對資訊型的簡報。若你的簡報類型為說服型，則可試著完成下面這個句型（畫底線處為簡報目標）。

建立主要目標句型（說服型）　　　　　　　　　MP3 **02**

My presentation is successful if the audience...
如果聽眾⋯⋯，那我的簡報便成功。

My presentation is successful if the audience <u>chooses my firm as their legal counsel.</u>
如果聽眾選擇我公司作其法律顧問，那我的簡報便成功。　　● counsel (n.) 法律顧問

My presentation is successful if my boss <u>agrees to allot money to the</u> <u>project I'm working on</u>.

如果我老闆同意撥錢給我正在進行的專案，那我的簡報便成功。

● allot (v.) 分配，撥給

My presentation is successful if the audience <u>agrees to use the results of</u> <u>my study to develop a new curriculum plan</u>.

如果聽眾同意用我的研究結果來發展新的課程計畫，那我的簡報便成功。

My presentation is successful if the audience <u>decides to switch from</u> <u>eating meat to eating fruits and vegetables</u>.

如果聽眾決定從吃肉改成吃蔬果，那我的簡報便成功。

My presentation is successful if the audience <u>decides to stand up and</u> <u>fight for legalization of same sex marriages</u>.

如果聽眾決定挺身爭取同性婚姻合法化，那我的簡報便成功。

2 創造核心訊息

當你在準備簡報時，或許自認為內容有很多精彩之處，主要重點也很多，但不管簡報長短如何，一個重要的準則是必須創造出一個「核心訊息」(core message)。

何謂核心訊息？此即聽眾在簡報結束後可以「帶著走」(take it with them) 並反覆回味的東西。也就是說，如果聽眾只能記住簡報的一個訊息，那麼核心訊息便是你最希望聽眾在簡報結束後回想內容時，會想到的

那個「唯一」的東西！請注意，此處強調的是「唯一」，亦即你只能在眾多的簡報內容中挑選一項核心訊息，並將此訊息反覆向聽眾強調，讓他們牢記在心。

核心訊息通常與你的簡報目標息息相關。舉例來說，在上面的例句 The purpose of my presentation is to let the audience understand the importance of energy conservation.（我簡報的目標是讓聽眾了解節約能源的重要性。）中，你的核心訊息應該就是：

● Energy conservation is vital to life.
節約能源攸關生存。

也就是說，儘管你的簡報旁徵博引了許多資料，內容也十分豐富，但「節約能源攸關生存」就是你希望聽眾牢牢記住的核心訊息。

又例如在上面的例句 My presentation is successful if the audience decides to switch from eating meat to eating fruits and vegetables.（如果聽眾決定從吃肉改成吃蔬果，那我的簡報便成功。）中，你的核心訊息就應該是：

● Eating fruits and vegetables is better than eating meat.
吃蔬果比吃肉好。

核心訊息的功能

　　你或許會問：「為什麼核心訊息如此重要呢？」，因為殘酷的事實是，大多數的聽眾不管在聆聽簡報當下吸收到多少資訊，或者在聆聽簡報時感受到多大的震撼，在簡報結束後通常不會刻意去複習筆記或反覆研究你的簡報檔案。可以肯定的是，他們在一段時間後會忘記許多簡報的細節！不過如果你的核心訊息夠清楚，他們還是會明確記得你說到核心訊息時的那個「感覺」。神奇的是，只要這個感覺存在，他們便能夠牢記你的核心訊息，久久不忘。這也是為什麼成功的講者通常會在簡報的不同時間點（例如在一開始、在中間、在結束等的時候），利用不同的方式（例如用肯定句、問句、重複同一句子、改動句子的某些字、舉不同例子等），反覆重申核心訊息，讓聽眾即使想忘記也很難！

Memo

Unit 4 熟悉簡報流程

簡報可能單獨進行，也可能包含在一場會議之中，不管如何，簡報通常包含以下三大部分。

> Q 開場 (opening)
> Q 主體 (body)
> Q 結束 (closing)

下兩頁 (pp. 18~19) 的流程圖包含一般簡報的流程、時間分配、講者應完成的步驟、注意事項，以及流程細節的相關章節。當然，根據不同的簡報性質及目的，某些步驟也可視情況省略或變更順序。

由下兩頁圖表中的時間分配以及應完成步驟可以清楚知道，簡報最重要的部分還是在「主體」(body)。不過這並非絕對，還得要看個別簡報的性質、形式及主題來做調整。在每個步驟 (step) 旁也列出了此部分內容在本書的章節及頁碼，方便你在時間緊迫時挑選合適的部分率先閱讀。在你完成簡報前的準備工作後，便可以著手製作簡報檔案，此即 Chapter 2 的內容。

Step 1　暗示簡報即將開始 ▸ Chapter 3, Unit 1 (p. 61)
簡報開始前須確定聽眾都已安靜下來，並準備好聽簡報。

Step 2　感謝聽眾 ▸ Chapter 3, Unit 2 (p. 63)
若簡報是包含在一場會議中，則須感謝主辦單位、與會人員，甚至是在場重要人士。

Step 3　自我介紹 ▸ Chapter 3, Unit 3 (p. 67)
除了講者的簡介，有時還要包含所屬機構或單位的介紹。

Step 4　陳述引言 ▸ Chapter 3, Unit 4 (p. 73)
引言的目的是引起聽眾的注意力及興趣，愈有創意愈好。

Step 5　說明簡報目的與主題 ▸ Chapter 3, Unit 5 (p. 81)
清楚地告訴聽眾簡報的目的與主題，以及想要達成的目標。

Step 6　說明簡報架構與流程 ▸ Chapter 3, Unit 6 (p. 85)
說明簡報的結構、流程、所需時間、有無問答時段等。

Step 7　連接到簡報主體的第一個主要重點 ▸ Chapter 7 (p. 239)
使用轉換語將開場與主體的第一個主要重點做連接。

結束　　　時間分配占 10 ～ 20%

Step 1　陳述結論與摘要 ▸ Chapter 5, Unit 1 (p. 141)
再次陳述簡報的主要重點，並反覆強調簡報的核心訊息，以加強聽眾的記憶。

主體　　時間分配占 60 ～ 80%

Step 1　陳述內容，由第一個主要重點依序往下一個主要重點陳述

▶ Chapter 4, Unit 2 (p. 111) 及 Chapter 7 (p. 239)

條理分明地說明每個主要重點，並在每個主要重點的轉換之間，利用轉換語來連接。

Step 2　根據簡報內容的長短，陳述數個主要重點

▶ Chapter 4, Unit 2 (p. 111)

主要重點的數量大約在三～五個。少於三個會讓簡報內容顯得薄弱；超過五個則內容顯得龐雜而難以吸收。

Step 3　陳述主要重點時，提供支持細節　▶ Chapter 4, Unit 1 (p. 101)

每個主要重點須有相關的支持細節（含例子或理由）支持。

Step 4　介紹並說明圖表　▶ Chapter 6 (p. 175)

詳細解釋每張圖表，對於所提出的相關數據、資料等，都必須引用資料出處。

Step 2　進行問答時段　▶ Chapter 5, Unit 2 (p. 153)

問答時段的好壞常常關係到整個簡報的成敗，必須事先準備可能被詢問的問題並想好要如何回答。

Step 3　結束簡報並向聽眾道別　▶ Chapter 5, Unit 3 (p. 169)

再次感謝聽眾。

Chapter 2
簡報檔案的製作

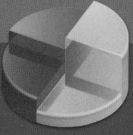

English Public Speaking
and Presentation

Without structure and order there is chaos.

—Francis D. K. Ching, *Design Drawing*

沒有結構與次序，便是一團混亂。

——程大錦（建築教育家及作家）《設計圖學》

　　現代社會講求創意，但常常忽略形式；簡報內容雖然也重視創意，但在追求創意的同時，還必須兼顧結構與次序，不然便如同上面引言所說的，會是一團混亂。由此可知，簡報必須結構清楚、架構完整，且簡報檔案的呈現方式應簡單明瞭，不應過於繁複，這樣聽眾才能充分吸收講者想要傳達的訊息。本章將會詳述簡報檔案製作的流程，包含如何利用大綱建立結構清楚且架構完整的簡報檔案、檔案製作的重要原則，以及一個良好的簡報檔案所應包含的元素。

　　另外，目前最常見的簡報檔案為 Microsoft 的 PowerPoint，因此本書所舉的例子仍以 PowerPoint 為主。除了 PowerPoint 之外，目前市面上還有為數不少的免費或付費的簡報檔案製作軟體，其中較受歡迎的有 Prezi 及 Emaze，兩者都可讓簡報檔案更生動，有興趣的讀者可以自行參考。

你在完成簡報前的準備工作（包括了解聽眾、確定簡報形式、建立簡報目標，以及熟悉簡報流程）後，便要開始製作簡報檔案，其中第一步便是要思考如何建立簡報的「大綱」(outline)。我們在 Chapter 1 中提到，簡報最重要的部分還是在「主體」(body)，因此建立大綱指的便是建立簡報主體的大綱。

1 記錄想法與靈感

要建立大綱，首先必須將腦中關於簡報的想法及靈感盡可能地記錄下來。以下是兩種幫助你蒐集想法及靈感的方式。

- 列出法 (list)
- 心智圖 (mind map)

A. 列出法

Step 1：列出所有想法

首先在一張空白的紙張（或在電腦螢幕上）將自己可能在簡報中用到的東西，或者可讓你達成簡報設定目標的相關事項，不管順序、形式等，先全部列出來。在列出這些東西的同時，你也可上網或到圖書館找相關資料，甚至請教師長或專家。將資料蒐集完備、列出所有想法及靈感後，便可以開始進行 Step 2，亦即將列出來的東西去蕪存菁並分類。

Step 2：去蕪存菁並分類

在將東西去蕪存菁並分類時，最好將簡報的主要重點維持在三～五項，原因是若主要重點過多，會使簡報顯得過於複雜，甚至失去重點，聽眾也會因為簡報內容過於龐雜而難以吸收。此外，每個主要重點的分量最好平均，以維持結構的平衡；也就是說，若你有 30 分鐘可以講三個主要重點，那麼每個主要重點的講述時間應大致平均，亦即各約 10 分鐘，而不要一個主要重點講 5 分鐘、一個 15 分鐘、另一個 10 分鐘。最後，在排序與分類的過程中，你會發現有些想法或靈感雖然很好，但受限於簡報時間或其他因素必須刪除，這時便要果斷割愛、無須留戀。完成 Step 2 後，便可以進行到 Step 3，即建立簡報大綱。

Step 3：建立簡報大綱

建立簡報大綱最重要的是安排主要重點的順序。一般而言，若簡報的內容與時間有關（例如介紹公司過去五年的銷售業績），則可以按照年分的推移來安排順序。同樣地，若簡報的內容與空間有關（例如介紹某個知名遊樂園，則可以按照左到右、前到後、外層到裡層等順序逐一介紹。更多關於資訊型及說服型簡報主要重點的順序安排，可參考 Chapter 1, Unit 2「確定簡報形式」(p. 7) 的內容。

除了一般標準的按照時間、空間等排序，你還可以考慮將聽眾比較熟悉的內容放在前面，再進入到比較陌生的領域，讓他們不會一開始聆聽時便感到有壓力。有了條理分明且次序井然的大綱後，簡報便具備了良好的結構。

Exercise

解答請見 ▶ p. 302

1. 你任職於餐飲業，剛接到老闆的要求，即必須為自家泰式料理餐廳「泰花園」(Thai Garden) 用英語向客戶做簡報，主題是「泰花園餐廳很適合親朋好友一起用餐」。請用「列出法」寫下 15 項你可以想到的想法和靈感。

_____

_____

_____

_____

_____

2. 你剛接到老師的學期報告作業，即必須用英語介紹台北這座城市，簡報的主題是「台北很適合居住」。請用「列出法」寫下 15 項你可以想到的想法和靈感。

_____

_____

_____

_____

_____

B. 心智圖

　　心智圖又稱樹狀圖或思維地圖，是一種利用圖像來幫助使用者思考、表達思維的輔助工具。建立簡報大綱時，你可以利用心智圖來幫助自己將資訊做系統性的整理。若要做心智圖練習，首先必須準備一張紙，接著在紙的正中間畫個圈圈，寫下簡報的主題，然後根據腦中所出現的與主題相關的字詞及彼此間的關聯性，分為不同的叢集，接著再層層向外擴展。畫心智圖的好處是可以讓你很清楚地看出不同想法與靈感間的關聯，以及階層性（例如主要重點、次要重點及次次要重點之間的階層性）。以下為心智圖大致的形式。

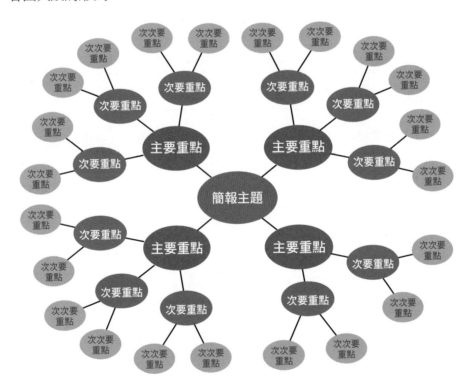

　　請注意，不管你是用列出法或心智圖的方式來建立簡報大綱，都必須時時思考你已經訂出來的簡報目標（請見 Chapter 1, Unit 3, p. 11），如此安排或規畫出來的簡報才不會離題或失焦！

解答請見 ▶ p. 303

Exercise

1. 你任職於餐飲業，剛接到老闆的要求，即必須為自家泰式料理餐廳「泰花園」(Thai Garden) 用英語向客戶做簡報，主題是「泰花園餐廳很適合與親朋好友一起用餐」。請用「心智圖」畫出你的想法和靈感。

2. 你剛接到老師的學期報告作業，即必須用英語介紹台北這座城市，簡報的主題是「台北很適合居住」。請用「心智圖」畫出你的想法和靈感。

2 簡報大綱的基本結構

　　記錄下簡報的想法與靈感後，你便可以這些東西為基礎，建立簡報大綱。由於簡報最重要的部分在主體，因此其結構必須清楚，也要符合邏輯。以下為主體的基本結構。不同顏色的字代表不同階層，例如藍字代表第一個階層，即「主要重點」(main point)；綠字代表第二個階層，即「次要重點」(sub-point)；紅字則代表第三個階層，即「次次要重點」(sub sub-point)。

　　請注意，根據簡報內容的不同，有些簡報只需要用到第一個階層的主要重點，有些則需要用到多個階層。此外，每個主要重點之下的次要重點與次次要重點的數目最好不要相差太多，以免主要重點之間的內容分量差異過大。以下為簡報大綱的基本結構。

主要重點 1 (main point 1)
　　次要重點 1 (sub-point 1)
　　　　次次要重點 1 (sub sub-point 1)
　　　　次次要重點 2 (sub sub-point 2)
　　次要重點 2 (sub-point 2)
　　　　次次要重點 1 (sub sub-point 1)
　　　　次次要重點 2 (sub sub-point 2)

主要重點 2 (main point 2)
　　次要重點 1 (sub-point 1)
　　　　次次要重點 1 (sub sub-point 1)
　　　　次次要重點 2 (sub sub-point 2)

次要重點 2 (sub-point 2)

　　次次要重點 1 (sub sub-point 1)

　　次次要重點 2 (sub sub-point 2)

主要重點 3 (main point 3)

　　次要重點 1 (sub-point 1)

　　　　次次要重點 1 (sub sub-point 1)

　　　　次次要重點 2 (sub sub-point 2)

　　次要重點 2 (sub-point 2)

　　　　次次要重點 1 (sub sub-point 1)

　　　　次次要重點 2 (sub sub-point 2)

Exercise

解答請見 ▶ p. 304

根據本章之前在「列出法」及「心智圖」中請你練習的兩個簡報主題，請進一步建立各自的英語簡報大綱。

1. 泰花園餐廳適合與親朋好友一起用餐

_____

_____

_____

_____

_____

2. 台北適合居住

_____

_____

_____

_____

3　決定簡報題目

　　當你經過以上過程建立簡報大綱後，便可以思考如何為簡報訂定題目 (topic)。你或許會認為，簡報題目不是應該在最一開始便決定嗎？其實不然，因為根據我的經驗，實務上常發生的情形是，講者就算一開始決定好了題目，通常在經過記錄想法與靈感、建立大綱的過程後，或多或少會再回頭修改題目，甚至換個題目，因此建議你在一開始只要先確定簡報的目標 (goal) 及相關主題 (topic) 即可，接著再著手建立主體 (body) 部分的大綱 (outline)，之後再決定簡報題目，最後再進行開場 (opening) 與結束 (closing) 或其他更細部的內容。以下為建議的簡報製作流程。

　　建立簡報目標與主題 ➡ 建立簡報大綱 ➡ 決定簡報題目 ➡ 其他

　　以本章上述兩個簡報主題為例，在建立大綱後，便可嘗試訂定簡報題目。例如第一個簡報題目可訂為：

● Thai Garden: An Ideal Place to Dine with Family and Friends
泰花園餐廳：親朋好友聚餐的理想去處

第二個簡報題目則可訂為：

● Taipei: An Ideal Place to Live
台北：理想的居住城市

Exercise 解答請見 ▶ p. 306

根據本章之前在「簡報大綱的基本結構」中請你列出的兩個簡報大綱，請進一步為它們訂定更有創意的英語簡報題目。

1. 泰花園餐廳

_____

_____

_____

_____

2. 台北

_____

_____

_____

_____

精簡明確的簡報題目

在聽眾不認識講者與不知道簡報內容的情況下，簡報題目的好壞常常是其決定是否聆聽簡報的關鍵，因此能成功訂定出吸引聽眾的題目很重要。訂定簡報題目就如同一家公司為其產品訂定 slogan（口號，醒目的廣告語）一般，愈精簡明確愈好。以下是一些熱門品牌或商品的 slogan，都帶有上述幾個特點，也因此能讓消費者留下深刻且長久的印象！你在訂定簡報題目時，不妨也試試看。

MacBook	The world's thinnest notebook 全世界最薄的筆記型電腦
iPod	1,000 songs in your pocket 一千首歌在口袋裡
Google	The world's information in one click 一鍵通世界
Starbucks	A third place between work and home 工作與家庭之外的第三空間

Unit 2 簡報檔案的製作原則

許多人製作簡報檔案時常有個迷思，認為投影片的內容愈豐富、色彩愈多變、各式各樣的特效愈多，愈能吸引聽眾的興趣，也愈能顯示自己的準備充分。其實事實並不然，有時甚至剛好相反！以下為製作簡報檔案時應遵守的三個原則。

- ◎ 不要將所有資訊放在投影片上
- ◎ 投影片版面力求簡約
- ◎ 善用圖表簡化複雜概念

1 不要將所有資訊放在投影片上

講者常犯的一個錯誤是，將簡報講稿 (script) 整個放到投影片 (slide) 上，然後在聽眾面前逐字逐句唸出講稿。站在講者的角度，將整篇講稿放到投影片上不僅可以確保自己不會忘稿，還可以幫助聽眾理解自己的簡報內容，何樂而不為？然而，站在聽眾的立場，要跟著講者逐字逐句去看密密麻麻的文字，實在是一件很吃力的事，不僅乏味，注意力也容易渙散。所以請記得，只有將投影片上不必要的字刪掉，重要的字才會凸顯出來！

因此，良好的投影片應該只放簡報的重點和輔助圖片，資訊的傳遞仍須靠講者本身，而非投影片上一大堆令人望之卻步的內容。也就是說，

講者自身良好的口語表達能力才是簡報成功的關鍵；而且只有簡單的投影片，才能將聽眾的焦點放回講者自己身上！以下是一張關於電子菸 (e-cigarette) 的投影片。很明顯地可以看出，講者只是將講稿原封不動地放在投影片上。

What is an electronic cigarette?

An electronic cigarette uses an electronic nicotine delivery system (ENDS). It is a battery-powered vaporizer which produces a similar feel to tobacco smoking. Electronic cigarettes produce an aerosol, commonly called vapor, rather than traditional cigarette smoke, which the user inhales. In general, an e-cigarette has a heating element that atomizes the refillable liquid known as e-liquid. E-liquids usually contain a mixture of propylene glycol, nicotine, and flavorings. Some e-liquids lack nicotine. E-liquid without propylene glycol is also available.

要如何改進這張投影片的缺失呢？首先，講者應將投影片的字體及顏色簡化，使投影片清楚易讀。最重要的是，講者應該將原先複雜的講稿去蕪存菁，簡化成「條列式重點」(bullet point)，並輔以簡報主角「電子菸」的圖片。下面便是修改後的投影片，視覺效果明顯增強許多。

What is an Electronic Cigarette?

- Electronic nicotine delivery system
- Battery-powered vaporizer
- Aerosol (a.k.a. vapor)
- Refillable liquid (a.k.a. e-liquid)
  - Propylene glycol
  - Nicotine
  - Flavorings

2 投影片版面力求簡約

製作投影片時應使用相同或類似的主題顏色，避免放入多餘或複雜的圖片；版式和背景不要太花俏，也不要使用與簡報主題不符的版式和背景。此外，除非有必要，否則應該盡量減少使用特效，例如讓字體晃動、變大變小、旋轉等，也不要加入額外的音效，以免造成簡報時的干擾。

另外要注意的是，投影片的字體最好選擇一般常見且常用者，以方便聽眾閱讀。至於圖片的選擇則盡量以簡單明瞭為主，切忌放上任何無意義的圖片，以免使聽眾混淆。

以下為一張關於 2012 年 Finland（芬蘭）在 PISA（國際學生能力評量計畫）表現的投影片，投影片的主要內容為左上方的表格 (table)，然而這張表格的顏色過多、字體過小，令人不知道應該將注意力放在何處。此外，表格以外的地方充斥著不相干的圖畫及圖片，也令人眼花繚亂。

Finland's Performance in PISA in 2012
GLOBAL EDUCATION LEAGUE TABLE

Overall Rank*	Country/Economy	Mathematics Score	Reading Score	Science Score
1st	Shanghai (China)	613	570	580
2nd	Singapore	573	542	551
3rd	Hong Kong	561	545	555
8th	Taiwan	560	523	523
5th	South Korea	554	536	538
12th	Finland	519	524	545
26th	United Kingdom	494	499	514
36th	United States	481	498	497

Source: 2012 Program for International Student Assessment, OECD

要如何改進這張投影片的缺失呢？首先，講者應該只要保留左上方的表格，刪去其他內容。此外，表格文字的顏色應該統一，只要特別強調 Finland 即可，如此便可以凸顯這張投影片的重點，整個版面也會顯得簡潔許多。以下便是修改後的投影片。

Finland's Performance in PISA in 2012
GLOBAL EDUCATION LEAGUE TABLE

OVERALL RANK*	COUNTRY/ECONOMY	MATHEMATICS SCORE	READING SCORE	SCIENCE SCORE
1st	Shanghai (China)	613	570	580
2nd	Singapore	573	542	551
3rd	Hong Kong	561	545	555
4th	Taiwan	560	523	523
5th	South Korea	554	536	538
12th	**Finland**	**519**	**524**	**545**
26th	United Kingdom	494	499	514
36th	United States	481	498	497

Source: 2012 Program for International Student Assessment, OECD

3　善用圖表簡化複雜概念

要將複雜的簡報內容簡化最好的方式便是用圖表 (diagram/chart/figure) 來表達。例如將複雜的生產過程用流程圖 (flow chart) 表達、將複雜的公司人事結構用組織圖 (organization chart) 表達等。圖表的種類眾多，包含線圖、條形圖、餅圖、表格等，不同圖表有其各自的功能與使用時機，目的都是幫助聽眾理解複雜的資訊。

除了圖表外，照片、圖畫、漫畫等也多能引起聽眾的興趣，善用這些視覺輔助工具，便能大大幫助聽眾了解你想要傳達的資訊，但前提是這些東西必須符合簡報主題！

　　以下的投影片是關於彩色蔬果 (colorful foods) 對人體健康的益處，內容包含各式不同顏色的蔬果種類、所含的營養素、對人體的幫助等，然而這樣的資訊若純粹用文字表達，便會顯得鬆散，字數也偏多。

要如何改進這張投影片的缺失呢？最好的方式便是製作表格 (table)，將所有的資訊分門別類，並輔以相對應的顏色，讓聽眾一目了然。以下便是修改後的投影片。

有關如何介紹及說明各式圖表，本書 Chapter 6 會做更詳細的介紹。

 善用輕薄短小的多媒體材料

　　不可否認，以往成功的簡報多取決於豐富的簡報內容及講者良好的簡報技巧，但現今聽眾性質已有改變，例如年輕的聽眾多已經習慣聲光刺激，再加上注意力持久度 (attention span) 愈來愈低，因此身為講者的你必須善用多媒體 (multimedia)，例如音樂、短片等來增加簡報的多樣性，以滿足聽眾的需求。

　　使用音樂或短片時必須注意，長度最好不要超過 2.5 分鐘，因為根據統計，在影音網站 YouTube 上，人們觀看一個影片的平均長度為 2.5 分鐘，如果影片超過此長度，人們通常會選擇不看。這是為什麼現今簡報都有「輕、薄、短、小」的傾向。同樣地，這也是為什麼重要人物如美國總統雷根 (Ronald Reagan) 與歐巴馬 (Barack Obama) 的演說都很少超過 20 分鐘，因為時間一長，再好的講者也無法阻止聽眾分神！

Unit **3** 良好的簡報檔案元素

　　儘管性質、形式及主題不同，良好的簡報檔案通常有些共通的元素，以下為良好的簡報檔案必備的六項元素。

- 完整的架構
- 適當的投影片重點與標題
- 合宜的文字外觀
- 清楚的條列式重點
- 正確的文字
- 銜接順暢的投影片

1 完整的架構

　　通常一個架構完整的簡報檔案按照邏輯順序會包含以下幾張投影片。

- 標題頁 (cover page)
- 大綱頁 (overview/outline)
- 主體頁 (body)
- 結論頁 (conclusion)
- 參考資料頁 (reference)
- 聯絡資料頁 (contact information)

A. 標題頁

　　標題頁通常出現在簡報檔案的第一頁，包含簡報題目 (topic)、簡報者姓名 (name)、機構名稱 (affiliation)、職稱 (title/position)、簡報日期 (date)，甚至是簡報者的聯絡方式 (contact information) 等。

　　其中要注意的是，簡報題目的英文字第一個字母通常必須大寫，包含名詞、動詞、形容詞、副詞、代名詞等。此外，題目中的冒號「:」及破折號「—」後面接的第一個字也必須大寫。介系詞、連接詞、不定詞、冠詞等則必須小寫，除非這些字包含或超過五個字母（例如題目中若有 about, among, during, between, through 等字，則第一個字母便必須大寫）。以下是幾個簡報題目的大小寫寫法。

- Memory in Sight-Impaired Adults: A Case Study
  視障人士的記憶：案例研究

- Taiwan's Public Housing Projects—Bridging the Gap Between Rich and Poor?
  台灣的公共住宅計畫──消弭富人和窮人之間的差距？

- Automotive and Industrial Manufacturing: Annual Report 2015
  汽車和工業製造：2015 年年度報告

　　以下是標題頁範例。在這個標題頁中，講者列出了簡報題目、機構名稱、講者姓名、職稱、簡報日期，以及聯絡方式。

❶ 簡報題目　　❸ 講者姓名　　❺ 聯絡方式

❷ 機構名稱　　❹ 職稱　　　　❻ 簡報日期

B. 大綱頁

　　大綱頁通常出現在簡報檔案的第二頁,包含的內容是整個簡報的主要重點 (main point)。根據需要,有些講者也會將次要重點 (sub-point) 放進大綱頁中。一般而言大綱頁都是以條列式重點 (bullet point) 呈現。

　　以下是大綱頁範例。在這個大綱頁中,講者列出了四個主要重點及最後的結論 (conclusion),以及第一個主要重點的四個次要重點。

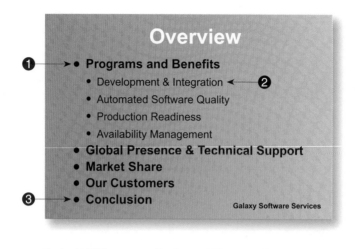

❶ 主要重點　　❷ 次要重點　　❸ 結論

C. 主體頁

　　這個部分是簡報中的主要內容頁面，頁數不一定，端看簡報需要。請注意，這部分投影片的排列順序必須與大綱頁中排列的順序一致。以下是主體頁範例。

排序方式與
大綱頁一致

D. 結論頁

此頁通常接在所有的主體頁之後，作為整個簡報的結尾。

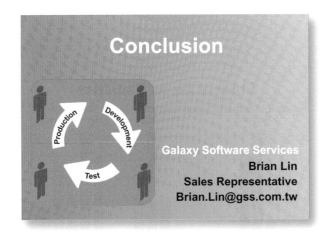

E. 參考資料頁

此頁應詳細列出簡報中所有引用到的資料出處，包含書籍、雜誌、網頁等，以方便有興趣的聽眾於事後查詢。若簡報當中沒有引用任何資料，則此頁可以省略。

F. 聯絡資料頁

此頁通常出現在簡報的最後一頁，內容為講者的聯絡方式，包含電子郵件、電話等。若講者已經在標題頁列出聯絡資訊，則此頁可以省略。

2 適當的投影片重點與標題

簡報檔案中，主體頁的每張投影片都應該有一個清楚的重點，也應該只包含一個重點。不過根據我多年的教學經驗，實務上常有講者在一張投影片中放入許多重點，這樣不僅讓投影片本身顯得雜亂，也讓聽眾不知

該將注意力放在何處。例如下面第一張圖的主體頁投影片便包含三個重點（即三個統計資料），並不適當。在此建議將每個重點（即每個統計資料）分開，製作成三張投影片，每張投影片只包含一個重點（即一個統計資料），例如下面第二張圖。

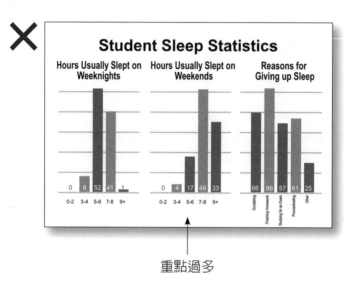

重點過多

只包含一個重點

此外，講者也應該善用投影片的「標題」(title)，讓聽眾知道投影片的重點；而且每張投影片的標題最好使用簡短的「字詞串」(phrase)，而不是完整的句子 (sentence)。

例如下面投影片的標題是 Our company has outstanding global presence and technical support.，爲一個冗長的完整句子。

這裡建議修改成下面投影片中的字詞串 Global Presence & Technical Support，這樣明顯簡潔許多。

除了使用字詞串，你也可以善用「問句」來當作投影片的標題。以問句形式呈現的投影片標題，除了可以激起聽眾的興趣、讓聽眾專心並思考，甚至也可以鼓勵聽眾參與討論。請注意，當你決定用問句作標題，則必須在接下來的講稿中提出此問句標題的答案。舉例來說，如果你的投影片標題是 What Are the Key Concepts of Global Education?（全球教育的主要概念爲何？），那麼在問句的下方或下一張投影片中，便必須列出數個 key concepts（主要概念）作爲答案，如同以下投影片所示。

「問句」形式的標題

What Are the Key Concepts of Global Education?

- Global citizenship
- Conflict resolution
- Diversity
- Human rights
- Interdependence
- Social justice
- Sustainable development
- Multiple perspectives

參考答案

3　合宜的文字外觀

製作投影片時，文字的字型、大小等都要合宜，例如每張投影片最好使用同一種字型，而且最好是常見且容易閱讀的字型。若不得已必須使用其他字型，最好不要在同一張投影片中使用超過三種字型。

此外，應盡量避免使用全部大寫、斜體、粗體等字型的英文字。還有，投影片中所有使用的文字大小以 28 級或 28 級以上爲佳，最好不要小

於24級，以免造成聽眾在閱讀上的困難。至於標題的字級則應採用更大級數，一般不要小於40級。

以下投影片範例皆使用同一字型，標題文字大小為50級，右側文字則為28級，皆符合標準。或許你會問：「下面圖形中的文字似乎過小？」，這是因為這部分的文字屬於圖片的一部分，呈現時是看整體的感覺，因此不在規範內！

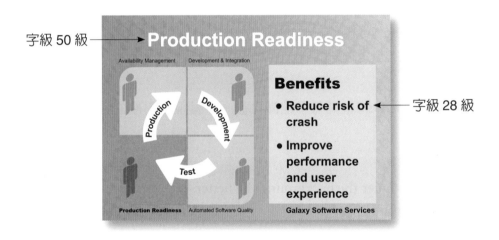

字級 50 級 ——

字級 28 級

4 清楚的條列式重點

主體頁的投影片若以文字為主，則最佳的呈現方式是條列式重點。使用條列式重點時請注意以下規範：(a) 每個條列式重點最好不要超過八個字；(b) 每個條列式重點應自成一行；(c) 每張投影片的條列式重點不要超過八行。

此外，條列式重點的呈現方式通常爲字詞串 (phrase)，盡量不要使用完整句子，以免文字過多；也因爲條列式重點爲字詞串，而非完整句子，因此一般並不需要在結尾處打句點「.」。當然，條列式重點也可爲句子或問句，不過不管以何種方式呈現，最好使用統一的格式，不要一行用句子，一行用問句，一行用字詞串等。舉例來說，如果你的講稿 (script) 中有下面這個完整句子：

- The first suggestion is that the simpler the background of your painting the better.
  第一個建議是您圖畫的背景愈簡單愈好。

那麼你可以將整個句子縮減之後，再呈現在對應的投影片 (slide) 上。例如：

- The simpler the background the better.
  背景愈簡單愈好。

不過更好的方式是用條列式重點的字詞串呈現出來。例如：

- The simpler, the better
  愈簡單愈好

以下四個投影片範例都是主體頁的內容，每一張右側的條列式重點各有兩項，而且都是以原形動詞的字詞串開始，也因此，整體投影片的格式一致，看起來賞心悅目。

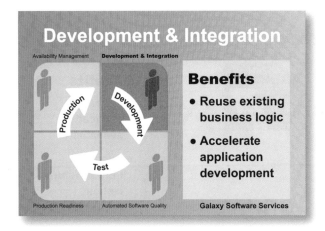

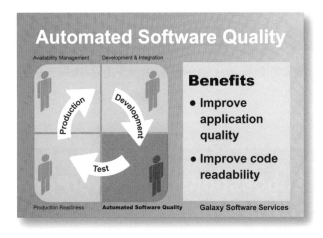

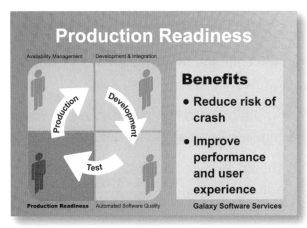

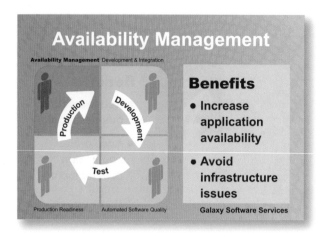

解答請見 ▶ p. 307

Exercise

以下是某位講者的投影片。這張投影片雖然是以條列式重點呈現,但卻是使用完整的句子,因此文字過多。請修改投影片,以「字詞串」的方式呈現要點。

Suggestions for PowerPoint Presentation Slides

- It's a good idea to use headings to show the main points of the slide.

- Both the Chinese and English must follow formal typing rules.

- Paying attention to the layout, such as word spacing, line spacing, fonts, etc.

- You should also use animation to make your presentation livelier.

_____

_____

_____

_____

_____

5 正確的文字

簡報的投影片可以事前準備，因此正確性十分重要，請你務必再三檢查，不能有任何錯誤。檢查時請特別注意拼字、標點符號、字母間距等。

舉例來說，連字號「-」與破折號「—」在英文中常有誤用或混用情形，例如許多人會將連字號寫成破折號，請見下面兩例。

✔ a well-established company
✘ a well—established company
　一間富規模的公司

✔ the world's best-known singer
✘ the world's best—known singer
　世界最知名的歌手

或將原本應用破折號的地方寫成連字號，請見下例。

✓ The two products—one from Company A and the other one from Company B—are the most popular.

✗ The two products-one from Company A and the other one from Company B-are the most popular.

這兩項產品——一個是 A 公司的，另一個是 B 公司的——最受歡迎。

連字號顧名思義是將兩個字連成一個字；破折號的目的則是在一個句子中插入一個額外的概念，而這個概念的前後便可以用破折號來區隔，兩者差別甚大，使用時要特別小心。

除此之外，標點符號必須緊跟著前面的字母，兩者之間不應該有空格 (space)，而在標點符號之後則必須有空格，請見下例。

✓ Speakers should use photos, cartoons, or graphs to trigger the interest of the audience.

✗ Speakers should use photos ,cartoons ,or graphs to trigger the interest of the audience .

✗ Speakers should use photos , cartoons , or graphs to trigger the interest of the audience .

講者應使用照片、卡通或圖片來引起聽眾的興趣。

當投影片出現錯字時

簡報檔案應力求 error-free（無錯誤），但如果你在簡報場合中才發現投影片上有錯字，該怎麼辦呢？這時你應該勇於承認，並向聽眾說 Sorry about the typo.（抱歉打錯字了。）來表達自己的歉意。

6 銜接順暢的投影片

　　簡報檔案是由多寡不一的投影片組合而成，在上一張投影片與下一張投影片之間，以及每個主要重點之間，你可以做適當的連接，即使用「轉換語」(transition)，讓整個簡報聽起來更流暢自然。

　　舉例來說，你在一個關於「低頭族」（即重度手機使用者）的簡報中製作了兩張投影片。第一張（如投影片 1）為低頭族常常低頭傳訊息，頭低得愈低，對頸部的傷害便愈大。第二張（如投影片 2）的內容則是幾個讓低頭族可以不要專注在手機的撇步 (tip)。這時你可以在這兩張投影片之間加上一個「轉換語」，這樣一來這兩張投影片之間的關聯就會變得更加緊密。

投影片 1

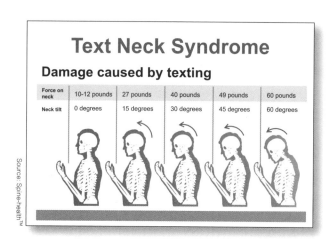

53

● Now that you know how texting could damage your spine, you should try to stay away from your phone. Let's take a look at some tips to distract you from your phone.
既然您知道傳訊息會傷害脊椎，那就應該離手機遠一點。讓我們來看看一些幫助您不要一直盯著手機的撇步。

投影片 2

Tips to Distract You from Your Cellphone

● Don't check your phone right before going to bed or after waking up.

● Read a paper book at night instead of a book on a smart device.

● Keep your phone in your pocket or in your purse while you are driving or walking.

● Give yourself a maximum amount of time to spend on devices each day.

　　由於轉換語的運用十分重要，本書在 Chapter 7 還會詳述簡報中的轉換語，以及如何有效連結簡報各個部分。

　　在本章中我們詳述了製作簡報檔案的方式，包括建立大綱及結構、製作原則，以及良好的簡報檔案所必備的元素。書末的附錄提供一個完整的簡報檔案範例 (p. 324)，請好好參考！最後，在製作簡報檔案的過程中，務必謹記「KISS 原則」(KISS principle)，也就是 Keep It Simple and Straight（保持簡單及明瞭）！

讓簡報照顧到每位聽眾

　　人們學習事情的方式不盡相同，這些不同方式被稱為「學習風格」(learning style)。同樣地，聽眾根據學習風格的不同，一般也可以分為視覺學習者 (visual learner)、聽覺學習者 (auditory learner)、動覺學習者 (kinesthetic learner) 三種類型。據統計，視覺學習者通常最多（約占 40%），而聽覺學習者與動覺學習者則較少（約各占 30%）。因此，當你在製作簡報檔案時最好能讓這三種人都能受益。舉例來說，當資訊是用圖表、圖片、大綱等方式呈現時，視覺學習者最容易理解，因此簡報中應多加入這些元素。此外，當資訊是用聲音呈現時，聽覺學習者最容易記憶，因此簡報中可以適時加入音檔或影片檔。最後，動覺學習者在自己動手做事情時學得最好，因此若你在簡報中使用道具，或提供實際的產品讓這類聽眾觸摸、使用，則效果最佳！

 🎧 MP3 **03**　　　　　　　　　　　　　　　　解答請見 ▶ p. 308

以下是兩張投影片的講稿，請分別為其製作一張良好的投影片，並將講稿的要點以條列式重點呈現。

1. 背景說明 講者是 TasteOfLove 餐點供應公司的行銷人員，想藉由這張投影片向潛在客戶介紹公司的「五道菜餐點」菜單。

　　 任務要求 請製作一張可呈現此菜單內容的投影片，標題名稱是 Five-Course Menu。

This is a sample of our five-course menu for your special event. As you all know, a five-course meal starts with soup, followed by an appetizer, a salad, the main course, and then a dessert. Here at TasteOfLove we like your menu to be exactly what you want it to be, so if you don't see any particular items on the menu that you know the guest of honor loves, let us know and we will customize the menu just to your liking. OK, here is our menu. As you can see, for the first course, the soup course, you can choose from Tomato Basil Soup and Clam Chowder. For the second course, the appetizer, you can choose either Goat Cheese Risotto Balls or Pork Potstickers. There are also two types of salad for you to choose from, Caesar Salad and Fruit Salad. As for the entrée, we offer three choices: Smoked Salmon, Roasted Chicken Breast, or Grilled Rib Eye Steak. Finally, for dessert, our two options are Bread Pudding and Chocolate Torte. This menu is $35 per person, plus tax and gratuity, and includes non-alcoholic drinks. Also, we offer full service for all parties and no room charge or corkage fees.

這是我們為您的盛宴所準備的五道菜菜單。大家都知道,五道菜餐點始於湯品,接著是開胃菜、沙拉、主菜,然後甜點。本公司 TasteOfLove 希望為您準備的餐點是您真正想要的,所以如果您在菜單上看不到您的貴賓喜歡的特定餐點,請讓我們知道,我們會根據您的喜好客製餐點。好,這就是我們的菜單。如您所見,對於第一道湯品,您可以從番茄羅勒湯和蛤蠣濃湯中擇一。對於第二道,開胃菜,您可以選擇山羊奶酪燴飯球或豬肉鍋貼。沙拉也有兩種選擇:凱撒沙拉和水果沙拉。至於主菜,我們提供三個選擇:煙燻鮭魚、烤雞胸肉或烤肋眼牛排。最後,我們的兩個甜點選項是麵包布丁和巧克力果仁蛋糕。此菜單是一人份 35 美元,外加稅和小費,包含非酒精性飲料。我們為所有的派對提供全套服務,沒有加收包廂費或開瓶費。

- course (n.) (一道) 菜　appetizer (n.) 開胃菜　customize (v.) 客製　entrée (n.) 主菜　gratuity (n.) 小費　charge (n.) 收費　corkage fee (自備酒所付的) 開瓶費

2. 背景說明 講者是品酒協會的講師，想藉由這張投影片向協會會員介紹基本品酒的程序及方式。

任務要求 請製作一張可呈現基本品酒程序及方式的投影片，標題名稱是 Basic Wine Tasting Procedure。

So, you've arrived at a winery and are ready to taste the fruits of the winemaker's labor. But how do you "taste" wine if you're only a casual wine drinker? Don't worry. I'm here to tell you about the basic wine tasting procedure. The first thing you should do is pour some wine into a clean, clear glass. Hold the glass by the stem. If you only plan to sample the wine before moving on to another, pour just enough for a few sips. After that, you can observe the wine's color and clarity by viewing the glass against a white background or light. Tilt the glass away from you and note the color of the wine from the edges to the middle. Then, swirl the wine glass around for a few seconds to let the wine "breathe." This will allow oxygen into the wine and bring out its natural aromas. After that, you can sniff the wine, first with your nose a few inches from the glass, then feel free to insert your nose into the glass and breathe deeply. You can repeat the sniffing several times if you want. Then, you can sip the wine by "chewing" it or rolling it over your tongue to cover your taste buds. Make sure you do it gently for a few seconds. Then, it comes to the last step of wine tasting—swallowing the wine. And remember, winery staff are helpful and will guide you through the wine-tasting process. So if you have any questions, feel free to ask.

您現在來到了一家釀酒廠，準備好品嚐釀酒師傅辛勞的成果。但如果您只是一般的葡萄酒愛好者，要如何「品」酒呢？不用擔心。我就是要告訴您

基本的品酒程序。您應該要做的第一件事是把葡萄酒倒進乾淨清透的玻璃杯。手握住玻璃杯腳。如果您只打算在品嚐另一種酒之前試試眼前的這酒，那就只要倒一點點，足夠啜飲幾口就好。之後您可以把酒杯襯著一個白色的背景或對著光，以觀察酒的顏色和清晰度。將玻璃杯朝您的身體外傾斜，並從邊緣到中間注意酒的顏色。然後，旋轉酒杯幾秒鐘讓酒「呼吸」。這個動作會讓氧氣進入酒裡，帶出其天然的香味。在那之後，您可以嗅酒，首先用您的鼻子離酒杯幾英寸的地方聞，然後可以將鼻子埋入酒杯，深深呼吸。您可以重複嗅幾次，如果您想要這樣做的話。然後，您可以利用「咀嚼」的方式，或讓酒滾動翻過舌頭覆蓋味蕾的方式啜飲葡萄酒。請記得輕輕地做個幾秒鐘。然後就是品酒最後的步驟——吞嚥酒。請記住，釀酒廠的工作人員會幫助並引導您完成品酒過程。所以如果有任何疑問，可以隨時提問。

● winery (n.) 釀酒廠　winemaker (n.) 釀酒師　stem (n.)（高酒杯的）腳
　tilt (v.) 傾斜　swirl (v.) 旋轉　aroma (n.) 香味　sniff (v.) 嗅聞
　feel free 無拘無束　taste bud 味蕾

Chapter 3

簡報開場用語

English Public Speaking
and Presentation

Well begun is half done.

—Aristotle

好 的 開 始 是 成 功 的 一 半 。

—— 亞 里 斯 多 德 （古 希 臘 哲 學 家）

　　簡報要成功，「好的開始」是關鍵因素！誠如上面英文名句所述，如果你能在簡報一開始便引起聽眾興趣、創造愉悅氣氛，甚至可以順利地講數分鐘不忘稿，便可帶給自己極大信心，之後的簡報也可更順利地進行。

　　那麼要怎麼做才會有個好的開始呢？完成簡報前的準備工作之後，在製作簡報檔案的同時，你便可以開始撰寫講稿。內容完成後，建議你試著背誦前一～三分鐘的內容，這一～三分鐘的內容應已包含本章的所有內容，即暗示簡報即將開始、感謝聽眾、自我介紹、陳述引言、說明簡報目的與主題，以及說明簡報架構與流程。若你可將這部分的講稿熟記，甚至背誦，臨場便可以侃侃而談。有了好的開始，你的自信便會增加，要順利完成簡報便不是難事！

　　以下為簡報開場的步驟及用語。如本書之前所言，根據個別簡報性質、形式及主題不同，某些步驟可視情況省略或變更順序。

簡報開場的「氣勢」很重要，因此一踏上講台或簡報位置時請不要馬上開口！應該先站定，面帶微笑環顧全場數秒，等聽眾的注意力都集中在你身上後再開始說話。不過因為場合不同，有時你會發現自己要開始簡報時，聽眾尚無法專心聆聽，或者仍在從事其他活動，這時便要委婉地暗示他們，簡報即將開始。以下為相關用語。

🎧 MP3 **04**

Please take your seats.
請各位就坐。

Ladies and gentlemen, please be seated.
各位先生女士，請就坐。

Ladies and gentlemen, if I may have your attention.
各位先生女士，請注意。

Is everyone ready? It's about time to start the presentation.
大家都準備好了嗎？簡報差不多要開始了。

It looks like it's just about time, so let's get started.
看來時間差不多了，我們開始吧。

I know everyone is on a tight schedule, so let me begin.
我知道大家時間都很趕，那我就開始吧。

真人重點示範影片 1
YouTube 搜尋作者和書名

I see we're all here. Shall we get started?

看來大家都到了。那我們開始如何？

It looks like some people have still not come yet, but let's get started anyway.

看來有些人還沒到，不過我們還是開始好了。

當聽眾的注意力都集中在你身上之後，便可以進行開場。一般而言，講者都會先感謝聽眾，包含會議參與人員、主辦單位，甚至重要人士。你可以用最簡單的 good morning（早安）、good afternoon（午安）、good evening（晚安）等打招呼，展現自信及輕鬆的態度。在簡短打招呼之後，便可以將所有聽眾統稱爲 ladies and gentlemen（各位先生女士），但如果你知道在場重要人士的姓名及頭銜，最好能一一點名，並將目光投視到他們的身上，讓他們感受到尊重。不過若你不太確定其姓名或頭銜，那最好不要冒險亂說，因爲說錯姓名或頭銜是一件很不禮貌的事！

 MP3 **05**

1 簡短打招呼

Good morning, ladies and gentlemen.
各位先生女士，早安。

- -

Dr. Young, Mr. Chen, ladies and gentlemen. Welcome.
楊博士、陳先生、各位先生女士，歡迎。

- -

Distinguished guests, good evening.
各位貴賓，晚安。

- -

Director Young, honorable guests, ladies and gentlemen.
楊處長、各位貴賓、各位先生女士。　　　　　　● honorable (adj.) 可敬的

- -

真人重點示範影片 2
YouTube 搜尋作者和書名

2 向聽眾道謝

Thank you for finding the time to come today.
謝謝您今天撥冗參加。

Thank you all for coming on such short notice.
謝謝大家在這麼臨時通知的狀況下過來。　　　　　　● short notie 臨時通知

I appreciate the opportunity to be here with you today.
很感謝今天有這個機會可以與大家相見。

Thank you for coming. It's my pleasure to share with you my research findings.
感謝光臨。很高興能和您分享我的研究發現。

Thank you for being here. It's a great pleasure to be able to attend this conference.
謝謝您大駕光臨。能夠參加這個討論會，我感到十分高興。

Thank you for giving me the opportunity to address such a distinguished audience.
感謝您給我這個機會在貴賓面前演說。　　　　　　● distinguished (adj.) 卓越的

Thank you for attending this session. I'm excited to present our research results to you.
感謝您參加這個場次。能夠向您報告我們的研究結果，我感到很興奮。

I'd like to give a word of thanks to Ms. Rivers of the Marketing Department for helping to set up this presentation.

我想感謝行銷部門的 Rivers 女士幫忙安排這場簡報。　　　● set up... 安排…

I know things must be hectic in the HR Department right in the middle of the hiring season, and I thank everyone for taking the time to come today.

我知道人資部門正處於僱人季節,應該忙翻了,因此很感謝大家今日撥冗參加。　　　　　　　　　　　　　　　　　● hectic (adj.) 忙碌的

正式與非正式語言

　　以上所提供的招呼及感謝用語較適合使用於正式場合。然而,根據不同情況,講者有時可以使用比較非正式的語言,以營造輕鬆的氣氛。舉例來說,在對自己部門的同事做簡報時,用語便可以輕鬆一點,以免讓同事感到拘謹。以下為不同正式程度的招呼和感謝用語。

範例 1(打招呼)

正式	Good morning, ladies and gentlemen. 各位先生女士,早安。
半正式	Good morning, everyone. 大家早安。
非正式	Good morning to you all. 你們大家都早啊。 How are you all? 大家都好嗎?

正式	Thank you for your time this morning.
	謝謝您今天早上撥冗參加。
半正式	I'm pleased to be here.
	我很高興在這裡。
非正式	Glad to be here.
	很高興在這裡。

身為講者，自我介紹很重要，因為這是讓聽眾認識你的最好方法。不過介紹的長度不需太長，只要將自己的名字、所屬機構、職稱、業務內容等清楚告訴聽眾即可。要注意的是，就算聽眾對你早已熟知，基於禮貌還是必須陳述自己的名字。若你是在公司內部做簡報，也需告知聽眾你的部門與職稱。若你不是當地人，最好也說明一下自己來自何處。

 MP3 **07**

1 自我介紹

以下是講者簡要介紹自己的名字、所屬機構及職稱的說法，你可以視實際情況替換或修改。

My name is Jennifer from the Marketing Department.
我是行銷部門的 Jennifer。

My name is Demi McLean, and I'm with the Investment Banking Department.
我是投資銀行部門的 Demi McLean。

Before we get started on the presentation, allow me to briefly introduce myself. I'm a sales rep with AG Technology in Silicon Valley.
在我們開始簡報之前，請容我簡單地自我介紹。我是矽谷 AG Technology 的業務代表。

● rep (n.) 代表 (= representative)

I am Chung Mei-Ching, Associate Professor in the Department of Mechanical Engineering at National Taiwan University. I am from Taipei, Taiwan.

我是 Chung Mei-Ching，台灣大學機械系的副教授。我來自台灣台北。

My name is Natalie Hope. I'm from Desktop Solutions, and I'll be speaking on behalf of Mr. Anderson today.

我是 Desktop Solutions 公司的 Natalie Hope，今天我將代表 Anderson 先生來做簡報。

● on behalf of... 代表⋯

I'm Rick Fan, representing Legisco. I'm a senior analyst, and I am here to speak on behalf of my boss, Ms. Linda Black.

我是 Legisco 公司的 Rick Fan。我是一名資深分析師，代表我的老闆 Linda Black 女士來發表談話。

  MP3 **08**

2 結合自我介紹及其他

以下例句結合了打招呼、自我介紹、簡報主題介紹等用語，你可以視實際情況替換或修改。

Good morning, ladies and gentlemen. My name is Karen Rector. I'm here from express.com to discuss how our services work and how they can benefit your company.

各位先生女士，早安。我是 express.com 公司的 Karen Rector，來這裡和各位討論本公司的服務是如何運作，以及此服務可以為貴公司帶來什麼好處。

● benefit (v.) 有益於

Good morning. Thanks for having me here today. I'm Amy Klapton of JP Marketing, and I'm here to present our company profile.

早安，感謝今天邀請我來這裡。我是 JP Marketing 公司的 Amy Klapton，來這裡介紹本公司的概況。

● profile (n.) 概況

I'm delighted to be here today. I'm Louis Chang, VP of the Risk Management Department, Fortune Capital Co. My talk today is about Internet security and its effect on your company's future.

我很高興今天來這裡。我是 Louis Chang，Fortune Capital 公司風險管理部門的副總裁。我今天是來告訴大家有關網路安全以及其對貴公司未來的影響。

● VP 副總裁，副社長 (= vice president)

Good afternoon. My name is Sarah Gomez. I'm a sales manager with Connected Technology in Canada, and I'm here today to talk about our latest technology and what it can do for your company.

午安。我是 Sarah Gomez。我是加拿大 Connected Technology 公司的銷售經理，今天在這裡告訴大家本公司最新的技術，及這項技術能為貴公司做什麼。

 MP3 **09**

3 介紹所屬機構背景

　　從上面的例子可以看出，多數講者在介紹其所屬機構（包含公司、學校等）時通常只會講出其名稱，不會介紹太多；但在某些場合，講者所屬機構的背景與相關資料對聽眾而言很重要，這時便必須花點時間多做介紹，但時間也不宜過長，以免聽眾覺得不耐煩。

Our primary market is older citizens, especially seniors who have been retired for more than five years.

我們的主要市場是老年人，尤其是退休五年以上的年長者。

● senior (n.) 較年長者 (= elder)

Our company is proud to be one of five major players in the automobile manufacturing industry.

我們公司非常自豪，能夠在汽車製造業的五強中占有一席之地。

We distinguish ourselves in the marketplace by focusing primarily on our customers' ever-changing taste buds.

我們與市場上其他公司有所區隔，焦點主要放在客戶不斷變化的口味。

● distinguish (v.) 使具有特色　taste bud 味蕾

UCA is one of the leading technology universities in the nation. At present, our university consists of five colleges, 16 departments, and 32 graduate institutes.

UCA 是全國領先的科技大學之一。目前我們大學包含五個學院、16 個科系，以及 32 個研究所。

Our businesses include the sale and trading of securities, investment banking services, venture capital, and brokerage services.

我們的業務包括證券銷售和交易、投資銀行服務、風險投資及經紀服務。

● securities (n.) 證券　venture (n.) 風險投資　brokerage (n.) 經紀業

Our headquarters are located in downtown Chicago. We have more than 500 research professionals, in 80 branch offices, managing over $30 billion in client assets.

我們的總公司設在芝加哥市中心。我們有超過 500 位專業研究員、80 個分支機構，並管理超過 300 億美元的客戶資產。

● headquarters (n.) 總公司　professional (n.) 專家　assets (n.) 資產

Our school's programs cover a wide array of disciplines across science, arts, and the humanities, with up to 3,500 courses available each semester.

我們學校的課程涵蓋各式學科，橫跨科學、藝術和人文學科領域，每學期有多達 3,500 門課程可供選擇。　● array (n.) 一系列　discipline (n.) 學科　up to... 多達…

Before we get started on the presentation, allow me to briefly introduce our company. Our company was founded in 1920 and employs more than 350 people. We are a manufacturer of high-quality, luxury yachts for the rich and famous.

在開始簡報前，請允許我簡要介紹一下我們公司。本公司創於 1920 年，員工超過 350 人。我們是為富商名流打造高品質豪華遊艇的製造商。

● found (v.) 創辦　employ (v.) 僱用　luxury (adj.) 豪華的

Let me explain who we are and what we do. Hope for Paws is a non-profit organization dedicated to helping animals who suffer negligence and abuse. We have a huge network of rescuers from across the nation, and we mainly rely on donations from animal-lovers like you.

讓我解釋我們是誰以及我們是做什麼的。Hope for Paws 是一個非營利組織，致力於幫助被忽視及被虐待的動物。我們在全國有龐大的救援人員網絡，主要依靠像各位這樣的動物愛好者的捐款。

● non-profit (adj.)（機構）非營利的 (= nonprofit)　dedicate (v.) 致力於　negligence (n.) 疏忽　donation (n.) 捐款

Allow me to briefly introduce our university. We were established in 2001, and we now have five colleges and nine schools with over 20,000 students and faculty. We are a dynamic, young university located at the heart of Asia. Our goals are to pursue excellence and promote creativity for our society and the world.

請允許我簡要介紹一下我們大學。我們是在 2001 年成立，現在有五個學院和九個研究所，超過兩萬名學生及教職員。我們是一所有活力的年輕大學，位於亞洲的中心位置。我們的目標是爲社會與世界追求卓越並提倡創造力。

● faculty (n.) 教職員　dynamic (adj.) 充滿活力的

英語非母語時

在國際場合用英語做簡報時，對於英語非母語的講者或多或少都會有壓力，許多人甚至會在簡報前先爲自己有限的英語能力向聽眾道歉。其實這是不必要的，因爲在國際化的社會，任何人都可自由地用英語這個通用的語言交流。如果你真的擔心自己的英語能力或口音會造成聽眾的困擾或誤解，則可以利用以下兩個好用句。

As you can tell, English is my second language, so I'd appreciate your patience with my not-so-perfect English.
如您所知，英語是我的第二語言，所以感謝您包容我那不甚完美的英語。

My English is limited, so please bear with my accent. If you can't understand it, please do let me know.
我的英語能力有限，所以請多包涵我的口音。如果您不能理解我的口音，請務必讓我知道。

● bear with... 忍受⋯　accent (n.) 口音

講完上述資訊後，你便可以正式進入簡報的內容。簡報的內容通常由「引言」(hook) 開始，hook 的意思是「鉤子」，由此可知引言的目的主要是引起聽眾對簡報的興趣，使其「上鉤」。引言有時也稱為開場白 (opening statement)，不管名稱為何，它們都位於簡報內容的最前端，通常會決定簡報整體氣氛的好壞，因此愈有創意、愈能吸引聽眾的注意力愈好。不過要注意的是，引言應該要與簡報內容息息相關，不然聽眾會聽得一頭霧水，不知道你引言的目的為何。

一般而言，簡報的引言形式通常包含以下三種。

> **Q** 問問題 (ask rhetorical questions)
> **Q** 說故事 (tell stories)
> **Q** 印象式發言 (give striking statements)

A. 問問題

指的是講者問聽眾一個或多個問題，目的為引導聽眾思考簡報主題，以及引發聽眾的興趣及好奇心。這類問題稱為「修辭性問題」(rhetorical question)，或者更白話來說就是「不需要回答的問題」，原因在於講者的目的只是在激發聽眾思考，而不是要求他們真的回答問題。因此在這類問題提出之後，講者通常會接著或在之後的簡報中提供答案，亦即不需要聽

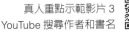
真人重點示範影片 3
YouTube 搜尋作者和書名

真人重點示範影片 4
YouTube 搜尋作者和書名

眾費心回答。當然，如果講者希望與聽眾互動，也可以讓聽眾回答所提問的問題，增加聽眾的參與感。無論如何，講者所提問的問題必須與簡報內容相關。

B. 說故事

指的是講者說一則或數則能引發聽眾切身感受的故事，並藉此引導到簡報主題。這類故事可長可短，可以是新聞或寓言，也可以是聽眾尚未聽過或早已耳熟能詳的故事，或者也可以是講者親身經歷的故事。同樣地，這類故事必須與簡報內容相關。

C. 印象式發言

指的是講者利用意想不到的統計數字 (statistics)、驚人的事實 (fact)，或與一般大眾想法相左的資訊 (information) 來引起聽眾的注意，甚至是強烈的情緒反應。這類的數據、事實、資訊等通常能在聽眾的腦海中留下深刻的印象，而這也是講者使用它們的目的。同樣地，這類印象式發言必須與簡報內容相關。

以上三種引言方式可以在簡報中個別使用，也可以同時使用。舉例來說，你的引言可以只有「說故事」，也可以包含「問問題」及「印象式發言」，端看你如何搭配運用。

除了上述三種方式，另一種引言的方式也很常出現（尤其在歐美文化中），那便是利用「幽默」(humor)。然而，這種方式在使用時的困難度較高，並非每次都能成功。舉例來說，假使聽眾聽不懂講者的笑話，或覺得笑話不好笑，那場面便會有點尷尬。此外，使用幽默時必須看清楚場合，如果聽眾來自不同的文化或語言背景，更要小心使用，以免冒犯到他

人，弄巧成拙。對於英語非母語的你而言，除非很有把握，不然不建議使用這種方式！

　　以下分別提供三種引言方式的好用句。每個例句左上方的小標題主要是說明簡報的主題或場合。

 問問題用語

領導技巧

Would you rather be a follower of a group or the leader? Why?
您寧願當團體中的跟隨者還是領導者呢？為什麼？

親子教育

As a parent, do you think it is better for children to grow up in the countryside or in a big city?
身為父母，您認為讓孩子在鄉下或在大城市長大哪個較好呢？

公司年度產品彙報

Does anyone know how many new products our company developed last year? And the year before?
有人知道我們公司去年研發出多少個新產品嗎？前年呢？

企業在亞洲布局

Have you ever wondered how some manufacturing companies are staying one step ahead even in this tough economy? How do they do that?

您有沒有想過爲什麼有些製造業公司在這個艱困的經濟環境中，仍然可以搶得先機呢？他們是怎麼做到的？　　　　　　　　　　　● tough (adj.) 艱困的

台灣的觀光行銷

Think about this situation: A person you know is planning to move to Taiwan. What do you think this person would like and dislike about living in Taiwan?

試想以下這個情況：一個您認識的人打算搬到台灣來住。您認爲這個人會喜歡與不喜歡台灣的什麼地方呢？

保險保單的行銷

Consider for a moment: Is it better to enjoy your money when you earn it or is it better to save your money for a rainy day?

請試想一下：您認爲賺了錢就花掉比較好，還是把錢存起來以備不時之需比較好呢？　　　　　　　　　　　● rainy day 不時之需，未雨綢繆

品酒會

I would like to start my presentation by asking you to name the top five winemakers in our marketplace. Can anyone tell me?

簡報開始之際，我想請您說出我們這個行業中五位頂尖的釀酒師。有任何人可以告訴我嗎？

說明　一般來說，「問問題」的引言方式通常不要求聽衆回答問題，但如果講者真的希望聽衆回答，也可以明確告訴聽衆，就像這個例句最後所使用的問句 Can anyone tell me?（有人可以告訴我嗎？）。

● name (v.) 說出…的名字　marketplace (n.) 市場

MP3 **11**

2 說故事用語

年輕人就業輔導

While in Taipei last month, I was having lunch with the head of the HR Department from a well-known, five-star hotel. She was complaining about how frequently their young workers switch jobs, and how careless and irresponsible they can be.

我上個月在台北和著名五星級飯店人資部門的負責人共進午餐。她抱怨他們年輕的員工頻繁轉換工作,做事不小心且不負責任。

● HR 人力資源 (= human resources)　irresponsible (adj.) 無責任感的

成功者的人格特質

A few years ago, I was at a trade show in Germany and I met a sales rep from ASUS. He was a shy, young man trying his best to sell me his company's latest laptop. Last week, I ran into him again at a press conference, and he has risen to be the Director of International Sales. How did he do it? What's the secret of his success?

幾年前我在德國的一個貿易展上認識了一名華碩的業務代表。他是個害羞的年輕人,想盡辦法要賣我他們公司最新的筆記型電腦。上週我在一個新聞發表會上再次遇到他,他已經躍升為國際銷售總監。他是怎麼做到的?他成功的祕訣是什麼?

● press conference 新聞發表會,記者招待會

教師培訓課程

This is a true story. A teacher asked her 5-year-old student: "Peter, what do you call a person who keeps on talking when people are no longer interested?" Little Peter responded: "A teacher?" This tells us the importance of integrating communication skills into teacher training programs.

這是個真實的故事。一位老師問她五歲的學生:「Peter,你會怎麼稱呼一個當旁人都已經沒興趣聽時,卻還一直在講話的人呢?」小 Peter 回答說:「是『老師』嗎?」這個故事告訴我們將溝通技巧融入教師培訓課程的重要性。

● integrate (v.) 使融合

3　印象式發言用語

禁用歧視性語言的重要性

In today's games, Team Idiots are playing Team Cripples, while Team Moron will take on Team Ugly.

在今天的比賽中,傻瓜隊要對上殘廢隊,而白癡隊會對上醜八怪隊。

說明　idiot(傻瓜)、cripple(殘廢)、moron(白癡)、ugly(醜陋的)皆為歧視性語言,本不應該用在簡報中,講者在引言中故意使用這些字眼,目的是引起聽眾的驚訝與震撼,以凸顯社會上使用歧視性語言的嚴重性,進而達到簡報的目的。

防曬產品發表會

Do you know that people with pale skin are eight times more likely to get skin cancer than people with dark skin?

您知道皮膚白皙的人得到皮膚癌的機率是膚色深的人的八倍嗎?

說明　講者在引言中利用一個統計數字來引起聽眾對簡報主題的興趣。

職場年齡歧視

A report that just came out revealed that people under 30 are twice as likely to get a job interview than people over 40.

一則剛刊登的報導顯示,30 歲以下的人得到面試的機會是 40 歲以上的人的兩倍。

說明　講者在引言中利用一個統計數字來引起聽眾對簡報主題的興趣。

青少年霸凌

Today we have around 100 high school students here. One hundred students. Well, that's how many students will be bullied verbally or physically in Taiwan during the 20 minutes I'll be speaking to you. More than 7,000 every day; more than 200,000 every month. This is how serious youth bullying is.

今天我們這裡有大約一百名中學生。一百名學生。嗯，他們代表了我在對各位談話的這 20 分鐘內，台灣有多少名學生會被口頭或身體霸凌。每天有超過七千人、每個月有超過 20 萬人被霸凌。這凸顯出青少年霸凌是多麼嚴重的一件事情。

說明 講者在引言中利用許多統計數字來引起聽眾對簡報主題的興趣。

● bully (v.) 霸凌　verbally (adv.) 口頭上

女性性騷擾及性侵害

Before I begin the talk, please take a moment and think of the four women closest to you. Who comes to mind? Your mother? Your wife? Your daughter? Your sister? Your best friend? Now guess which one will be sexually molested or assaulted during her lifetime. This may sound scary and unbelievable, but according to the Department of Justice, one in every four women in our country will be sexually molested or assaulted sometime during her life.

在我談話之前，請花點時間想想四個和您最親近的女人。您會想到誰呢？您母親？您妻子？您女兒？您姐妹？還是您最好的朋友？現在請猜一猜，哪一位將在她的一生中遭受性騷擾或性侵害。這可能聽起來很可怕，也難以置信，但是根據司法部的資料，我國每四位女性中有一位將會在她生命的某個時候遭到性騷擾或性侵害。

說明 講者在引言中利用「問問題」，也利用「印象式發言」中的統計數字來引起聽眾對簡報主題的興趣。

● come to mind 想起來，浮現腦海　molest (v.) 騷擾，猥褻　assault (v.) 攻擊

職場性別歧視

We all know that women are far from treated equally on the job, but do you know how bad the situation is, even in the U.S.? Well, women typically hold lower-paying, lower-status jobs than men. And they only account for eight percent of upper-level managers in large corporations. Worse yet, although half of the employees in the largest, most prestigious firms around the United States may be women, as few as 5% or less actually hold senior positions.

我們都知道女性在職場上所獲得的待遇與男性差別甚大，但您知道情況有多麼糟糕，即使是在美國嗎？女性通常比男性做更低薪、地位更低的工作。而且她們只占大企業高階經理人數的 8%。更糟的是，雖然美國各地規模最大、最負盛名的公司有一半的僱員可能是女性，實際上她們其中只有 5% 或更少的人擔任高階職務。

　說明　講者在引言中除了利用「問問題」，也利用「印象式發言」中的統計數字來引起聽眾對簡報主題的興趣。

● far from... 完全不⋯，遠非⋯　account for...（在數量、比例上）占⋯

prestigious (adj.) 有聲望的

本書在 Chapter 1 中提到準備簡報的首要工作之一便是「建立簡報目標」，而其中一個重要的準則便是創造一個核心訊息 (core message)。之所以要這麼做，乃是因為講者必須在簡報一開始時明確告訴聽眾這個簡報的目的 (purpose) 及主題 (topic)。舉例來說：「講者想傳達什麼訊息給聽眾？」、「講者希望聽眾思考什麼？」、「講者希望聽眾感受什麼？」、「聽眾聽完簡報後要做什麼事？」等，亦即讓聽眾知道他們為什麼要在這裡聽簡報。

 MP3 **13**

1 說明簡報目的與主題

說明簡報目的與主題的用語必須能反映簡報的整體內容，此外最好也能讓聽眾知道他們可以從講者的簡報中得到怎樣的收穫。雖然這聽起來很複雜，但說明簡報目的與主題時應盡量簡單、明瞭，最好能在一、兩句話中將這些資訊表達出來。

....

Today I want to talk about giving an inspirational speech to youngsters. You'll learn how to plan such a speech and deliver it confidently.
今天我想談談如何對青少年發表鼓舞人心的演說。您將學到如何規畫這種演說，以及如何有自信地發表出來。　　　　　　●inspirational (adj.) 鼓舞人心的

....

The purpose of my presentation is to inform you about our initiatives in building peaceful inter-communal relations in Kenya, by sharing with you the case study of Linwood County.

我簡報的目的是以林伍德縣爲例，告訴您有關我們在肯亞所建立的跨社區和平關係的倡議活動。

● initiative (n.) 倡議活動　case study 個案研究

The purpose of this presentation is to identify six key measures to assess how the Taiwan healthcare system is performing.

這個簡報的目的是在找出六個主要方法，以評估台灣醫療保健系統的表現。

● key (adj.) 主要的　assess (v.) 評價

My objective this evening is to convince you that people who work at home are more productive than people who work in offices.

我今晚的目的是要說服各位，在家工作的人比在辦公室工作的人更有生產力。

● convince (v.) 說服　productive (adj.) 有生產力的

As you know, the reason we are here today is to discuss how we can maintain profitability under this challenging and uncertain economic environment.

如您所知，我們今天齊聚在此的原因，是要討論如何在這個充滿挑戰和不確定的經濟環境下仍能持續獲利。

● profitability (n.) 獲利（狀況）　challenging (adj.) 具有挑戰性的

We have gathered here this afternoon to take a look at how we can streamline our production process to minimize costs and bring our products to market in a more timely manner.

我們今天下午齊聚在此，是爲了看看如何能簡化我們的生產過程，以便將成本降到最低，並更及時地將產品推向市場。

● streamline (v.) 使簡化　minimize (v.) 使減到最少　timely (adj.) 及時的

The topic of my presentation today is "five reasons to outsource," and I'm going to show that outsourcing your e-mail marketing campaigns can save time, improve efficiency, and lower costs.

我今天的簡報題目是「五大委外的理由」，我會向各位顯示，外包您的電子郵件行銷活動可以節省時間、提升效率，並降低成本。

● outsource (v.) 外包，委外　campaign (n.) 活動

 MP3 **14**

2　以聽眾利益為重點

　　根據簡報性質及場合的不同（通常在商業簡報中較常見），有時候講者會希望在一開始就讓聽眾知道「您能從我的簡報中獲得什麼利益」，這時便可以利用以下的說法，將原本位於簡報結尾處的內容率先說出來。舉例來說，下面例句中的紅字處便是講者希望聽眾知道的利益。

The information you receive today will help you lose 10 pounds in just 10 days.

您今天得到的資訊將會幫助您在短短十天內減掉十磅。

By the end of this presentation, you'll understand why home security systems matter.

在簡報的最後，您將會了解為何居家安全系統是如此地重要。

● matter (v.) 有重要性

The information I am giving you today should enable you to sleep better and even fight insomnia.

真人重點示範影片 5
YouTube 搜尋作者和書名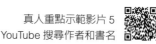

我今天要給您的資訊應該可以讓您睡得更好，甚至對抗失眠。

● insomnia (n.) 失眠

By the end of this presentation in half an hour, you'll have gained a better understanding of our school's exchange programs.

在簡報的最後，也就是半小時後，您會對本校的交換學生計畫有更深入的了解。

Over the next 20 minutes, you're going to hear about something that will change your ideas about the whole grains diet.

在接下來的 20 分鐘，您所聽到的資訊將會改變您對全穀粒飲食法的看法。

After listening to my ideas, I am sure you will agree with my proposal to move our garment factories to India in order to cut down costs.

聽完我的想法後，我確信您會同意我的提案，把公司的服裝工廠遷往印度，以降低成本。

● cut down... 削減…

In my presentation today I'm going to show you how our latest antivirus software helps protect your PC, Mac, Android phone, and even tablet.

在今天的演說中，我要告訴您本公司最新的防毒軟體將會如何保護您的個人電腦、Mac、Android 手機，甚至平板電腦。

● tablet (n.) 平板電腦 (= tablet computer)

做簡報時，除非主辦單位有事先宣布，不然講者通常需要向聽眾說明簡報的架構與流程，包含主要重點、所需時間、是否有問答時段 (Q&A session) 等。口頭說明簡報架構時，通常也會搭配簡報檔案中的大綱頁 (overview/outline) 投影片，詳細內容可以參考 Chapter 2, Unit 3「良好的簡報檔案元素」(p. 39)。

此外，如果是在會議中進行簡報，便可能需要說明整個會議或簡報的流程，這時候建議你製作一頁 agenda 的投影片。agenda 一般稱為「討論事項」或「進行事項」，作用就是告訴聽眾整個會議或簡報的議程。你或許會問：「為什麼要這麼麻煩呢？」，這是因為聽眾通常不喜歡未知的事情，如果不知道簡報接下來會怎樣、時間要多長，他們便會不安，甚至不耐煩，所以建議你在簡報一開始時就將這些資訊說明清楚。

 MP3 **15**

1 說明簡報所需時間

I'll be speaking for about 30 minutes.
我的簡報約 30 分鐘。

My presentation will last about 30 minutes.
我的簡報會持續大約 30 分鐘。

真人重點示範影片 6
YouTube 搜尋作者和書名

真人重點示範影片 7
YouTube 搜尋作者和書名

It won't take more than 30 minutes.
簡報不會超過 30 分鐘。

My talk should take around 30 minutes.
我的談話大概會花 30 分鐘。

The presentation will take approximately 30 minutes.
簡報大概會花 30 分鐘。　　　　　　　　　　　　● approximately (adv.) 大概

 MP3 **16**

2　用列舉法說明簡報架構與流程

　　列舉法 (listing) 就是利用 one, two, three, first, second, third, then, next, finally 等字來將所要說的資訊清楚地列出來。善用這些說法可以幫助聽眾更加了解你的簡報架構與流程。

There are four things we need to cover today. One is...; two is...; three is...; and four is...
今天的簡報要涵蓋四件事。一是……；二是……；三是……；四是……

I have divided my talk into three parts. In the first part,... In the second part,... And in the final part,...
我將談話分成三部分。在第一部分……。在第二部分……。以及在最後一部分……

Today I have three main points. First, I will talk about... Next, I will show you... And finally, I intend to discuss...

我今天有三個主要重點。第一,我會談到……。接著我會讓您知道……。最後,我打算討論……

My presentation is divided into three parts. First, I'll spend a couple of minutes introducing... Second, I'm going to talk about... Finally, I'll discuss...

我的簡報分成三部分。第一,我會花兩三分鐘的時間介紹……。第二,我會談到……。最後,我會討論……　●a couple of... 兩三個…,幾個…

I will start off by giving you background information on... I will then go on to talk about... At last, I will highlight... And if there is some time left, I'll elaborate more on...

我在一開始時會給您……的背景資訊。然後我會接著談論……。最後,我將強調……。如果還剩一些時間,我將進一步闡述……

●start off 開始　highlight (v.) 強調　elaborate (v.) 闡述

 MP3 **17**

3 說明簡報架構與流程用語

Here is an overview of my presentation.
這是簡報的概要。

Here on this slide you can see an outline of my presentation.
您在這張投影片上看到的是簡報的大綱。

Before I start, I'd like to give you an overview of the presentation.
我開始前想先說一下簡報概要。

As you can see, I've divided my talk into three parts. First, causes of hypertension. Second, symptoms of hypertension. Last, ways to fight hypertension. There will be a 5-minute Q&A at the end.
如您所見，我將我的談話分成三個部分。首先是導致高血壓的成因。第二是高血壓的症狀。最後是對抗高血壓的方法。在結束前會有五分鐘的問答。

● hypertension (n.) 高血壓

I'll begin by describing the background to this fund-raising campaign, and then go on to explain the progress we've made so far, and end with a discussion on the campaign's follow-up phase and activities.
我一開始會先描述這個資金籌募活動的背景，接著解釋我們到目前為止已取得的進展，然後以討論此活動的後續階段及活動作結。

● fund-raising (adj.) 籌款的　follow-up (adj.) 後續的　phase (n.) 階段

I'd first like to explain our marketing campaigns, which include both short-term and long-term activities, and then later discuss the overseas promotion issues, including promotions in the following three countries: Thailand, Singapore, and South Korea.
首先我想說明我們的行銷活動，包括短期和長期的活動，之後討論海外推廣事宜，包括下列三個國家的推廣：泰國、新加坡與南韓。

● short-term (adj.) 短期的　long-term (adj.) 長期的

The first part of my presentation will cover our company's overall operations last year, including customer services, distribution, marketing, community relations, and corporate services. The second part will focus on this year's prospects.

我簡報的第一部分將涵蓋我們公司去年的**整體營運**，包括客戶服務、銷售、市場行銷、社區關係和企業服務，第二部分則將集中在對今年前景的報告。

● distribution (n.) 銷售（量） prospect (n.) 展望

There are three main points I would like to discuss. First, I will show you in detail why I think it's a good idea to set up a new office in Vietnam where the corporate tax rate is low. After that, I will lay out the requirements and procedures to do so. Next, I will discuss the potential problems for doing so and their solutions.

我要討論的主要重點有三個。首先，我會詳細告訴您為什麼我認為在越南這個企業所得稅率低的國家設立新的辦事處是個好主意。之後我會一一陳述要這麼做的必要條件和過程。接著我將討論這麼做的潛在問題及解決方法。

● in detail 詳細地 set up... 設立… lay out... 闡述… requirement (n.) 必要條件

Exercise

請參考上述各式用語，並根據下面大綱頁投影片的內容，寫出實際的講稿，以說明簡報流程與架構。簡報題目的名稱是 More than Running: Orienteering（不只是跑步：定向越野運動）。

Outline

- **Introduction to Orienteering**
  - ✓ History & Origins
  - ✓ Rules

- **Equipment needed**
  - ✓ Orienteering map
  - ✓ Control description sheet & control card
  - ✓ Compass

- **Tips when participating**

- **Conclusion**

MP3 **18**

4 簡報開場用語彙整

　　到目前為止，本章介紹了簡報開場的各式用語，包含以下六個部分（即六個步驟）。

Step 1 暗示簡報即將開始	● 簡報開始前先確定所有聽眾都已準備好聆聽簡報。
Step 2 感謝聽眾	● 在一場會議中做簡報時，應感謝主辦單位、參與人員、在場重要人士等。
Step 3 自我介紹	● 進行自我介紹，有時候也會介紹所屬機構、單位等。
Step 4 陳述引言	● 為了引起聽眾的注意力與興趣，愈有創意愈好。
Step 5 說明簡報目的與主題	● 說明這次簡報的目的與主題，以及簡報想要達成的目標。
Step 6 說明簡報架構與流程	● 說明簡報的架構、流程、所需時間、是否有問答時段等。

如果你能好好運用這些說法，相信一定可以為你的簡報帶來一個很棒的開始！以下兩個範例結合了這些步驟的用語，句子前面都會註明步驟，你可以對照參考。正如同前面所說，根據個別簡報性質及目的的不同，某些步驟可視情況省略或變更順序。

範例 1

Step 1 Well, it's about time. Why don't we get started? **Step 2** Good afternoon, everyone. Thank you all for being here. **Step 3** My name is Lisa Chen, senior project manager from the Marketing Department. **Step 4** As some of you might have heard, our team has been working on the Nestle Gold Blend Coffee Limited Edition promotional campaign for several months. To be honest, it's not an easy task to come up with yet another brilliant commercial ad for our biggest client, and our teams have been burning the midnight oil. And, you want to know what kept us going all night at work? Of course, the numerous free samples of Gold Blend Coffee that our generous client gave us! **Step 5** Anyway, today I would like to briefly explain three of the ideas we have come up with so far in the hopes that we can select the best one. **Step 6** I'll first go over the three options, and then explain the pros and cons of each one. If you have any questions, feel free to ask at any time. At the end of my presentation, I'll show you three short video clips we have made for each of the ideas so you can get a better idea as to how the commercial may look. After my presentation, we should hopefully be able to select the best idea together. The entire presentation should take no more than one hour. Okay. Let's move on to our first idea.

嗯，時間差不多了，我們就開始吧？大家午安，感謝各位的出席。我是 Lisa Chen，市場行銷部的資深專案經理。可能有些人已經聽說過，我們小組花了好幾個月的時間在雀巢金牌咖啡限量版的促銷活動上。老實說，要再產出我們最大客戶另一個高明的廣告實在不容易，我們的小組可是日以繼夜地都在工作。而您想知道我們如何可以徹夜工作嗎？答案當然就是我們大方的客戶給我們數不盡的金牌咖啡樣品啦！總之，今天我想簡短地向各位解釋我們目前所想出來的三個行銷點子，希望能從中選出最好的一個。首先我會將三個選項都說一次，然後解釋每一個選項的利與弊。如果您有任何問題，可以隨時提出來。在簡報的最後，我會給您看三個我們根據每個想法製作的短片，讓您對電視廣告大概是什麼樣子有個比較清楚的概念。在我的簡報結束後，希望我們可以一起選出其中最好的點子。我整個簡報應該不會超過一小時。好，就讓我們進入第一個點子吧。

promotional
campaign
促銷活動

come up with...
想出（主意等）

ad (n.) 廣告
(= advertisement)

burn the
midnight oil
熬夜

sample
(n.) 樣品

the pros and
cons
利與弊

Outline

- **Background info**
  - ▶ What is a working holiday?
  - ▶ Working holiday destinations

- **Detailed info**
  - ▶ Types of jobs available
  - ▶ Estimated expenditure and income
  - ▶ Eligibility criteria

- **Conclusion**
  - ▶ Benefits

- **Q&A**

Working Holiday

Step 1 Please be seated. It's about time to start the presentation. **Step 2** Good morning, ladies and gentlemen. Welcome. I appreciate the opportunity to be here with you this morning. **Step 3** I am Daniel Guo, a consultant with Education&Travel, **Step 5** and I am here to talk about working holidays in New Zealand. **Step 3** Before I begin, please allow me to briefly introduce my company. Education&Travel was founded in 1993, and we are the world leader in international education. As of this year, we have successfully sent over 20,000 clients overseas for study, travel, and, of course, working holidays. **Step 4** And the reason I can stand here to introduce this wonderful experience to you is because I myself was once a participant in a working holiday. In fact, I joined the program to New Zealand six years ago, and the agent I chose to help me fulfill my dream was of course, Education&Travel. **Step 6** Here is the outline today. I'll start by sharing with you some background information on working holidays, including what they are and their various destinations. I'll then go into the details of the program, including the types of jobs available, the estimated expenditure and income, and the eligibility criteria. I'll end my presentation by highlighting the benefits of participating in such a program. My talk should last no more than 30 minutes. I'm sure you'll have a lot of questions after my presentation, so there will be a 15-minute Q&A session after my talk.

請就座。差不多該開始進行簡報了。各位先生女士早安。歡迎。我很感謝今天早上有這個機會可以在這裡。我是 Education&Travel 公司的顧問 Daniel Guo。我今天要來談談紐西蘭的打工度假。在我開始之前，請容我介紹一下我們公司。Education&Travel 成立於 1993 年，是國際教育的世界領導品牌。到今年為止，我們已經成功地送超過兩萬名客戶到國外唸書、旅遊，當然還有打工度假。而我之所以可以站在這裡向您介紹這個超棒的經驗，是因為我本人也曾經是打工度假的一員。事實上，我六年前加入這項計畫到紐西蘭，而我選擇幫我完成夢想的代辦公司想當然爾就是 Education&Travel。這是我今天的大綱。我會先告訴您打工度假的背景資訊，包括打工度假是什麼，以及不同的打工度假地點。我接著會介紹這項計畫的細節，包含可以從事的各種工作類型、預估的花費及收入，以及符合去打工度假的資格標準。我會以參與這項計畫的好處做個結束。我的談話應該不會超過 30 分鐘。我相信在簡報後您會有很多問題，所以講完後會有 15 分鐘的問答時段。

working holiday
打工度假

as of...
到（日期）為止

agent
(n.) 代理商

destination
(n.) 目的地

expenditure
(n.) 支出，花費

eligibility
(n.) 資格

criterion
(n.)（判斷等的）標準

具有神奇力量的「三的法則」

　　科學家發現人們最能輕易回想起來的訊息數量介於三～四個之間。因此簡報中「三的法則」(rule of three) 很重要。美國總統歐巴馬 (Barack Obama) 便是這個法則的愛用者，例如在他 2009 年第一次總統就職演說稿中，便出現了多個使用「三的法則」的句子，例如下面例句中所標示的 (1), (2), (3)（句末標示該句在就職演說影片中所出現的時間）。

I stand here today [1] humbled by the task before us, [2] grateful for the trust you have bestowed, and [3] mindful of the sacrifices borne by our ancestors. (34:23)
今天我站在這裡，為眼前的重責大任感到謙卑，對各位的信任心懷感激，並對先賢的犧牲銘記在心。

[1] Homes have been lost; [2] jobs shed; [3] businesses shuttered. (36:12)
許多人失去房子，丟了工作，生意也垮了。

Starting today, we must [1] pick ourselves up, [2] dust ourselves off, and [3] begin again the work of remaking America. (40:13)
從今天起，我們必須跌倒後再站起來，拍掉身上灰塵，並再次展開重造美國的工程。

美國總統歐巴馬 2009 年就職演說

...those of us who manage the public's dollars will be held to account; to [1] spend wisely, [2] reform bad habits, and [3] do our business in the light of day. (42:14)
……我們那些管理大眾金錢的人都將負起責任──明智地花錢，改掉惡習，並正大光明地做事情。

[1] The capital was abandoned. [2] The enemy was advancing. [3] The snow was stained with blood. (51:33)
首都棄守，敵人進逼，雪沾染血。

　　下次做簡報時，別忘了嘗試「三的法則」！舉例來說，如果要說明公司產品的優勢，就從眾多優勢中挑選其中最重要的三個來陳述。或者，如果要說明支持安樂死 (euthanasia) 或死刑 (death penalty) 的理由時，也應該挑選三個最具有說服力的理由來陳述，甚至在一句話中將此三個理由簡要地陳述出來。

Chapter 4
簡報主體用語

Unit 1 提供支持細節

Unit 2 陳述內容

Unit 3 表達約略值與縮略語

Unit 4 引用資料出處

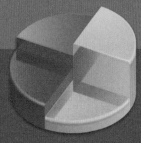

English Public Speaking
and Presentation

Examples make statements clearer, give readers more information, and decrease the chances that the fact or idea will be wrongly applied to real-life situations.

—Anonymous

例子讓所陳述的東西更清楚、給讀者更多資訊，並減少了事實或想法被錯誤地應用在現實生活的機會。

──佚名

　　誠如上面引言所述，一個人說話時若要讓對方清楚明瞭自己的意思，例子 (example) 會是最佳利器。因此在簡報中，若你提出了一個「陳述的東西」(statement)，最好在其後一併提供「支持細節」(supporting details)，以幫助聽眾更清楚理解所獲得的資訊。

　　本書在 Chapter 2 裡曾提到簡報中最重要的部分在「主體」(body)，因此這個部分的結構十分重要。不過光有良好的結構還不夠，正如同地球上多數生物構造一般，有了骨頭還要有肉，才能稱得上完整；對簡報而言，若說「結構」是骨頭，那「支持細節」就是肉。本章的目的便是詳述各種提供支持細節的方式與用語，請你務必好好運用。此外，本章也會說明簡報的主體部分常會使用到的約略值 (approximate value) 與縮略語 (abbreviation/acronym) 的說法，以及如何引用資料出處 (source)。善用這些說法都能幫你的簡報大大加分！

提供支持細節

　　Chapter 2 裡提到做簡報時必須明確陳述「主要重點」(main point)，以及主要重點後面的「次要重點」(sub-point)、「次次要重點」(sub sub-point) 等，其實這些主要重點後面的東西都統稱為「支持細節」(supporting details)，目的就是在「支持」(support) 前面的主要重點。

主要重點 1 (main point 1)
　　次要重點 1 (sub-point 1)
　　　　次次要重點 1 (sub sub-point 1)
　　　　次次要重點 2 (sub sub-point 2)
　　次要重點 2 (sub-point 2)　　　　　　　　支持細節
　　　　次次要重點 1 (sub sub-point 1)　　　(supporting details)
　　　　次次要重點 2 (sub sub-point 2)

主要重點 2 (main point 2)
　　次要重點 1 (sub-point 1)
　　　　次次要重點 1 (sub sub-point 1)
　　　　次次要重點 2 (sub sub-point 2)　　　支持細節
　　次要重點 2 (sub-point 2)　　　　　　　　(supporting details)
　　　　次次要重點 1 (sub sub-point 1)
　　　　次次要重點 2 (sub sub-point 2)

主要重點 3 (main point 3)

    次要重點 1 (sub-point 1)

        次次要重點 1 (sub sub-point 1)

        次次要重點 2 (sub sub-point 2)

    次要重點 2 (sub-point 2)

        次次要重點 1 (sub sub-point 1)

        次次要重點 2 (sub sub-point 2)

支持細節 (supporting details)

你或許會問：「爲什麼良好的支持細節很重要？」，那是因爲一個人若說話只有陳述的東西，而沒有提供例子、理由等支持細節，則對方便無法得到足夠或具體的資訊，甚至無法被說服。例如當你說：

- Lillian is beautiful.
  Lillian 很漂亮。

聽衆可能不見得完全清楚你所謂的 beautiful 定義爲何，因此一定會追問 Why?（爲什麼？）、How so?（哪一點很漂亮？）、What made you say so?（你憑什麼這麼說呢？）。可知光有 Lillian is beautiful. 這個陳述的東西還不夠，你還必須加上一些支持細節，例如下面例句中的紅字處便是支持細節。

- Lillian is beautiful because she has a heart-shaped face with huge eyes and delicate cheekbones.
  Lillian 很漂亮，因爲她有一雙大眼睛與細緻的顴骨，以及一張心形臉。

很明顯地，有了以上的支持細節，便可以很清楚且具體地告訴對方你所謂的「Lillian 很漂亮」是什麼意思，對方除了能夠得到充分的資訊外，也能決定是否被你說服。由此可知，支持細節不僅可以幫助你「背書」(endorse) 所說的話，也可以避免聽眾曲解你的話語。

支持細節一般會包含「例子與理由」(example and reason)。提供例子與理由時通常有兩個選擇，一個是提供「短的例子與理由」(brief example and reason)，另一個則是提供「長的例子與理由」(extended example and reason)。短的例子與理由通常包含在一句話中，例如在下面例句中，紅字處是短的例子與理由，黑字處則是陳述的東西 (statement)。

- Warm paint colors, like red or pink, can give your home a warm and cozy feeling.
  溫暖的油漆顏色，如紅色或粉紅色，可以帶給您的家溫暖和舒適的感覺。

  - cozy (adj.) 舒適的

- I love sweets, for example, chocolate, brownies, and pies.
  我愛吃甜食，例如巧克力、布朗尼及派餅。

- I refuse to work with Ben because he is lazy, irresponsible, and never on time.
  我拒絕和 Ben 一起工作，因為他懶惰、不負責任，且從來不準時。

另一方面，長的例子與理由則通常需要另外用一句話或幾句話才能說完，例如在下面段落中紅字處為長的例子與理由（共四句話），黑字處則為陳述的東西。

When going to a job interview, it is important to wear your best outfit. For example, you should wear a suit made from the same cloth that consists of at least a jacket and trousers. You should also wear a tie with simple patterns and bright colors. Also, your shoes should coordinate in color and style with your clothing. Don't wear brand new or casual footwear.

去面試工作時，穿上您最好的服裝很重要。舉例來說，您應該穿上由相同布料製成的一套西裝，至少包含一件外套和一件長褲。您還應該繫一條圖案簡單且色彩鮮豔的領帶。此外，鞋子的顏色和風格應該要與衣服互相搭配。不要穿全新或休閒的鞋子。

● pattern (n.) 圖案　coordinate (v.)（衣服、布料等）搭配

解答請見 ▶ p. 311

Exercise

以下有兩個「陳述的東西」，請你加上「支持細節」，使其意義更加清楚與具體。第一題請提供三個「短的例子與理由」；第二題請提供三個「長的例子與理由」。

1. The number of divorces in Taiwan has been increasing in recent years.

近年來台灣的離婚數字一直在增加。

(a) _____

(b) _____

(c) _____

2. E-mail will never replace traditional hand-written letters.

電子郵件將永遠不會取代傳統的手寫信件。

(a) _____

(b) _____

(c) _____

1　提供例子與理由

　　正如本章之前一再重申的，在簡報中舉例非常重要，尤其要舉明確且易懂的例子，例如聽眾日常生活中熟悉的事物。以下是常用的特定句型或用語。

for example,... 舉例來說，…	such as... 例如…	due to... 由於…
for instance,... 舉例來說，…	like... 像是…	owing to... 由於…
include.../including... 包含…	because... 因為…	for the reason of... 基於…的理由

以下是在英語簡報中提供例子與理由時常用的例句。

My garden is at its best during warm months, for instance, May, June, and July.

我的花園在溫暖的月分狀況最好，例如五月、六月和七月。

My report will explain in depth the reasons for the recent Asian market growth.

我的報告會深入解釋近期亞洲市場增長的原因。　　　　　　　　● in depth 深入地

Owing to the recession, we have no choice but to cut back on our overseas staff.

由於經濟衰退，我們沒有選擇，只能削減我們的海外員工。

● recession (n.)（經濟的）衰退　cut back on... 削減…

He dropped out of school for the reasons of personal health and financial difficulties.

他基於個人健康及經濟困難的理由而輟學。

Our sales increased last quarter due to higher pricing and favorable currency conditions.
我們上一季的銷售增加，是因為定價較高和有利的貨幣匯率。

● favorable (adj.) 有利的　currency (n.) 流通貨幣

I'll explain in full detail why we prefer proposal A to proposal B. The first reason is... The second,...
我會詳細解釋為什麼我們喜歡 A 提案更勝於 B 提案。第一個理由是……。第二，……

Products made of rice, such as rice crackers, rice noodles, rice milk, and rice vinegar, are very popular in Europe now.
像是米果、米粉、米漿、米醋等由米製成的產品，目前在歐洲都很受到歡迎。

Tropical islands, like Fiji, Tahiti and the Maldives, are ideal vacation destinations for many Japanese families.
諸如斐濟、大溪地、馬爾地夫等的熱帶島嶼，是許多日本家庭理想的度假地點。

● destination (n.) 目的地

There are many kinds of pet grooming services, including shampooing, blow drying, styling, ear cleaning, and paw hair shaving.
寵物美容服務包括許多項目，如清洗毛髮、吹乾、做造型、清耳朵、剃爪毛等。

● grooming (n.) 梳洗

Countries in Latin America—Mexico and Peru for example—were under Spanish colonization in the 19th century.
像是墨西哥、秘魯等的拉丁美洲國家，在 19 世紀時被西班牙殖民統治。

● colonization (n.) 殖民

Let me give you a couple of examples of a business using information systems to attain operational excellence. First,... Second,...

讓我舉兩個使用資訊系統而達到卓越經營的例子。第一，……。第二，……

- a couple of... 兩個… operational (adj.) 經營上的

Here are two reasons why I think China's economic growth is slowing down, and why the slowdown is set to continue. First,... Second,...

我有兩個理由來解釋為何我認為中國的經濟成長正在放緩，而且這個放緩的情勢會繼續下去。第一，……。第二，……

- slowdown (n.) 放緩，減速

A good example of the boom in online shopping is that people nowadays purchase music online rather than going to record stores to buy CDs.

一個關於線上購物熱潮的好例子便是人們現在都在網路上購買音樂，而不是去唱片行買 CD 了。

- boom (n.) 興盛

There are many different types of street artists; for example, musicians, jugglers, living statues, painters, and people who sell hand-made crafts.

街頭藝人有許多不同的類型，例如樂手、雜耍者、活雕像、畫家，以及賣手工藝品的人。

- juggler (n.) 玩雜耍的人

I don't think Sally Chu should receive $1 million in damages for her fall for the following two reasons. First,... Second,...

我不認為 Sally Chu 應該因為跌倒受傷而獲得一百萬美元的賠償。理由有二，第一，……。第二，……

MP3 **20**

2 將概念具象化

　　在本章我們學到支持細節的重要性，這是因為在簡報中，講者形容事物時通常過於抽象或者不夠精確，導致聽眾無法真正了解意涵。以下舉兩個例子來說明，讓你更了解「將概念具象化」的意思。

● This pen is very light.
這枝筆很輕。

● The blender is small.
這台果汁機很小。

　　這兩個句子對聽眾並沒有太大的意義，因為他們不會理解你所謂的「輕」、「小」是多輕、多小。身為講者，你唯有將這些概念具象化，舉出確切的例子（最好是聽眾日常生活中會接觸到的東西），對聽眾才有意義，例如：

● This pen is as light as <u>a straw</u>.
這枝筆就如同一根吸管那樣輕。

● The blender is smaller than <u>a fanny pack</u>.
這台果汁機比一個腰包還小。

　　這時聽眾便可以藉由你所舉的實際例子（即 a straw 和 a fanny pack）來理解你真正想要表達的意涵。以下是其他有用的舉例方式，紅字處是所舉的具象化例子。

More than 1.5 million tons of waste is generated in Taiwan each year. Guess how much space it takes up? Well, it's about five baseball stadiums.

台灣每年製造超過 150 萬噸的垃圾。猜猜它們占用多少空間？大約是五座棒球場的大小。

Taiwanese people consume 250,000 pieces of fried chicken fillet every day. If you pile them up all together, it's about the height of 10 Taipei 101 buildings!

台灣人每天吃掉 25 萬片炸雞排。如果將它們都堆在一起，就有大約十座台北 101 大樓的高度！

The average house price of a three-bedroom apartment in Taipei is over NT$26 million, which means you have to work hard for 16 years without spending a penny before you can afford such an apartment.

台北三房公寓的平均房價超過新台幣兩千六百萬，這意味著您必須不花一分一毫努力工作 16 年，才能負擔得起這樣一間公寓。

下次做簡報時，別忘了舉例，而且還要試著將所舉的例子具象化！

簡報主體的內容可能包羅萬象，不過無論是資訊型、說服型或其他形式的簡報，其陳述的方式都有類似的模式可依循。以下是各種不同陳述方式的英語簡報句型或用語，包含強調重要性、比較不同東西、提供選擇方案、提供想法和建議，以及給予承諾。

1 強調重要性

講者一定很清楚自己簡報的重點，當然也會希望將自己認為重要的資訊清楚地傳達給聽眾。如果要強調內容某處的重要性，你可以利用以下這三個特定句型。

強調重要性句型 MP3 **21**

I'd like to call your attention to...
我想請您特別注意……

I'd like to emphasize the importance of...
我想強調……的重要性。

I'd like to take a few minutes to highlight...
我想花幾分鐘來強調……

以下是使用這三個特定句型的句子，所強調的內容出現在句子的後半部（即畫底線處）。

I'd like to call your attention to <u>the significance of this case and its impact on the entire nation.</u>

我想請您特別注意這個案件的重要性及其對整個國家的影響。

I'd like to emphasize the importance of <u>ethics in a politician's personal and professional life.</u>

我想強調道德在政治人物的私人和職業生活中的重要性。　　●ethics (n.) 倫理，道德

I'd like to take a few minutes to highlight <u>the incredible rescue work we did in Southeast Asia last year.</u>

我想花幾分鐘來強調我們去年在東南亞所做的令人難以置信的救援工作。

●incredible (adj.) 難以置信的

　　此外，若你想特別強調自己所提供的資訊對聽眾有何特定利益，則可以用以下這個句型。

強調有特定利益句型　　　　　　　　　　　 MP3 **22**

> ..., which means (that) ～
> ……，這意味著～

　　以下是使用這個句型的句子，所強調的特定利益在 which means (that) 之後（即畫底線處）。

This bike has a built-in automatic lock/unlock system, which means that <u>you can not only save time but also be sure the bike won't be stolen.</u>

112

這輛自行車內建有自動上鎖／解鎖系統，這意味著您不僅可以節省時間，還可以確保自行車不會被偷。　　　　　　　　　　　　　　　● built-in (adj.) 內建的

This cellphone is connected to your house via Bluetooth, which means that you can turn on the air con or run a hot bath at the touch of a button.

這款手機透過藍牙連接到您的房子，這意味著您只要按下一個按鈕，便可以打開空調或在浴缸放熱水。　　　　　　　　　● via (prep.) 經由　air con 空調

Our newest printer has an "economic" print mode, which means it lowers the cost of printing by 30% and cuts the printing time by 50%.

我們最新的印表機有「經濟」列印模式，這意味著它會降低 30% 的列印成本並減少 50% 的列印時間。

2　比較不同東西

做簡報時，若要讓聽眾更了解你所說的內容，或者要加深聽眾的印象，一個很好用的方式便是藉由「比較」(comparison)。舉例來說，你可以藉由比較讓聽眾對你所提出的數字有感覺。當你說 Jacob made $80,000 this year.（Jacob 今年賺了八萬美元。），聽眾並無法得知八萬美元是多或是少，這時你便可以藉由比較讓聽眾了解此數字的意義。例如：

● Jacob made $80,000 this year, double from last year.
　Jacob 今年賺了八萬美元，和去年相較翻了一倍。

這時聽眾便能從 double from last year 中理解，Jacob 今年所賺的錢比去年多很多，所以今年的經濟狀況應該不錯。以下是比較時常用的句型或用語。

MP3 **23**

比較用語	
compared with... 與⋯相比	the difference between ... and～ ⋯與～的差別
in comparison to... 與⋯相比	...beyond comparison ⋯無可比擬
when you compare... 當您比較⋯	

以下是使用這些比較句型的句子。

The difference between our school and theirs is that we have a more diverse student body.
我們學校和他們之間的區別是我們的學生族群更多樣。

● diverse (adj.) 多樣性的　body (n.) 群體

In comparison to Joseph's proposal, I think Carey's will be easier to execute and cost us half as much.
與 Joseph 的提案相比，我認為 Carey 的提案更容易執行，花費也只要一半。

● execute (v.) 執行

When you compare our company's home theater system to LG's within the same price range, ours is clearly superior.

當您比較我們公司與 LG 相同價格範圍的家庭劇院系統時，我們公司的（家庭劇院系統）明顯優異許多。

● superior (adj.) 優異的

Compared with Taiwanese students, American students usually have less homework and get out of school a few hours earlier each day.

與台灣學生相比，美國學生的作業通常較少，每天也提早幾個小時放學。

I'm confident to say that the specs of our notebook are beyond comparison.

我很有自信地說，我們筆記型電腦的規格無人能比。

● specs (n.) 產品規格 (= specifications)

3 提供選擇方案

　　進行簡報時，尤其是商業簡報，講者常常需要提出不同的方案供聽眾選擇，或者告知聽眾某事物的優點和缺點，以下是常用的句型或用語。

選擇方案用語 MP3 **24**

Let's break down the pros and cons...
讓我們分別來看利與弊……

Let's talk about the ... options of ～
讓我們來談談～的……選項。

Let's look at the ... options of ～
讓我們看看～的……選項。

...possible options are open to us.
我們有⋯⋯可能的選項。

There are ... options available.
有⋯⋯可能的選項。

There are a few alternatives...
有一些替代方案⋯⋯

There are two possibilities to consider...
有兩個可以考慮的可能性⋯⋯

There are ... ways to go on this issue.
對於這項議題，有⋯⋯可進行的方式。

the pros and cons of...
⋯的利與弊

the advantages and disadvantages of...
⋯的優點與缺點

以下是使用這些提供選擇方案句型的例句。

There are two ways to go on this issue. One is to... The other is to...
對於這項議題，有兩種可進行的方式。第一種是⋯⋯。另一種是⋯⋯

It seems we have two alternatives. First, we could... Second, we could...
看來我們有兩個替代方案。第一，我們可以⋯⋯。第二，我們可以⋯⋯

● alternative (n.) 替代方案

How can we do this? There are a few alternatives. We could... Or we could... At last...

這個我們可以怎麼做呢？有一些替代方案。我們可以……。或者我們可以……。最後……

What options are on the table for us now? Let's see... First off, we could... Second, we could...

我們現在眼前有哪些選項呢？讓我們看看……。首先，我們可以……。第二，我們可以……

● option (n.) 選項　on the table 公開的

At the moment, two possible options are open to us. First, we could... Alternatively, we could...

目前我們有兩個可能的選項。首先，我們可以……。或者，我們可以……

● alternatively (adv.) 可供選擇地

Now, let's talk about three courses of immediate action we can consider. One is to... Another is to... And the last option is to...

現在，讓我們談談可以列入考慮的三個立即行動選項。一是……。另一個是……。最後一個選項是……

● course (n.) 做法

As it turned out, there are a couple of possibilities for us to consider. On the one hand, we could... On the other hand, we could...

事情發展至此，我們有兩個可能性可以考慮。一方面，我們可以……。另一方面，我們可以……

There are a number of options available at this point. Let me explain them one by one. For starters... Another would be to... Otherwise, we could... As a last resort, we could...

目前有幾個可能的選項。讓我一個一個解釋。首先……。另一個選項可以是去……。不然我們可以……。作為最後手段，我們可以……

說明 for starters 為口語說法，意思是「首先，一開始」，也可以用 for a start, for openers, to start/begin with, first of all, in the first place 等替換。

● as a last resort 作為最後手段

Regarding our plan to cut our dependence on imported water, let me break down the pros and cons. The advantages include... On the other hand, the main disadvantage is that...

關於我們減少對進口水依賴的方案，讓我分別談談利與弊。優點包括……。反之，主要的缺點是……

● dependence (n.) 依賴　break down... 個別來檢視…

I have identified some advantages and disadvantages of our new strategy. Let me talk about the advantages first. One is..., another is..., and finally... Now let's turn to the disadvantages. First... Second...

我已經點明了我們新策略的一些優點和缺點。讓我先談一談優點。一是……，另一個是……，最後……。現在讓我們轉而談缺點。第一……。第二……

● turn to... 轉向…

4　提供想法和建議

　　做簡報時，當講者提出不同的方案供聽眾選擇，或是告知聽眾某事物的優點與缺點，通常也會表達一下自己的想法，並進一步提供相關建議。以下是提供想法與建議常用的句型或用語。

提供想法或建議句型 MP3 **25**

In my opinion,... 在我看來，……	We need to... 我們需要……
I believe that... 我相信……	We ought to... 我們應該……
I recommend that... 我建議……	It's imperative that... 絕對要……
I would like to offer... 我想提供……	Now is the time... 現在是……的時候。
This is why I want to... 這就是為什麼我想……	It's (high) time... 是到了……的時候。

以下是提供想法與建議時常用的例句。

Today we need to decide if these terms are acceptable.
今天我們需要決定是否能接受這些條款。　　　　● terms (n.)（契約或談判等）條款

It's imperative that we cut costs and increase sales.
我們絕對要降低成本及增加銷售。　　　　● imperative (adj.) 絕對必要的

Now is the time to start planning our training courses for next year.
現在是開始規畫我們明年培訓課程的時候了。

I'd say that our school's website needs to be greatly improved.
我認為我們學校的網站需要大幅改進。

I believe this is the way to go, and ASUS would be my first choice.
我相信這是最好的方式，而華碩將是我的首選。

This is why I want to make a proposal that I think could benefit our company.
這就是爲什麼我想提出一個我認爲有利於公司的提案。

In my opinion, most of the health foods on the market are overrated and overpriced.
在我看來，市面上大多數的健康食品被高估，定價也過高。

● overrate (v.) 高估　overprice (v.) 將…定價過高

We ought to think about our hiring policy a little more before making a decision.
我們應該多考慮一下我們的聘僱政策後再做決定。

It's high time that the company did something about the security of our e-mail system.
是到了公司爲我們電子郵件系統的安全問題做點事的時候了。

說明　It's time... 的後面接原形動詞時，表示講者認爲「該是做某事的時候」；但接過去式動詞時，表示講者不單只是表示做某事的時候到了，還暗示「現在才做某事已經有點晚了」。本句型若加上 high，則更強調「現在正是適合的時機」。在這個例句中，講者暗示了公司早該處理卻沒有處理，現在則是最該處理的時機。

Regarding the issue of premature infant death, I'd like to offer a couple of thoughts.
關於早產兒死亡的問題，我想提出兩個想法。　　● premature (adj.) 早產的

After reviewing these options, I believe the best way to solve the problem is to open dialogues with our customers.

檢視完這些選項之後，我認為解決這個問題最好的方式是開啟與我們客戶的對話。

Instead of promoting our existing products, I recommend that we develop new product lines.

與其促銷我們既有的產品，我建議開發新的產品線。

5 給予承諾

　　進行簡報時，尤其是商業簡報，講者常常會在提出建議之後，順理成章地一併提供聽眾某種承諾，以下是給予承諾時常用的句型或用語。

承諾句型 MP3 **26**

I promise that... 我承諾……	I can say with confidence that... 我可以很有自信地說……
I can promise you that... 我可以向您承諾……	I can give you my word that... 我答應您……
I am sure (that)... 我確定……	Let me assure you that... 讓我向您保證……
I am confident that... 我有自信……	You can trust us to... 您可以信任我們……

There should be no problem (for ～) to... （對～來說）……應該沒問題。	There should be no problem that... ……應該沒問題。

以下是一些給予承諾的例句。

Let me assure you that we have quoted the lowest possible price.
讓我向您保證，這是我們的最低報價。　　　● assure (v.) 向…保證　quote (v.) 報（價）

I can say with confidence that this project will be a great success.
我可以很有自信地說，這個專案將會大大成功。

I promise that you will be 100% satisfied with our service.
我保證您會完全滿意我們的服務。

I can promise you that after you try our massage therapy you'll feel 10 years younger.
我可以向您承諾，試過我們的按摩治療後，您會感覺年輕十歲。

There should be no problem for us to find a solution by next Monday.
我們在下週一之前找到解決方案應該沒有問題。

You can trust us to do everything in our power to fix this problem for you.
您可以信任我們，我們會盡全力來為您解決這個問題。

I'm confident that we can come to an agreement which will be beneficial to both parties.

我有信心我們將會達成有利於雙方的協定。

● beneficial (adj.) 有益的　party (n.) 參與方，當事人

I'm sure you'll be very happy with the additional functions we have developed for the product.

我確信您會很滿意我們為產品所開發的額外功能。

I can give you my word that we can deliver the parcel to you at your home residence on time.

我答應您，我們可以準時將包裹寄到您的住家。　● residence (n.) 住所

利用「口語」強調重點

在本章中，我們提到利用特定句型強調重點。想要強調簡報內容的重要性，除了可以利用特定句型，還可以利用「口語」強調，亦即利用「重讀」某些字的方式來強調重點。以下是三種有效的做法。

1. 強調原本不會重讀的 be 動詞

英文中根據詞性重要性的不同，有些字會重讀，有些字會輕讀；一般而言，會重讀的字包含名詞、一般動詞、形容詞、副詞、疑問詞等，會輕讀的字則有 be 動詞、連接詞、介系詞等。然而，藉由重讀一般不會重讀的 be 動詞，你便是在向聽眾暗示你在強調所說的內容。

記得在重讀句中的 be 動詞時，不要將 be 動詞和其他字縮寫，而是要單獨說出來。舉例來說，不要說 we're，而要說 we are；不要說 I'm，而要說 I am。此外，「重讀」的意思是，在句中說到這些字時要「音量加大」、「音調提高」、「速度放慢」。以下紅字處為特別重讀的字，當你在練習時，請同時聆聽本書所附的 MP3。

We are the best company for you to partner with.
我們絕對是您合作夥伴的最佳選擇。

Apple is still our biggest competitor in all aspects.
就各方面而言，蘋果公司絕對仍是我們最大的競爭對手。

There is still a chance that this school will close.
這所學校絕對仍然有可能關閉。

I am confident that we can eventually come to an agreement.
我絕對有自信我們最終能達成協議。

2. 強調助動詞

　　與 be 動詞相同，英文句子中的助動詞通常不是重要詞性，因此不會重讀。不過如果要特別強調，則可以特意將助動詞重讀，例如以下幾個例句所示。紅字處是特別重讀的字，練習時請一併聆聽本書所附的 MP3。

Yes, we can and will succeed!
是的，我們一定可以、也一定會成功！

She had left before we closed the shop.
她在我們關店前早就離開了。

To our surprise, the president did show up at last night's farewell party.
我們很驚訝校長竟然真的出現在昨晚的歡送會。

I would very much appreciate if you could speed up the delivery process.
如果您可以加速運送過程，我絕對會非常感激。

3. 強調否定字

　　一般而言，否定字在句子中因爲帶有語意上「否定」的重要性，因此會重讀。在簡報時，如果要特別強調，你可以將這些否定的字以不縮寫的方式說出來，例如將 didn't 說成 did not、將 isn't 說成 is not，以達到強調的目的。下面提供幾個例句，其中紅字處是特別重讀的字，請同時搭配本書所附的 MP3 練習。

He is not the right person for this job.
他絕對不是這份工作的合適人選。

The Dean did not practice what he preached.
院長就是說一套、做一套。

We must not forget the consequences of climate change.
我們絕對不能忘記氣候變遷的後果。

If you don't make a decision now, I will not be able to offer you this incentive price again.
如果您現在不做決定，我就絕對無法再爲您提供這麼有誘因的價格。

　　如果想訓練英語聽說能力，並進一步了解英文中哪些字必須重讀，哪些字必須輕讀，以及如何聽懂英文的關鍵字，可參考《黃玫君的觀念英文聽力：從聽出關鍵字開始》一書。

不同性質與內容的簡報常會出現數字與各式機構的名稱，若你在說這些字時發音錯誤或唸出不是一般約定俗成的說法，便會讓聽眾對你的專業產生質疑，因此你必須知道該如何正確用英文表達這些說法。

1 約略值

簡報時常會用到數字或百分比，尤其在說明圖表時，這時你當然可以將每個數字，甚至數字中的小數點都說得精確，但這麼做不僅你說起來費力、聽眾聽起來也費力，這時倒不如告訴聽眾一個約略的數值 (approximate value)，反而令他們更容易記憶。

舉例來說，當你要說 35.24% 時，便可以說成 around one-third（約三分之一）；要說 998,543 時，便可以說成 almost a million（將近一百萬）。以下是其他相關的可能說法，你可以根據實際情況靈活運用。

表達約略值用語		MP3 **28**
98.52%	➡	almost all... 幾乎所有的…
92%	➡	most.../most of the... 大部分的…
73%	➡	almost three-quarters of... 幾乎有四分之三的…

48%	⇒	about half of... 將近一半的…
53%	⇒	just over half of... 超過一半一點點…
107	⇒	more than a hundred... 超過一百的…
1,003	⇒	a little over a thousand... 一千多一點的…

2 縮略語

英文中有許多縮略語 (abbreviation/acronym)，做簡報時若使用到這些縮略語，最好能將它們說明清楚，以確保聽眾了解你在說什麼。以下是一些說明縮略語的說法。

解釋縮略語用語　　　　　　　　　　🎧 MP3 **29**

...stands for ～ …代表～	..., or ～ ,... …，或（簡）稱為～，…
...refers to ～ …指的是～	..., also known as ～ ,... …，也稱為～，…
...is an acronym for ～ …是～的（首字母）縮略語	..., aka/a.k.a. ～ ,... …，也稱為～，…

以下是常見的縮略語在句子中的用法。練習時請特別注意聆聽下面例句中 OEM, NATO, YOLO, AIDS, HIV, NCAA 的唸法。

OEM stands for original equipment manufacturer.
OEM 代表原始設備製造商。

● equipment (n.) 設備，器材　manufacturer (n.) 製造商，生產商

NATO is an acronym for North Atlantic Treaty Organization.
NATO 是北大西洋公約組織的首字母縮略語。

● acronym (n.) 首字母縮略詞　treaty (n.) 條約，協定

YOLO refers to the phrase "you only live once," which was popularized by Canadian rapper Drake.
YOLO 指的是 you only live once（你只活一次）這個詞，是由加拿大饒舌歌手 Drake 唱紅的。

● popularize (v.) 使流行　rapper (n.) 饒舌歌手

Acquired immunodeficiency syndrome, or AIDS, is caused by a virus called HIV.
後天免疫缺乏症候群，或稱爲愛滋病，是由一種叫作 HIV 的病毒所引起的。

● acquired (adj.) 後天的　syndrome (n.) 症候群

The National Collegiate Athletic Association, also known as the NCAA, organizes the athletic programs of many universities in the U.S. and Canada.
美國大學體育聯合會，也稱爲 NCAA，在許多美國和加拿大的大學舉辦體育活動。

● collegiate (adj.) 大學的　athletic (adj.) 體育的

要注意的是，上面句子中 OEM, NATO, YOLO, AIDS, HIV, NCAA 的唸法各有不同。英文的縮略語中，較常見的是把每個字母分開來唸，也有些是將所有的英文字當成一個單字來唸，還有一些情況是將縮略語中的一部分分開唸、一部分合起來唸。當然，還有一些縮略語的唸法屬於約定俗成，亦即其唸法是大眾長久以來所使用，而沒有特別的發音規則或理由，例如下面 NCAA 的唸法是 N-C-double A，而 NAACP 的唸法是 N-double A-C-P。你最好事先查清楚不同縮略語的發音方式，以免在簡報時唸錯或誤唸。

字母分開唸的唸法

- OEM (original equipment manufacturer)
  原始設備製造商

- PTA (Parent-Teacher Association)
  家長教師聯誼會

- WHO (World Health Organization)
  世界衛生組織

- PMS (premenstrual syndrome)
  經前症候群

視作單字的唸法

- NATO (North Atlantic Treaty Organization)
  北大西洋公約組織

- NASA (National Aeronautics and Space Administration)
  美國太空總署

- SARS (severe acute respiratory syndrome)
  嚴重急性呼吸道症候群

- NAFTA (North American Free Trade Agreement)
  北美自由貿易協定

- YOLO (you only live once)
  你只活一次

- AIDS (acquired immunodeficiency syndrome)
  後天免疫缺乏症候群（簡稱愛滋病）

部分分開、部分結合的唸法

- APEC (Asia-Pacific Economic Cooperation)
  亞洲太平洋經濟合作會議（簡稱亞太經合組織）

- ISO (International Organization for Standardization)
  國際標準化組織

- JPEG (Joint Photographic Experts Group)
  聯合圖像專家群

約定俗成的唸法

- NCAA (National Collegiate Athletic Association)
  美國大學體育聯合會

- NAACP (National Association for the Advancement of Colored People)
  美國全國有色人種促進會

Unit 4 引用資料出處

做簡報時，講者多會引用各種資料，此種方式稱爲 oral citation（口頭引述）。簡報所引用的資料出處 (source) 種類眾多，可以是某本專業期刊 (journal)、某本書 (book)、某本雜誌 (magazine)、某次演說 (speech)、某個訪談 (interview)、某項問卷調查 (questionnaire)，甚至是某個網站 (website) 的資料等。建議你適時在簡報中引用資料出處，這樣不僅可以提高你簡報的可信度，還可以顯示你的專業！

1 引用資料出處應注意事項

身爲一個負責任的講者，若你在簡報時引用資料，則必須清楚告訴聽眾資料的來源與出處。以下是四個必須注意的重點。

A. 引用資料時必須考慮可信度

在種類眾多的資料中，一般而言專業期刊及書籍的可信度較高，網站上的資料則較不可信，除非是國家或機構的官方網站 (official website)，因此簡報所引用的資料最好不要全部來自網路。

B. 引用資料的方式應根據出處而有所不同

一般而言，若你引用的是期刊文章、書籍、雜誌等平面資料，則應該說出作者的姓名、期刊名 / 書名 / 雜誌名、特定文章的名稱等，年分則可視需要而定，但不需要說出頁碼等細節。若來源是某次演說，則應該說出講者姓名、演說主題、時間等資訊。若來源是訪談或問卷調查等，則應該說出主持人、受訪者、訪談 / 問卷調查的主題等。若來源爲網站，則應該

說出網站的名稱（非網址），且若爲官方網站，則需要說出機構名稱，因爲這樣更可以增加資料來源的可信度。

C. 適時增加所引用資料的可信度

若你所引用的對象不是家喻戶曉的人物或機構，則最好在引用資料時稍加說明一下此人或此機構的資歷 (credentials)，這樣可以讓聽眾覺得你所引用的資料有分量，而不是隨便引用。例如，與其只說 I'd like to quote Dr. Thomas Lee,...（我想引用 Lee 博士的話，……），你可以說 I'd like to quote Dr. Thomas Lee, who is a famous Korean behavioral psychologist and has published several books on animal behavioral psychology,...（我想引用 Lee 博士的話，他是韓國知名的行爲心理學家，出版過數本關於動物行爲心理學的書籍，……）。這樣一來不熟悉 Lee 博士的聽眾便可以藉由你的介紹知道這個人的背景，增加你引用這個人所說的話的可信度。

D. 引用資料的用語必須與簡報整體結合

雖然引用資料的好處不少，不過仍然建議你在引用時，不要因爲過於細節的用語而打斷簡報的流暢度。請記得，所有相關的細節資料都可以在簡報檔案中的「參考資料頁」(reference) 中列出，不必一一詳述，只要在簡報中簡要提到就行了。

2 引用資料出處用語

以下是引用資料出處常見的句型或用語，你可以視情況加入相關的人名、機構名等。此外，這些句型或用語中的現在式動詞也可以視情況改成過去式。

According to...
根據……

In (one's) book/article/autobiography/speech,...
在（某人的）書／文章／自傳／演說中，……

Cited in the...
引用……

...says/explains that ～
…說／解釋～

...goes on to say ～
…接著說～

...states/reports that ～
…說／報導～

As stated/reported by...
如……所說／報導

...writes/suggests/insists/claims/argues that ～
…寫／建議／堅持／宣稱／主張～

以下是在簡報中引用資料出處的說法。

Becky White wrote in her 2010 novel titled *Solitude* that...
Becky White 在其 2010 年名為《孤獨》的小說中寫到……　　● solitude (n.) 獨居

Neil Gilbert, author of *Restoring Social Equality*, states that...
《重建社會平等》一書的作者 Neil Gilbert 說……

● equality (n.) 平等

According to an article about migrant workers in last month's *Time* magazine...
根據上個月《時代》雜誌上一篇有關移工的文章……

● migrant (adj.) 移居的

According to Lisa Lin, women's softball coach, whom I interviewed last week...
根據我上週訪問的女子壘球教練 Lisa Lin 的看法……

According to statistics included on the U.S. Department of Justice Drug Enforcement Administration website report on Viagra...
根據美國司法部藥品管制局網頁上關於「威而剛」報告裡的數據……

● enforcement (n.) 實施　administration (n.) 行政機關

In the latest Gallup poll cited in the March 3rd issue of *People* magazine...
在三月三日那一期《時人》雜誌所引用的最近一次蓋洛普民意調查……

說明 本句為第二手資料的引用，亦即講者雖然要引用蓋洛普民意調查的資料，但本身是從《時人》雜誌上面看到此資料，而非自己找到或看到蓋洛普民意調查的資料。

● Gallup poll 蓋洛普民意調查

From a survey that our researchers took last month of your opinions...
根據我們研究者上個月向您所做的意見調查……

In Suarez's book *Learning in the Global Era* published in 2013, she defined global education as...

在 Suarez 於 2013 年出版名為《全球化時代的學習》一書中，她定義全球教育
為……
• era (n.) 年代

Film critic Ian Long, in a 2015 *Cinema Scope* magazine article titled
"Global Discoveries on DVD" writes...
影評人 Ian Long 在 2015 年刊在《寬銀幕》雜誌名為「全球 DVD 大發現」的
文章中寫到……
• critic (n.) 評論家

The Global Teacher Project, funded by the U.K. Department for
International Development, claimed that...
由英國國際發展署資助的「全球教師專案」聲稱……

In a speech on business ethics delivered to the European Chambers of
Commerce last May, Kevin Lin, CEO of Novell, said that...
Novell 公司的執行長 Kevin Lin 去年五月向歐洲商會就「商業道德」所發表的
演說中說到……
• chamber (n.) 協會

In the 2013 article "Building Information Modeling for Existing
Buildings" published in the academic journal *Automation in
Construction*, Julian Stengel suggested that...
Julian Stengel 在 2013 年發表在學術期刊《自動化建築》中名為「建構現有建
築物的資訊模型」的文章中建議……
• academic (adj.) 學術的

When discussing multicultural content, in their 1993 book titled
Multicultural Education: Issues and Perspectives, James Banks and
Cherry Banks presented four approaches for integrating multicultural
content into a course syllabus.

當 James Banks 和 Cherry Banks 討論多元文化內容時，在其 1993 年所出版的《多元文化教育：議題與觀點》一書中，他們提出了將多元文化內容融入課程大綱的四種方法。 ● perspective (n.) 觀點　approach (n.) 方法　syllabus (n) 課程綱要

在這一章中，我們學會了各式各樣的簡報主體用語。最後要提醒你的是，除了必須在簡報中引用資料的出處外，還必須像本書 Chapter 2 中所介紹，在簡報檔案中另外製作一張參考資料頁 (reference) 的投影片。如此一來，對你所引述的東西有興趣的聽眾才可以在簡報結束後，根據此資料頁找到資料。

Chapter 5
簡報結束用語

Unit 1 陳述結論與摘要

Unit 2 進行問答時段

Unit 3 結束簡報並向聽眾道別

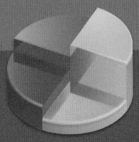

English Public Speaking
and Presentation

All's well that ends well.

—William Shakespeare

結尾好，一切都好。

——莎士比亞

　　以上英文名句為英國劇作家莎士比亞的劇作名稱，其意為「瑕不掩瑜」，亦即一件事若結局是好的，儘管中間有些小差錯，則整體而言還是好的，由此可知有個完美結尾的重要性。運用到簡報上，若你在簡報當中遇到一些小問題，但能漸入佳境並順利做完結尾，獲得聽眾肯定的掌聲，那整體而言便稱得上是一個成功的簡報！本章的三個單元將會教你如何圓滿地結束簡報，包括「陳述結論與摘要」、「進行問答時段」，以及「結束簡報並向聽眾道別」。

結尾因為是最接近簡報結束的時刻，因此是聽眾記憶最深刻的部分，請務必花心思準備，千萬不要草草結束。若你要確保達到原本設定的簡報目標，則必須重複簡報重點、強調聽眾應該牢記的部分（尤其是簡報的核心訊息），有時甚至還要促使聽眾採取行動。以下是相關的句型或用語，請多加演練。

1 陳述結論

一般而言，你可以利用以下這幾個句型或用語來向聽眾暗示簡報已經接近尾聲。

結論用語 🎧 MP3 **31**

In conclusion,...	To sum up,...	In brief,...
總之，……	總結來說，……	簡言之，……
In summary,...	In sum,...	In the past...
結論是，……	總之，……	在過去（時間單位）……
In a nutshell,...	In short,...	In closing,...
概括來說，……	簡言之，……	最後，……

以下是用於陳述結論時的好用例句。

真人重點示範影片 8
YouTube 搜尋作者和書名

In summary, the effects of the Chernobyl accident have been many and serious.

結論是，車諾比事故的影響有很多，也很嚴重。

In the past hour, I think everyone has become familiar with the history of Rome.

在過去一小時中，我想大家對於羅馬的歷史都已有所了解。

In conclusion, these are the options for overseas operations in the future and the subsequent benefits.

總之，這些就是未來海外營運的選項及隨之而來的好處。

● subsequent (adj.) 隨後的

To sum up, it took our company three years to get the products licensed and approved by the government.

總結來說，我們公司花了三年的時間才取得政府的產品執照與許可。

● license (v.) 發給許可證

In a nutshell, our company sells travel services through a network marketing business model.

概括來說，我們公司是透過網路行銷的商業模式來銷售旅遊服務。

● nutshell (n.) 概要

In short, we've looked into several possible reasons for why our new product failed to gain consumer acceptance.

簡言之，我們已經深入研究了幾個我們新產品無法讓消費者接受的可能原因。

● look into... 深入研究…

In brief, without a doubt, global warming is a serious threat to people, plants and animals, and the ecosystem, and we must do something about it.

簡言之，毫無疑問地，全球暖化對於人類、動植物及生態系統來說都是嚴重的威脅，而我們必須有所行動。　●without a doubt 毫無疑問地　ecosystem (n.) 生態系統

2　陳述摘要

　　除了陳述結論，你還可以將已說過的簡報重點再簡要地陳述一次，加深聽眾的印象。以下是用於陳述摘要時的好用例句或說法。

I'd like to finish by restating today's key issues.
我想重述今天主要的議題作為結束。

Before I finish, I'd like to run through the main points again.
在我結束前，我想再將主要重點複習一次。

I would like to finish by briefly summarizing today's main points.
我想將今天的主要重點以簡短的摘要作結。

Please allow me to finish my presentation by summarizing the benefits of our service.
請讓我簡述我們（公司）服務的好處來為簡報作結。

At the outset, I said that by the end of this presentation you would have changed your ideas about coloring books. I hope I've managed to deliver what I promised to you.

在開始時，我說過在簡報結束後，您對著色繪本的看法將會有所改變。我希望我有做到我所承諾過的。

● outset (n.) 開端　manage (v.) 設法　deliver (v.) 履行

As you leave here today, I would like you to remember that...

在您離開時，我想請您記住……

Before we finish, let's review the main purpose of this project...

結束前，讓我們再來溫習一下這個專案的主要目的……

I would like to finish by asking you to remember the following two things...

結束前，我想請您記住以下兩件事……

3　利用列舉法陳述摘要

　　正如同本書在 Chapter 3 中說明簡報架構與流程所使用的列舉法 (listing) 一般，當你陳述摘要時，也可以總結簡報所說過的內容，並利用列舉法簡潔地歸納要點。以下提供幾個好用的說法，紅字處便是使用列舉法的地方。

To sum up, we need to work on providing better services for our customers. To begin with, we must... Next, we should... Finally, it's time for us to...

總結來說，我們需要努力提供顧客更好的服務。首先，我們必須⋯⋯。接著我們應該要⋯⋯。最後，該是我們⋯⋯的時候了。

I would like to finish by emphasizing the importance of educating our youth to fight against cyber bullying. We can do so by first educating parents... In addition, teachers can...

我想以強調教導我們的年輕人對抗網路霸凌的重要性作結。要這麼做，我們首先可以教育父母們⋯⋯。此外，老師們可以⋯⋯　● cyber (adj.) 網路的　bully (v.) 欺凌

Before closing, I'd like to briefly go through my main points again. Our newest SoundPitch is especially useful for elders with serious hearing impairment. For starters,... Second,... Last but not least,...

在結束之前，我想簡短地複習一下我的主要重點。我們最新的 SoundPitch 對聽力嚴重受損的老人家特別有用。首先，⋯⋯。第二，⋯⋯。最後但同樣重要的是，⋯⋯

> **說明**　last but not least 常用在簡報的結尾，字面上的意思是「最後但並非最不重要（是）」，亦即告訴聽眾「最後但同樣重要（的是）」。

● go through... 重複⋯　impairment (n.) 損害

　　以下是幾段陳述摘要的內容，你可以擷取當中合適的部分套入簡報中，讓自己的簡報顯得更加簡潔洗練。

In conclusion, in today's seminar I showed you what I think can be done for our nation's troubled economy. I offered ideas for growth in different industries, and finally, I proposed changes that need to be implemented at the highest level.

總之，在今天的研討會中我讓大家知道我對國家問題重重的經濟該如何做的想法。我提供了刺激不同產業成長的想法。最後，我提出了政府高層應該要做的改變方法。

說明 此段向聽眾暗示簡報中總共談到三個重要議題：(1) what can be done for our nation's troubled economy；(2) ideas for growth in different industries；(3) changes that need to be implemented at the highest level。 ● implement (v.) 實施

I believe I have covered the issue of an aging population. Also, I've made it clear the seriousness of the problem, particularly in Taiwan. Lastly, I have stressed the heavy burden that will be borne by our next generation if we don't act soon.

我相信我已經說明了高齡人口的議題。還有，我也清楚說明了這個問題的嚴重性，特別是在台灣。最後，我也強調了如果我們不儘快做改變，下一代將會背負的沉重負擔。

說明 此段向聽眾暗示簡報中總共談到三個重要議題：(1) the issue of an aging population；(2) the seriousness of the problem；(3) the heavy burden borne by our next generation。 ● bear (v.) 負擔

I would like to end my presentation by reminding you of the key sales features of the new Airfryer. Remember: it is equipped with auto shut-off. It has less operating sound. And it comes with adjustable temperature. In sum, it is the best fryer on the market right now, and it will make our customers' lives a lot easier.

我想提醒您新型 Airfryer 的主要銷售特點，以為簡報作結。請記得：它配有自動斷電功能。它運作時聲音較小。它還可以調節溫度。總之，它是目前市面上最好的油炸機，而且它會讓我們顧客的生活容易許多。

說明 此段向聽眾暗示簡報中總共談到三個重要議題：(1) it is equipped with auto shut-off；(2) it has less operating sound；(3) it comes with adjustable temperature。 ● equip (v.) 配備 adjustable (adj.) 可調整的

I'll conclude now with a summary of my main points today. The first point is that the amount of sleep a person needs varies from one period of life to another. The second one is that continuous sleep deprivation will lead not only to a loss of mental efficiency, but also to disturbances of perception and hallucinations. Last but not least, the older people get, the more their performance and well-being suffer without sleep.

我現在想以簡述今天的主要重點作結。第一個重點是一個人所需的睡眠時間在生命的不同階段中有相當程度的變化。第二點是持續的睡眠剝奪不僅會導致心智效能的喪失，還可能導致知覺的擾亂與幻覺。最後，也同樣重要的一點是，年紀愈長，沒有睡眠對人的表現及身心健康損害就愈大。

> ● deprivation (n.) 剝奪　efficiency (n.) 效率　disturbance (n.) 擾亂
> perception (n.) 知覺　hallucination (n.) 幻覺

 MP3 **34**

4 促請聽眾行動

　　簡報結尾處除了可以陳述結論及摘要，也可以促請聽眾採取行動。根據簡報內容及目標的不同，行動的形式有很多種，例如要求來賓做某件事、邀請聽眾從事某種社會運動、請求客戶下訂單等。無論如何，要達到促請聽眾行動的目的，你的結論及摘要必須簡短但強而有力。以下是幾個好用例句，紅字處便是希望聽眾行動的內容。

Before urging you to initiate a campaign to support animal rights, I would like to briefly reiterate the main points I have presented today.

在促請您發起一場支持動物權利的活動前，我想簡要地重申我今天提出的主要重點。

> ● right (n.) 權利　reiterate (v.) 重申

I hope I've made clear the dangers of being a smartphone addict. What are you waiting for? Get rid of your cellphone now and start talking to the people you love and care about—face to face!

我相信我已經將智慧型手機成癮者的問題講得很清楚。您還在等什麼呢？現在就丟掉手機，開始和您所愛和所關心的人面對面談話！

● addict (n.) 有癮者　get rid of... 丟棄…，除去…　face to face 面對面，當面

For the reasons mentioned, I oppose the idea and the practice of capital punishment. Every day people die because of wrongful executions. Therefore, I ask you to please write your lawmakers or congresspeople to address this pressing issue.

根據之前提到的原因，我反對死刑的理念與執行。每天都有人因為錯誤的死刑而死。因此我請您寫信給您的立委或議員，以處理這項迫切的議題。

● capital (adj.) 死刑的　execution (n.) 執行死刑　address (v.) 處理，應付

I would like to finish my presentation by saying that our new phone has the highest power efficiency and the best performance on the current market. I'm looking forward to your order. Thank you very much.

總結我的報告，我想說，我們新的電話有目前市面上最高的電力效率和最佳的性能。期待您的訂單。非常感謝。

In brief, our goal is to achieve sales of $50 million in the fourth quarter. As you know, I need to give my supervisor a reply by the end of this week, so I really need your decision ASAP.

簡言之，我們的目標是在第四季達到五千萬美元的銷售額。如您所知，我在本週結束前要給老闆一個答覆，所以我真的需要您儘快決定。

● ASAP 儘快 (= as soon as possible)

5 以其他方式作結

　　除了上述幾種方式，你還可以利用其他結尾方式，讓簡報更加生動或與眾不同。以下數個例子分別是利用「提問」、「引述他人話語」、「預測未來」的方式來結束簡報。紅字處便是利用這些方式而傳達出來的內容，請多加體會。

提問

I would like to finish my talk by asking one simple question. If we don't start protecting the endangered Black Rhinos now, then what will their future be like in ten years?

我想問一個簡單的問題來為自己的談話作結。如果我們不從現在開始保護瀕臨滅絕的黑犀牛，那十年後牠們的未來會是什麼樣子呢？

● endangered (adj.) 瀕臨絕種的

....

So, as I close, please ask yourself, "What kind of retirement lifestyle do I want?" It's a very personal question, and I'm here to help you answer it.

因此，當我做結論時，請問問您自己：「我想要擁有何種退休生活方式？」這是個很私人的問題，而我就是來幫您回答這個問題的。

....

引述他人話語

I would like to conclude my presentation, not in my own words but in those of a great emancipator, also the President of the United States, Abraham Lincoln, "The best way to predict your future is to create it." Thank you, everyone.

我要結束演說，但不是用我自己的話，而是用一個偉大的解放者，也是美國總統林肯的話，即「預測未來最好的方法便是去創造它。」謝謝各位。

● emancipator (n.) 解放者

Well, before we wrap up the orientation, I'd like to share what Coco Chanel used to say to the people she worked with: "In order to be irreplaceable one must always be different." I wish you all the best. Welcome aboard.

好，在結束新進員工座談之前，我想引用服裝設計師可可‧香奈兒曾向她員工所說的話，即「一個人若要具有不可取代性，便必須永遠與眾不同。」祝您好運。歡迎加入本公司。　　　　● orientation (n.) 新人培訓　irreplaceable (adj.) 不可替代的

預測未來

Based on my analysis today, I am sad to say that acts of terrorism both large and small will be coming at us in unexpected ways we can't yet even imagine.

根據我今天所做的分析，我很難過地說，恐怖主義或大或小的攻擊將會以我們無法想像的方式朝著我們而來。

● terrorism (n.) 恐怖主義　come at someone 向（某人）逼近

What will the future hold for us if voters choose to vote for an extreme right-wing party? I'm confident to say that this country will be torn by division and will never move forward.

如果投票者選擇投給極右政黨，那我們的未來將會是如何呢？我可以很有自信地說，這個國家將會分裂，而且永遠無法進步。　　● tear (v.) 撕裂　division (n.) 分歧

　　關於「預測未來」的英文說法，本書在 Chapter 6, Unit 1「解釋圖表三步驟」中，會做更詳細且更完整的介紹 (p. 191)；當然，你也可以視需要先行研讀。

引用他人話語

🎧 MP3 **36**

　　簡報時有時會引用他人的話語，而且引用時一字不改。這時為了讓聽眾知道所引用的話語何時開始與何時結束，你可以在要引用的話語之前說 quote（開始引語），並在引用的話語結束後說 unquote（結束引語），這樣聽眾便明白這兩個字之間的東西就是你引用的話。舉例來說，在下面的例子中，口語上你可以這麼說（紅字處便是 quote 和 unquote 這兩個字使用的時機）。

> I would like to conclude my presentation, not in my own words but in those of a great emancipator, also the President of the United States, Abraham Lincoln, quote, the best way to predict your future is to create it, unquote. Thank you, everyone.

> Well, before we wrap up the orientation, I'd like to share what Coco Chanel used to say to the people she worked with, quote, in order to be irreplaceable one must always be different, unquote. I wish you all the best. Welcome aboard.

　　在實際簡報中，有些講者會只說 quote，而省略其後的 unquote 這個字。另外，有些講者會因為所要引用的話語很短（例如只有一句話），而省略了 quote 及 unquote 這兩個字。也有些講者會在引用話語時在聲音上做些變化（例如改變說話速度或聲調），或者乾脆將所引用的話顯示在投影片上，讓聽眾知道其正在引用話語。以上這些都是可行的方式，但為了保險起見，在正式場合中建議還是同時使用 quote 及 unquote 這兩個字。

要注意的是，有些講者會在引用他人話語時，以雙手做出「引號」的手勢（見下圖），以此代表自己正在引用話語，這是不適當的。爲什麼呢？其實這種手勢稱爲 air quote（引號手勢，空中引號），通常用來表示諷刺、挖苦或嘲弄，或表示所說的話帶有其他意思，因此不能使用在引用他人話語時，千萬別誤用！

引號手勢

一般英語簡報都會有「問答時段」(Q&A session)，一個好的 Q&A session 可以讓整體簡報加分，有時簡報最精彩的部分甚至就是在 Q&A session！這也是爲什麼目前一些西方的簡報都盡量縮短講者演說時間，留下充分的時間讓聽衆進行問答。

不過提到 Q&A session，多數講者都認爲這個部分的難度很高，因爲比較無法掌控聽衆的問題，也無從準備起，尤其如果必須以非母語的英語回應，通常會讓講者很緊張。但這並不是說你對於 Q&A session 只能聽天由命；要讓自己在 Q&A session 顯得專業，你可以在準備簡報內容時便先預期 (anticipate) 聽衆可能會問的問題，並將答案準備好，屆時若剛好被問到相同或相關的問題，便能從容不迫地回答。

至於 Q&A session 應該在何時進行？答案是「不一定」。一般而言，在場地較大或人數較多的場合中，你最好在簡報結束後再一併回答問題，以免場面顯得混亂。反之，在場地較小或人數不多的場合，因爲較具親密感，最好讓聽衆隨時發問，如此才不會顯得無禮或專橫。

此外，如果簡報時間較短，通常會統一在最後讓聽衆提問，反之，如果簡報時間較長，則可考慮讓聽衆隨時提問，不過如果是讓聽衆隨時發問，最好說明並限制問題數量及篇幅，不然有時聽衆的問題過於複雜，會讓你花太多時間回答，反而打斷簡報的流暢度。

真人重點示範影片 9
YouTube 搜尋作者和書名

還要注意的是，根據簡報類型的不同，Q&A session 進行的時機也可能會不同。如果是資訊型的簡報，你可以在結論前便開放提問，如此可以確保聽眾都了解簡報所提供的資訊內容。反之，如果是說服型的簡報（例如期望改變聽眾的觀念或希望聽眾採取某種行動等），那麼最好在簡報結束前再開放提問。

當然，你也可以根據個人習慣或喜好的不同決定 Q&A session 進行的時機；但無論如何，最好事先說明清楚，讓聽眾提問時有所依據。這裡要特別注意的是，身為講者的你擁有 Q&A session 的主導權，因此必須掌控好時間，並讓 Q&A session 順利進行。其次，當聽眾提問時不要打斷，儘管你可能已經預期到對方提問的內容，但還是應讓對方問完，這樣不只是尊重發問者，也是尊重其他聽眾。

 MP3 **37**

1 告知聽眾提問時機

I'll take questions at the end of my talk.
我會在談話接近尾聲時接受提問。

I'll answer questions at the end of the presentation.
我會在簡報最後回答問題。

If you have questions, please hold them until I have finished.
如果您有問題，請留到我結束時再發問。

Do you mind if I take questions at the end of my briefing?
您介意我在簡報結束後才接受提問嗎？
● briefing (n.) 簡報

I can take questions at any time.
我在任何時候都接受提問。

Don't hesitate to interrupt me at any time if you have questions.
別猶豫，如果有問題想問的話，可以隨時打斷我。

Feel free to stop me whenever you like if you have a question or comment.
如果您在任何時候有問題或想法的話，都可以打斷我。
● comment (n.) 評論

If you want to ask about anything, just let me know as I go along.
如果您有任何事情想問的話，在我簡報過程中讓我知道即可。
● go along 進行

I'm sure my talk will generate questions. Interrupt at any time if need be.
我相信我的談話會激發出問題。如果有需要，可隨時打斷我。

🎧 MP3 **38**

2　請聽眾開始提問

暗示簡報結束

I think I'll close here.
我想我就此結束。

I'd like to stop here.
我想在此打住。

Thank you for your attention.
謝謝您的聆聽。

That concludes my talk for today.
以上是我今天的談話。

This is a good time to end my part of the presentation.
現在是結束我這部分簡報的好時機。

Now, this brings me to the end of my presentation.
現在到我結束簡報了。

邀請聽眾提問

Are there any questions?
有任何問題嗎？

Do you have any suggestions?
您有任何建議嗎？

Does anyone have any questions?
有人有任何問題嗎？

If you have any questions, I'd be happy to answer them now.
如果您有任何問題，我現在很樂意回答。

Now, I'd like to take a few moments to answer your questions.
現在我想花點時間回答您的問題。

I'd be glad to answer any question you might have.
我會很樂意回答您的任何問題。

Please raise your hand if you have questions.
如果您有問題的話，請舉手發問。

I'd like to open things up for questions and discussion.
我想開放提問和討論。

　　進行 Q&A session 中，在聽眾問完問題時，為表示禮貌，你不妨謝謝聽眾的提問。此外，若聽眾提問的聲音很小聲，你可以重複一次他 / 她的問題，以便讓所有聽眾都能聽清楚。再者，如果你聽不到聽眾的問題或不清楚聽眾的提問重點，應該再次向聽眾確認，千萬不要題目沒聽清楚就急著回答，以免答非所問。下面提供一些相關用語或說法。

🎧 MP3 **39**

3　感謝聽眾提問

Thank you for your question.
謝謝您的問題。

That's a very good question.
那是個很好的問題。

You have asked an important question.
您問了一個很重要的問題。

You have brought up an interesting point.
您提出了一個有趣的觀點。　　　　　　　● bring up... 提出…

Let me explain more.
讓我進一步解釋。

Let me see if I can clarify it for you.
讓我看看是否能為您解惑。　　　　　　　● clarify (v.) 闡明

I'll try to explain it in layman's terms.
我會嘗試用一般人的說法解釋看看。　● layman (n.) 外行人　term (n.) 措辭，術語

I'm afraid I didn't explain that clearly. Perhaps an example will help clarify that.
恐怕我沒有將那件事解釋清楚。或許舉個例子會有助於闡明那件事。

🎧 MP3 **40**

4 聽不懂聽眾的問題時

Would you say that again, please?
能否請您再說一遍？

158

Would you mind repeating your question?
您介意重複您的問題嗎？

Sorry, I didn't quite catch that.
抱歉，我沒有聽得很懂（您的問題）。

Sorry, I don't quite know what you mean.
抱歉，我不太清楚您的意思。

Would you be a bit more specific?
您能否說得更明確一點？

Sorry, could you repeat the question? I couldn't quite hear you.
抱歉，能否請您重述一次問題？我聽不太到您所說的話。

🎧 MP3 **41**

5　確認聽眾的問題

Did I hear you correctly?
對於您的問題我有聽對嗎？

You said "endangered species," what animal are you referring to?
您提到「瀕臨絕種物種」，您指的是什麼動物呢？

When you said "the future," do you mean the near future or the long term?
當您說「未來」，您是指不久的未來還是長久的未來？

By "next decade," do you mean early or late in the next ten years?

您說「下個十年」，您是說下個十年的前半段或後半段？　　　● decade (n.) 十年

6 向聽眾坦承不會回答

Sorry, I have no idea.

抱歉，我完全沒概念。

I'm sorry, but I don't know the answer.

抱歉，我不知道答案。

That's a good question. You got me.

那是個好問題。您問倒我了。　　　● get (v.) 把⋯難倒

I could probably guess, but honestly I don't know the exact figure.

我可以試著猜猜，但老實說我不知道確切的數字。

To be honest, I'm not sure about the specs for that product.

老實說，我不確定那個產品的規格。

I'm not an expert on that subject, but I can forward your questions to my boss/colleague.

我不是那個主題的專家，但我可以將您的問題轉給我的老闆 / 同事。

MP3 **43**

7 無法及時回答時

Well, let me see...
嗯，讓我想想……
　說明　注意這裡的「...」表示語氣停頓。

Mmm ... interesting question...
嗯……這是個有意思的問題……
　說明　注意這裡的「...」表示語氣停頓。

Would you give me a minute to think about that?
能否給我一點時間思考一下那個問題呢？

That's a difficult question. Can I have a minute to think?
這個問題有點難。能否讓我想一下呢？

I'm afraid I can't answer your question off the top of my head.
我恐怕無法馬上回答您的問題。
　說明　off the top of one's head 是慣用語，意指「未經過仔細考慮或計算」，在這裡是表示講者無法馬上想出答案。

Let me talk to my supervisor and get back to you later.
讓我和上司談談後再回覆您。

I'll get in touch with you after looking into it more closely.
等我仔細研究後再與您聯絡。　　　● get in touch with... 與…聯絡　look into... 研究…

I don't know offhand, but maybe I can check and get back to you later?

我現在不知道答案，但或許我可以查過後晚點給您答覆？　●offhand (adv.) 立即

I'm afraid I don't have that information. But if you leave your e-mail address with me, I'll get back to you on that.

我恐怕沒有那項資訊。不過如果您將電子郵件留給我，我之後會回覆您。

I can't answer that question at the moment, but I can get the answer for you later. Can you leave your cellphone number with me?

我現在無法回答那個問題，但我可以稍後給您答覆。能否請您留您的手機號碼給我？

I'm not sure I completely understand your question. Perhaps we could discuss this face to face after the session.

我不確定是否有完全了解您的問題。或許我們可以會後當面討論一下？

 MP3 **44**

8 向聽眾確認回答是否妥當

Is that OK?

這樣回答可以嗎？

Are you clear now?

您現在清楚了嗎？

Does that answer your question?

我有回答到您的問題嗎？

Have I explained that clearly?

我有解釋清楚了嗎？

9 （不）同意聽眾的提問或意見

表示同意

You can say that again.

您說得沒錯。

I completely agree with you.

我完全同意您。

I accept your view without reservation.

我毫無保留地同意您的看法。　　　　　　　　　　　• reservation (n.) 保留

I'm inclined to agree with you.

我傾向同意您的看法。　　　　　　　　　　　• be inclined to... 傾向…

表示不同意

I don't agree with you on that.

那件事我不同意您的看法。

I'm afraid I have to disagree with you.

我恐怕無法同意您的看法。

Are you sure you have all the facts?
您確定已經有全面性的資料了嗎？

I'm sorry, but I can't accept your view.
抱歉，我無法接受您的看法。

I have some doubts about what you're saying.
我對於您所說的話有些疑慮。

I see what you mean, but I don't agree with you on a few points.
我了解您的意思，不過有幾點我無法同意。

I see your point, but have you considered the other side of the argument?
我了解您的觀點，不過您是否有考慮過另一方的論點呢？

I think we are at an impasse. Can we just agree to disagree on this issue?
我想我們是在死胡同裡打轉。在這個議題上，我們能否同意保留各自的意見呢？

說明　agree to disagree 是慣用語，用在兩方意見不同且無法達成共識時，意味雙方接受意見紛歧的事實，保留各自意見，亦即建立一個求同存異的管道。

● impasse (n.) 僵局

I can't go along with that for two reasons. First,... Second,...
那件事我有兩點理由無法同意。第一，……。第二，……　● go along 同意

10 回應無關或不必要的問題

It's not clear to me how this is related to our topic.
我不太清楚這個和我們的主題有什麼關聯。

I'm sorry, but this has little to do with our agenda today.
抱歉,這個和我們今天的議程沒什麼關係。

It doesn't have anything to do with the topic.
這個和主題沒有任何關聯。

說明 這種說法稍嫌直接,可能會使提問者不快,建議盡量避免。

Let's discuss it sometime later.
我們之後再討論這個吧。

I'm not in a position to comment on that.
我對那件事沒有立場發表意見。　　　　　　　　　　● position (n.) 立場

Why don't we put this issue to the side for now?
我們目前何不先將這個議題擱置一邊呢?

MP3 **47**

11 深入說明聽眾的問題

Why don't we go into the details now?
我們現在何不談談細節?

I can illustrate this by giving you another example.

我可以舉另一個例子來向您說明。
● illustrate (v.) 說明

....

Let me expand on some of the main points in our findings.

讓我闡述我們調查結果的一些要點。

....

Let me go into more detail about the learning strategy you mentioned.

關於您提到的學習策略，讓我更詳細解釋一下。

....

Let me tell you more about the adoption process you mentioned.

讓我告訴您更多關於您提到的領養程序。
● adoption (n.) 領養，收養

....

I'd like to clarify this point by referring to the chart on page 3 of the handouts.

我想藉由講義第三頁的圖表來澄清這一點。

....

Some additional background on this topic may help to clarify the point I'm trying to make.

關於這個主題的額外背景資訊，應該可以釐清我想要說的論點。

....

I'd like to expand on what I said about...

我想要闡述一下我說的有關……

....

I can further explain this by using ... as an example.

我可以進一步用……當作例子來解釋。

....

Perhaps I didn't make myself clear. What I meant to say was...

或許我沒有講得很清楚。我想說的是……

....

While we're on the subject of..., it's worth mentioning that ～
既然我們在……的話題上，值得一提的是～

Although it's not on the agenda, now that you've asked, I'd like to touch on the issue of...
雖然這個不在議程中，既然您問了，我想簡單談一下……的議題。

12　回應聽眾提問的其他說法

Let me rephrase that.
讓我換個說法。

● rephrase (v.) 將…重新表述

Let me put it another way.
讓我換另一種方式說。

I'd like to make one thing clear.
我想將某事說清楚。

I was just about to talk about that.
我正要講那件事。

I was just going to explain that.
我正要解釋那個。

Does anyone have a different opinion?
有人有不同的意見嗎？

Let me take this back to my office.
讓我將這個議題帶回辦公室詢問一下。

This is not a decision that I can make by myself.
這不是我個人可以做的決定。

We will get back to this issue later, so please let me finish.
我們晚點會再談到這個議題,所以請先讓我說完。

This question has a complex answer. My understanding is that...
這個問題的答案很複雜。我的理解是⋯⋯

結束了 Q&A session，簡報到此進入尾聲。這時候你應該尊重主辦單位的安排，在預定時間內結束整個簡報。有時候 Q&A session 會因為聽眾提問熱烈而延長，這時更應該向聽眾暗示簡報即將結束，而不是讓時間無限制地延長。

 MP3 **49**

1 暗示準備結束 Q&A session

There's not much time left.
沒剩多少時間了。

We only have until three o'clock.
我們的時間只到三點。

Let's call it a day.
我們結束吧。　　　　　　　　　　　　　　　　● call it a day 結束

Why don't we stop here?
我們何不就此結束呢？

Why don't we wrap up for today?
我們今天何不就此結束呢？　　　　　　　　　　● wrap up 結束

Let's go over what we've agreed on and then finish up here.
讓我們重新檢視彼此同意的地方，然後就結束吧。　● go over... 仔細檢查…

Any more questions? No? Well, in that case, thank you again for your attention.
還有問題嗎？沒有？嗯，那麼再次感謝您的聆聽。

....

Any other questions? No? OK then. Thanks for your interest in our product.
還有任何其他問題嗎？沒有？那好，謝謝您對本公司的產品有興趣。

....

If you have more questions, I would be happy to stay and answer them.
如果您還有問題的話，我很樂意留下來回答。

....

I'm happy to stay if there are any further questions. If not, I'll end here.
如果還有其他問題的話，我很樂意留下來。如果沒有，那我就此結束。

....

MP3 50

2　簡報結束時表示感謝

Thanks for coming tonight.
謝謝各位今晚的出席。

....

Thank you for being here today.
謝謝您今天的出席。

....

Thank you for having me this afternoon.
謝謝各位今天下午邀請我來。

....

It was my pleasure to be here today.

今天很高興能來到這裡。

I really enjoyed being here today. Thank you.

我今天真的很高興來到這裡。謝謝。

I'd like to thank you for giving me so much of your time.

感謝您給我這麼多時間做簡報。

I'd like to thank you for your input today. It has been very beneficial.

我感謝您今天的建議，這非常有幫助。　　　　● input (n.)（意見、資訊等的）投入

Once again, I want to extend my thanks to all of you for coming here this evening.

我想再次表達我對您今晚出席的謝意。

Thank you all very much for your attention, and I look forward to seeing you again.

非常感謝您的聆聽，我期待再次見到您。

I'm sorry for taking up so much of your time. You have my deepest gratitude.

占用您這麼多時間真是抱歉。我由衷地表示感謝。

說明　這句話通常用於講者占用太多會議時間（例如簡報長度遠超過原本表定時間），因而造成聽眾不便時。　　　　● take up... 占用（時間等）　gratitude (n.) 感謝

將聽眾的問題分類

在本章中，我們提到對講者而言，Q&A session 通常是最具挑戰性的部分，因為你無法完全預期聽眾會問什麼問題。不過聽眾的問題雖然難以預測，卻通常可以歸納成以下四大類。

1. 好的問題 (good question)

這類問題除了可以讓你再次闡述你的簡報重點，還能幫助你將想法更清楚地傳達給聽眾，甚至補充先前簡報內容的不足之處。

2. 困難的問題 (difficult question)

這類問題通常因為有難度，所以你可能會不知道答案，或無法當下立即回答。若遇到不知道答案的問題，最好誠實告知聽眾，並尋求其他方式以便日後回答。若無法當下立即回答，可以請聽眾給予你時間思考，或者也可以先反問提問者或詢問其他聽眾有無答案或想法，從中汲取靈感，以便提供提問者一些可以得到解答的方式。

3. 不相關或不必要的問題 (unrelated or unnecessary question)

這類問題之所以被提出，通常是因為提問者沒聽清楚你的簡報內容，或者你已經回答過此問題，又或者問題與簡報主題無關等。對於這類問題，你可以向提問者暗示自己並不需要回答。

4. 有敵意的問題 (hostile question)

這類問題通常出現在說服型的簡報中，因為提問者對議題有強烈意見，因此容易提出帶有敵意的問題。遇到這種情況時，你可以拒絕回答提問者的問題，並繼續做簡報或回答其他提問者的問題。切記此時千萬不能被激怒，仍必須保持風度和禮貌。

　　身為講者的你若能事先釐清聽眾的問題是屬於哪一類，便能比較容易決定臨場要如何回答。

Chapter 6
介紹並說明圖表

Unit 1 解釋圖表三步驟

Unit 2 各類型圖表介紹與說明

Unit 3 圖表相關用語

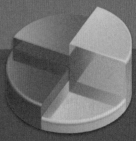

English Public Speaking
and Presentation

A picture is worth a thousand words.

—English proverb

一圖勝千言。

——英文諺語

以上的諺語說明了圖片力量的強大，有時甚至遠遠超過文字！運用在簡報中，圖片最大的優勢便在於將複雜的資訊視覺化，使之明白易懂，便於聽眾理解。

根據一項統計，在演說的場合，若資訊是以純粹口說的方式呈現，一天過後，聽眾大約只會記得所有內容的 10%，但若口說時有圖片搭配，聽眾記得的內容則上升到 65% 以上，很驚人吧？由此可知口說與圖片的結合力量有多強大；當然，若你能適時加上相關的影片 (video) 或動畫 (animation)，更能大大幫助記憶，讓聽眾甚至在一年後都能記起當初所接收到的資訊。

圖片的功能究竟多強大？以下幾張圖片可以提供你一點概念。首先請你先想想這三張圖片可能的主題 (topic) 及欲傳達的訊息 (message)。

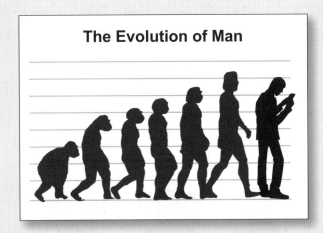

這張圖片的主題並非如圖中文字所顯示的 the evolution of man（人類的進化），而是現代人對手機的沉迷 (smartphone addiction)。其所要傳達的訊息是，如果人類一直低頭使用手機，總有一天便會退化到早期人類彎腰駝背的樣態。如果你在講述與手機成癮相關的主題時搭配這張圖片，相信無須多言，聽眾都會會心一笑。

圖片 2

這張圖片的主題是有關大陸一胎化政策 (one child policy) 對社會的影響，你在講述此一主題時，若能在人口結構、養老、社會與經濟安全等嚴肅議題中搭配這張圖片，相信聽眾都能對此一政策所造成的影響有更深刻的體會。

圖片 3

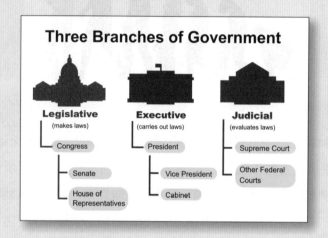

　　這張圖片的主題是關於美國政府立法 (legislative)、行政 (executive)、司法 (judicial) 三權分立及其職責。這樣一個複雜的主題若你只用口語說明，效果必定不佳，但如果能搭配這張清楚易懂的圖片說明，聽眾的理解力便可大大提升。

　　事實上，圖片和表格的種類繁多，簡報中根據性質、形式及主題的不同，所使用的圖表也會不同，你應該慎選，以期將簡報的效果最大化。本章首先介紹講者解釋圖表時必須遵循的三大步驟，並提示各類型圖表在介紹與說明時的技巧與用法，最後提供更多圖表實際的用語，供你運用於簡報實務上。現在就讓我們一起來學習！

　　本章在一開始時提到圖表力量很強大，可以幫助你將複雜且狀似雜亂無章的資訊做系統性的整理，讓聽眾易於理解並印象深刻。然而水能載舟，亦能覆舟，如果你無法將圖表解釋清楚，便會讓聽眾聽得一頭霧水，反而造成反效果。

　　一般來說，講者在使用圖表時最常犯的錯誤是「不多加解釋，草草帶過」。別忘了聽眾是第一次看到此圖表，因此必須仰賴你來獲得圖表的所有資訊。因此身為負責任的講者，你必須仔細解釋每張圖表及其所欲傳達的訊息。

　　一般來說，解釋圖表內容時通常包含以下三個步驟。

Step 1 做整體介紹	◉ 說明圖表類型、主題及內容概要、資料來源等
Step 2 描述與解說	◉ 描述圖表概況、說明圖例並解說順序、描述並解釋圖表
Step 3 提出見解	◉ 說明發生原因、做出評析、預測未來

　　請注意：根據圖表的不同，這三個步驟不一定完全適用，且順序也可能有所變動，例如你可能在一句話中即包含 Step 1 與 Step 2，或者 Step 2 與 Step 3，端視情況而定。

真人重點示範影片 10
YouTube 搜尋作者和書名

此外，在這三個步驟中，Step 1 與 Step 2 是你必須盡到的「基本」責任，Step 3 則是你身為講者的「價值」所在，亦即你個人對圖表的詮釋（包含說明發生原因、做出評析、預測未來等），這是聽眾最需要得到的資訊，因此建議你盡量將這部分的篇幅加大，並且充實這部分的內容。

以下是這二大步驟的相關用語，請務必學起來！

1 做整體介紹

說明圖表類型

This chart shows the life cycle of a butterfly.
這張圖顯示出蝴蝶的生命週期。

Please take a look at the bar graph on this slide.
請看這張投影片上的條形圖。

We can see from the timetable that...
我們可以從這張時刻表看出……

The diagram shows/describes/illustrates...
這張圖表顯示／描述／說明……

Figure 4 gives the results of the experiment.
圖表四是實驗結果。

The three kinds of buildings are depicted on this slide.
這張投影片描繪了這三種建築物。
● depict (v.) 描繪

This line graph shows total sales on a weekly basis.
這張線圖顯示出每週的銷售總額。

Let me share with you a chart that shows our sales trends for last year.
讓我跟您分享一個顯示我們去年銷售趨勢的圖表。

The next picture may be able to explain the phenomenon in more detail.
下一張圖片或許能夠將這種現象解釋得更清楚。

說明主題及內容概要

This table shows a detailed schedule for the plant construction.
這張表格顯示出工廠建造的詳細時程表。
● plant (n.) 工廠

This slide shows the relationship between gender and suicide behavior in Finland.
這張投影片顯示出芬蘭的性別與自殺行為之間的關係。

This chart shows the percentage of population by age group around the globe.
這張圖表顯示出全球各地人口按年齡所占的百分比。
● percentage (n.) 百分比

This is a pie chart showing the smartphone market share in China in the second quarter.
這是一張餅圖,顯示出第二季中國智慧型手機的市占率。

This bar chart shows the number of people visiting Taiwan in the last decade.

這張條形圖顯示出過去十年造訪台灣的人數。

For your reference, please take a look at this bar chart that shows our profits over the last fiscal quarter.

為了供您參考，請看這張條形圖，顯示出我們在上個財政季度的利潤。

● fiscal (adj.) 財政的

Please take a look at the diagram or refer to it in the back of your handouts for a detailed breakdown of the project.

關於這項專案的詳細分項，請看一下這張圖表，或翻到您講義的後面。

● refer to... 參考…　breakdown (n.) 分類

This line chart shows the number of new immigrants, or so-called "foreign brides," in Taiwan from 2001 to 2015.

這張線圖顯示出從 2001 年到 2015 年的新移民，或所謂的「外籍新娘」，在台灣的人數。　　　　● so-called (adj.) 所謂的

The table on this slide shows the comparison between our best-selling product Airfryer and our biggest competitor's Actifry.

這張投影片上的表格顯示出我們最暢銷的產品 Airfryer 與我們最大競爭對手 Actifry 比較的情況。　　● best-selling (adj.) 暢銷的　competitor (n.) 競爭者

To understand how light travels through human eyes, please take a look at this slide titled "The Structure of the Human Eye."

要了解光線如何穿越人的眼睛，請看這張名為「人眼構造」的投影片。

● title (v.) 為…加上標題

This line chart illustrates the market share of different search engines in the United States as measured by search queries.

這張線圖顯示出將美國各個不同搜尋引擎進行搜索查詢後，所測量出來的市占率。

● query (n.) 查詢

If you are ready to add a new member to your family, please pay attention to this chart illustrating the process of adopting a dog.

若您已經準備好增添家中的新成員，請注意這張用來說明領養小狗的流程圖。

This pyramid-shaped diagram represents the optimal number of servings to be eaten each day from each of the basic food groups in order to have a healthy diet.

這張金字塔圖代表了為了擁有健康飲食，每天必須攝取的每個基本食物群組的最佳份數。

● pyramid (n.) 金字塔　optimal (adj.) 最適宜的

Let's take a look at this industry profile pie chart. It's about the composition of the Toronto food and beverage processing industry by subsectors.

讓我們看看這個產業概況的餅圖。這是由多倫多食品飲品加工業的分部門所組成的。

● profile (n.) 概況　composition (n.) 組合　subsector (n.) 分部門，次部門

In order to understand how well Google is doing, we can first take a look at the market value of the largest Internet companies in the world. This slide shows the ranking of the 15 most valuable Internet companies by market capitalization.

為了了解谷歌是如何地成功，我們可以先看看這些世界上最大的網路公司的市值。這張投影片顯示了前 15 家最有價值的網路公司的總市值。

● ranking (n.) 排名　capitalization (n.) 資本估價

To illustrate how women are under-represented in higher-status, higher-paying occupations, let's take a look at this bar chart. This is the average earnings for full-time, year-round male and female workers by their education attainment.

為了說明女性在高地位、高所得職業中的比例是如何地低，讓我們來看看這張條形圖。這是全職且整年工作的男性和女性員工根據其教育程度所區分的平均收入。

● year-round (adj.) 整年的　attainment (n.) 成就

說明資料來源

This data was provided by the Ministry of Labor in 2015.

這份資料是 2015 年由勞工部提供的。

● ministry (n.)（政府的）部

The information is courtesy of the Office of Trade and Industry.

這項資訊來自於貿易及產業辦公室。

● courtesy of... 蒙…提供

The data is provided by the United Nations secretariat.

這份資料是由聯合國祕書處提供的。

● secretariat (n.) 祕書處

You can find this exact timetable on our website.

您可以在我們的網站上找到一模一樣的時刻表。

The data was obtained from Taiwan's Ministry of the Interior last month.

這份資料是上個月從台灣內政部取得的。

● interior (n.) 內部

I obtained this data from an online survey institute called Cellphone Today.

我是從一個名為 Cellphone Today 的線上調查機構得到這份資料。

2 描述與解說

描述圖表概況

The vertical axis shows millions of units sold.
縱軸（Y 軸）顯示以百萬為單位的銷售數額。　● vertical (adj.) 垂直的　axis (n.) 軸線

The horizontal axis represents the sales quarters.
橫軸（X 軸）代表銷售的季度。　● horizontal (adj.) 水平的

The X-axis shows the month and year.
X 軸顯示月分及年分。

The Y-axis represents the number of companies in thousands.
Y 軸代表以千為單位的公司數量。

The column in Table 4 shows the item numbers.
表格四的這個欄位顯示貨品號碼。　● item (n.) 一件商品

From the statistics given in the table, it can be seen that…
從這張表格的統計數據可以知道……　● statistic (n.) 統計數據

The X-axis represents the year, from 1990 to 2007, while the Y-axis shows the percentage of Americans who are obese.
X 軸代表從 1990 年到 2007 年的年分，Y 軸則顯示美國肥胖人口的百分比。

● obese (adj.) 肥胖的

On your left is the list of company names, and the market value of each company is shown on your right in billions of US dollars.

在您左邊的是公司名稱。在您右邊的是每家公司的市場價值，以十億美元爲單位顯示。

說明圖例

As the legend on the left indicates, the navy bar represents male and the red female.

如左邊的圖例所示，深藍色條形物代表男性、紅色（條形物）代表女性。

● legend (n.) 圖例 (= key)　navy (adj.) 深藍色的

The line with solid dots represents males while the line with hollow dots represents females.

有實心點的線代表男性，有空心點的線代表女性。

● solid (adj.) 實心的　hollow (adj.) 空心的

On the top of the chart, you can see the legend, with the blue line representing company A, black B, gray C, and red D.

您在圖表上方可以看到圖例，其中藍線代表 A 公司，黑線代表 B 公司，灰線代表 C 公司，紅線代表 D 公司。

The different colored segments represent the different smartphone brands that are currently selling in China.

（在這張餅圖中）不同的扇形顏色代表目前在中國銷售的智慧型手機品牌。

● segment (n.) 部分，切片

說明解說順序

I'll move counterclockwise in explaining the process of adopting a dog.

我會按逆時針方向解釋領養小狗的過程。　● counterclockwise (adv.) 逆時針方向地

I'm going to explain this diagram by beginning with the outer structure and moving to the inner structure.

我將從這張圖表的外部結構開始解釋，然後往內部結構移動。

I'll move from the upper left(-hand) corner and move clockwise in describing the four stages in a butterfly's life cycle.

我會從左上角按順時針方向移動來描述蝴蝶一生的四個階段。

● upper (adj.) 上方的，上面的　clockwise (adv.) 順時針方向地

As you can see, the food pyramid is divided into four horizontal sections, and I will go from bottom to top in explaining this diagram.

如您所見，食物金字塔被劃分成四個水平部分，我將從這張圖表的底部解釋到頂部。

● pyramid (n.) 金字塔

This is a diagram of the cross section of the eye with the front of the eye on the right and the optic nerve on the left. I will go from the right, where the cornea lies, to the left, where the optic nerve is, to describe how exactly light travels.

這是一張眼睛的截面圖，眼睛的前面在圖的右邊，眼睛的視神經在左邊。我會從右邊，也就是角膜所在處，向左邊，也就是視神經所在處，來確切描述光線如何穿越。

● cross section 橫截面　optic (adj.) 視覺的　cornea (n.) 角膜

描述與解說圖表

The pie chart shows that Intel has the largest market share.

這張餅圖顯示出英特爾具有最大的市場占有率。

This shows that consumer spending increased significantly in 2015.

這顯示出消費支出在 2015 年顯著增加。

The sales chart shows a distinct decline in the past few months.
這張銷售圖表顯示出在過去幾個月銷售顯著下降的情況。　　　● distinct (adj.) 顯著的

As revealed by this graph, the defect rate for this product has declined.
如這張圖表所示，這項產品的不良率已經下降了。　　　● defect (n.) 缺陷

This line graph shows the severity of the obesity problem in the United States.
這張線圖顯示出美國肥胖問題的嚴重性。　　● severity (n.) 嚴重性　obesity (n.) 肥胖症

As you can see from the organization chart, we're split into six operational divisions.
從這張組織結構圖可以看到，我們分成六個營運單位。

As can be seen in this figure, 68% of the participants correctly responded to the questions.
從這張圖表可以看到，68% 的參與者都正確回答了問題。

It is obvious that women with the same level of education as men earn less across the board.
很明顯地，教育程度相等的女性整體上都比男性賺得少。

From this chart, we learn that sales were mostly flat in the spring, and then jumped in the summer, but started to drop off in the autumn.
我們從這張圖表得知，銷售在春季大多平平，然後在夏季上升，但是在秋季開始下降。　　　　　　　　　　　　　● drop off 下降

As you can see, the obesity rate has risen from 12% in 2000 to 27% in 2015; it's clear that the obesity rate is on the rise.

如您所見，肥胖率已經從 2000 年的 12% 上升到 2015 年的 27%；肥胖率很明顯地呈現上升趨勢。

As you can see clearly, the male suicide rate is two times higher than that of the female rate throughout the years 1982 to 2015.
您可以清楚地看到，從 1982 年到 2015 年男性的自殺率都高出女性兩倍。

You can see from this chart that there is a tendency for customers to buy expensive products if they are told the items are in a limited edition.
從這張圖表可以看到，顧客傾向買貴的產品，如果他們被告知此產品是限量版的話。

● tendency (n.) 傾向

As you can see, the period from 2007 to 2009 was marked by a steady increase in new immigrant numbers; however, after that, the number has been dropping, with this year, 2016, hitting a record low.
如您所見，2007 年到 2009 年新移民的人數穩定增加；然而，在那之後，人數一直在下降，而在今年 2016 年時創新低。

● hit a record low 跌到歷史新低

 MP3 **53**

3 提出見解

說明發生原因

The increase in sales volume last quarter is the result of a discount in the retail price.
上一季的銷售數量增加是因為零售價格有折扣。

● volume (n.) 數量　retail (adj.) 零售的

The plummeting stock price is due to the fear of political instability in the Middle East.

股票價格的暴跌是由於對中東地區政治不穩定的疑懼。

● plummet (v.) 筆直掉下　instability (n.) 不穩定

There are two reasons for these students' success. One is sufficient family support, and the other is their own hard work.

這些學生的成功有兩個理由。一個是有足夠的家庭支持，另一個是自身的努力。

The reason Xiaomi is now China's biggest smartphone brand is mostly due to its low price.

小米之所以現在是中國最大的智慧型手機品牌，主要是因為價格低廉。

With these popular websites and services to suit web surfers' ever-changing needs, no wonder Google is deemed the Internet giant.

有這些受歡迎的網站和服務以滿足網友不斷變化的需求，難怪谷歌被視為是網際網路巨頭。

● suit (v.) 滿足（需要）　deem (v.) 認為

This sudden rise in profit between the second and third quarters was partly due to our major competitor pulling out of the African market.

第二季和第三季之間獲利突然上升，部分是由於我們主要的競爭對手退出非洲市場。

● pull out... 撤離⋯

做出評析

Obesity is not only serious but also costly in the U.S., and we have to find a way to fight it.

在美國，肥胖不僅是個嚴重的問題，也很耗費醫療資源，我們得想辦法對付它。

This figure shows evidence that supports Dr. Jacobson's theory that high-achieving students usually employ more learning strategies than low-achieving students.

這張圖表顯示出證據支持 Jacobson 博士的理論，即高成就的學生通常比低成就的學生使用更多的學習策略。　●high-achieving (adj.) 高成就的　employ (v.) 使用

From this diagram we learn that to have a healthy diet, we should try to eat a variety of food every day at the right amount.

我們從這張圖表得知，要有健康的飲食，應該試著每天適量地吃各式食物。

From this chart, we are proud to say that our Airfryer is the best fryer on the market, and it will make your life better and a lot easier.

從這張圖表我們可以很自豪地說，我們的 Airfryer 是市場上最佳的油炸機，它會讓您的生活變得更好，也輕鬆得多。

This huge salary gap clearly shows that sexism does exist in the workplace, and it's time we did something about it.

此一巨大的薪資差距清楚證明了性別歧視確實存在於職場，而且是該改變這個現況的時候了。　●gap (n.) 差距，隔閡　sexism (n.) 性別歧視

Despite the decrease in numbers, the overwhelming majority of these new immigrants have thus come to form a new demographic in Taiwan.

儘管人數有減少，但這些大量的新移民也因此構成了台灣新的人口結構。

●overwhelming (adj.) 勢不可擋的　demographic (n.) 人口統計（資料）

預測未來

This clearly shows that the world's population is aging, and it may have catastrophic consequences.

這明顯顯示出世界人口正在老化，而且它可能會引起災難性的後果。

●catastrophic (adj.) 災難性的

From this chart we can conclude that Google is the most valuable Internet company and will likely continue to be so for the next 10 years.
從這張圖表我們可以得出結論，谷歌是最有價值的網際網路公司，而且在未來的十年也很可能會如此。

Although the sharp decline during the last two quarters looks pretty scary, such a drop was industry-wide, and it is very unlikely to happen again in the future.
雖然過去兩季急劇下降的情況看起來相當可怕，但這種下降是整體產業的下降，而這種情形不太可能在將來再次發生。

From this figure we know that the number of wild Formosan black bears has been declining. And if we don't start conservation efforts, the species will be extinct in 20 years.
我們從這張圖表得知，野生台灣黑熊的數量一直在下降。而如果我們不開始努力保育，則該物種將在 20 年內滅絕。

●species (n.) 物種　extinct (adj.) 滅絕的

As you can see from the statistics, climate change is the single biggest environmental and humanitarian crisis of our time. If we don't act now to spur the adoption of cleaner energy sources, our future will be at stake.
從這些統計數字可看出，氣候變遷是我們這個時代最大的環境和人道主義危機。若我們不立刻行動來促進清潔能源的採用，未來將岌岌可危。

●humanitarian (adj.) 人道主義的　spur (v.) 推動　energy source 能源
at stake 處於危急關頭

在上個單元中介紹解釋圖表的三個步驟時，提到了一些不同類型的圖表。的確，圖表的類型很多，而且某些種類的圖表特別適合表現特定的資訊，因此使用時必須加以分辨。這個單元則將詳述簡報中常見的各式圖表及其功能、使用時機等，並提供範例讓你好好學習。

 MP3 **54**

1 線圖

線圖 (line graph/line chart) 可以表現數字的消長，因此常常用來顯示某事物隨著時間推移所產生的起伏變化。在簡報中，有關「趨勢」(trend) 的主題最適合使用線圖，例如公司產能增減、金融產品價格起伏、利率變動等。請注意，線圖多以座標 (coordinate) 顯示，但座標的基準不一定要從零「0」開始。

一般而言，說明線圖時通常會涵蓋以下幾個部分：標題、縱軸、橫軸、圖例、資料來源、趨勢解說等。以下提供與線圖相關的常見用語。

You can see the line rises steadily throughout the year 2015.
您可以看到這條線在 2015 年全年穩步上升。

It is apparent from the line chart that the market has been shrinking for three years.
從線圖可以明顯看出，三年來市場一直在萎縮。 ● shrink (v.) 縮小

Let's talk about female workers first, represented here by the solid line.

讓我們先來看看女性員工，即以這條實線來表示。

說明 solid line 是「實線」；broken line 是「虛線」；dotted line 是「點線」。

- -

According to the chart, our profits have risen for the fourth consecutive fiscal quarter.

根據圖表，我們的利潤已經連續四個財政季度上升了。

● profit (n.) 利潤　consecutive (adj.) 連續的

- -

As can be seen from the red line, our expenses for last quarter have risen 35%.

從這條紅線可看出，我們的開銷在上一季增加了 35%。　● expense (n.) 開銷，開支

- -

　　以下提供兩張線圖的範例，各包含一張投影片及其對應的講稿。講稿中所標示的 Step 1, Step 2, Step 3，即為本章 Unit 1 中解釋圖表內容的三個步驟。

Step 1 做整體介紹	● 說明圖表類型、主題及內容概要、資料來源等
Step 2 描述與解說	● 描述圖表概況、說明圖例並解說順序、描述並解釋圖表
Step 3 提出見解	● 說明發生原因、做出評析、預測未來

範例 1

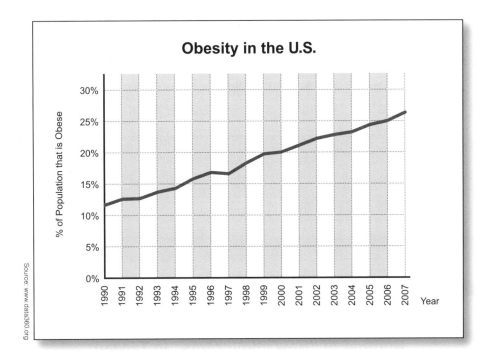

Obesity in the U.S.

% of Population that is Obese

Year

Source: www.data360.org

Step 1 This line graph shows the severity of the obesity problem in the United States. The statistics are obtained from data360. **Step 2** The X-axis represents the year, from 1990 to 2007, while the Y-axis shows the percentage of Americans who are obese. As you can see, the obesity rate has risen from 12% in 1990 to 27% in 2007. This is a 15% increase over the 17-year period. **Step 3** It's clear that the obesity rate is on the rise, and this is alarming. Although this chart only shows statistics up to the year 2007, the trend still continues, and as of 2014, more than one-third, or 78 million Americans are obese. Obesity is not only a serious problem, but also a costly one in the U.S., and we have to find a way to fight it.

這張線圖顯示出美國肥胖問題的嚴重性。這些統計數字取自 data360。X 軸代表從 1990 年到 2007 年的年分，Y 軸則顯示美國人肥胖的百分比。如您所見，肥胖率已從 1990 年的 12% 上升到 2007 年的 27%，在 17 年間增加了 15%。很明顯地，肥胖率呈現上升的趨勢，這十分令人擔憂。雖然這張圖表只顯示到 2007 年的統計數字，但是這個趨勢仍然持續當中，截至 2014 年，超過三分之一，也就是有 7,800 萬美國人罹患肥胖症。在美國，肥胖不僅是個嚴重的問題，也很耗費醫療資源，我們得想辦法對付它。

alarming
(adj.) 使人驚慌的

up to...
直到…

costly
(adj.) 昂貴的

■ 範例 2

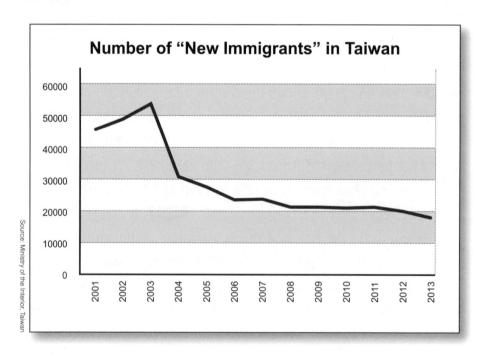

Number of "New Immigrants" in Taiwan

Source: Ministry of the Interior, Taiwan

196

Step 1 This line chart shows the number of new immigrants to Taiwan from 2001 to 2013. Many of these immigrants are so-called "foreign brides." The data was obtained from Taiwan's Ministry of the Interior last month. **Step 2** The X-axis represents the year, and the Y-axis shows the number of new immigrants. As you can see, the years 2001 to 2003 were marked by a steady increase in numbers; however, after that, the number has been dropping, with this year, 2013, hitting a record low. **Step 3** So what caused the influx between 2001 and 2003? It is because of the improvement in the cross-strait relationship and a change in government policies. On the other hand, interviews of newcomers were required from 2003. This measure was implemented to prevent "fake marriages." Since then, the number of new immigrants has gradually decreased. As a matter of fact, in 2003, as many as 3,800 "foreign brides" were forced to return to their homeland because of illegal marriage arrangements. Despite the decrease in numbers, the overwhelming majority of these new immigrants have thus come to form a new demographic in Taiwan.

這張線圖顯示出從 2001 年到 2013 年新移民在台灣的人數。這些新移民很多是所謂的「外籍新娘」。這項資料是上個月從台灣內政部取得的。X 軸代表年分，Y 軸則代表新移民的人數。如您所見，2001 年到 2003 年間數字穩定增加；然而在那之後，人數卻一直在下降，而在今年 2013 年則創下新低。是什麼原因造成 2001 年到 2003 年人口的大量湧入呢？這是因為兩岸關係的改善和政府政策的改變。另一方面，對新移民的面試自 2003 年開始實施。這項措施是為了杜絕「假結婚」。自此之後，新移民的數目已逐漸減少。事

influx
(n.) 流入

strait
(n.) 海峽

newcomer
(n.) 新來的人

illegal
(adj.) 非法的

實上，在 2003 年有多達 3,800 名「外籍新娘」因非法婚姻而被強制遣返。儘管人數有減少，但這些大量的新移民也因此構成了台灣新的人口結構。

解答請見 ▶ p. 312

Exercise MP3 **55**

1. 以下是一張線圖的投影片以及對應的講稿。請在講稿中標示 Step 1, Step 2, Step 3，代表解釋這張圖表內容的三個步驟。

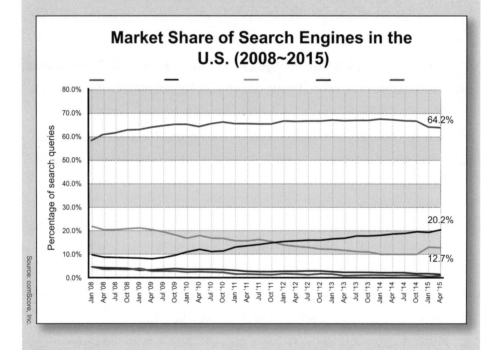

To understand more about the various search engines, please take a look at the statistics shown on this slide. The statistics are from comScore, Inc. This line chart illustrates the market share of different search engines in the United States as measured by search queries. The X-axis shows the quarterly timeline, from 2008 to 2015, and the Y-axis shows the percentage of search queries using each search engine. On the top of the chart, you can see the legend, with the blue line representing Google sites, black Microsoft sites, gray Yahoo, red Ask, and green AOL. As can be seen, it is obvious that Google has been the dominant search engine since 2008. It holds the majority of the market share, with more than 60% of the market most of the time and leaving the remaining four players far behind. Also, another interesting trend to observe is that although Yahoo used to be the second largest search engine, it has been surpassed by Microsoft since October 2011. No matter what, both companies have a lot of catchingup to do in comparison with their biggest rival, Google.

2. 以下是一張線圖的投影片及對應的講稿。請將這七段講稿依正確的順序排列。

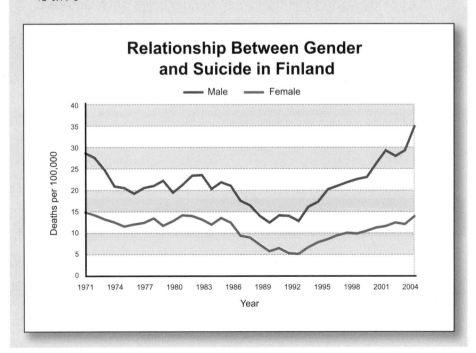

(1) The blue line represents males while the orange represents females.

(2) The second reason is that men usually take more dramatic measures than women when it comes to suicide. In other words, while women tend to show higher rates of non-fatal suicidal behavior, men have a much higher rate of completed suicides.

(3) The horizontal-axis shows the year, and the vertical-axis indicates the suicide rate.

(4) As you can see clearly, the male suicide rate is usually two times higher than the female rate, over the years 1971 to 2004.

(5) This slide shows the relationship between gender and suicide behavior in Finland.

(6) The first is that men usually experience higher levels of stress when trying to fulfill traditional gender roles such as being "emotionally tough" and being the "breadwinner" of the family.

(7) There are two reasons for the gap.

編號順序：_____ → _____ → _____ → _____ → _____ → _____ → _____

MP3 **56**

2 條形圖

　　條形圖 (bar graph/bar chart) 是以條形物 (bar) 的長短來比較事物數量的多寡。條形圖與線圖類似，都可以表現數字消長的趨勢，不過線圖通常含有時間推移的概念，條形圖則比較常用來比較不同事物的實際數量，

因此座標幾乎都是從零「0」開始。要注意的是，條形圖除了顯示整體的數量，還可以同時顯示其中的百分比，通常是顯示在長條的上方，以 % 表示。

　　一般而言，說明條形圖時通常會涵蓋以下幾個部分：標題、橫軸及縱軸、圖例、資料來源、比較、解說等。以下提供與條形圖相關的常見用語。

The final bar, representing last year, reaches $25,000.
最後的條形物代表去年，達到 25,000 美元。

As you can see, the red column in the second quarter was the high point of the year.
如您所見，在第二季的紅色柱狀物是那年的高點。　　　● column (n.) 柱狀物

The black bar depicts forecasted sales, and the shaded bar represents actual sales.
黑色條形物顯示預估的銷售額，灰色條形物則代表實際的銷售額。

● forecast (v.) 預測

In this bar chart, each sport is identified by a different color bar, as you can see in the legend.
如您在這張條形圖的圖例中所見，每項運動都由不同顏色的條形物來表示。

This bar graph reveals the customer ratings for our three product lines, shown in three different colors.
這張條形圖揭示了我們三個產品線的客戶評分，用三種不同的顏色表示。

以下是兩個條形圖的範例，各包含一張投影片及其對應的講稿。同樣地，這裡所標示的 Step 1, Step 2, Step 3，即為解釋圖表內容的三個步驟。

Step 1 做整體介紹	◉ 說明圖表類型、主題及內容概要、資料來源等
Step 2 描述與解說	◉ 描述圖表概況、說明圖例並解說順序、描述並解釋圖表
Step 3 提出見解	◉ 說明發生原因、做出評析、預測未來

範例 1

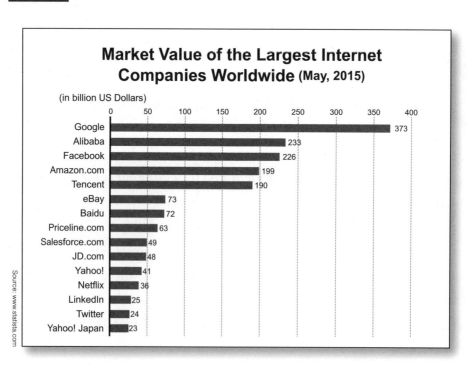

Step 1 In order to understand how well Google is doing, we can first take a look at the market value of the largest Internet companies in the world. This slide shows the ranking of the 15 most valuable Internet companies by market capitalization. **Step 2** On your left is the list of company names. The market value of each company is shown here in billions of US dollars. Apparently, Google comes out on top with market value of 373 billion US dollars, much more than the other Internet companies, including some well-known ones, such as Alibaba, Facebook, Amazon, and Yahoo. **Step 3** Now, please direct your attention to Yahoo. Both Google and Yahoo are portal websites; however, Google's market value is almost nine times as much as that of Yahoo. Isn't that amazing? One thing is for sure: Google must have done something right.

為了了解谷歌是如何地成功，我們可以先看看這些世界上最大網路公司的市值。這張投影片顯示了最有價值的前 15 家網路公司的總市值。在您的左邊是公司名稱。每家公司的市值是以十億美元為單位來顯示。很顯然地，谷歌以 3,730 億美元位居首位，遠遠比其他網路公司的市值高出許多，其中包括一些知名的公司，例如阿里巴巴、臉書、亞馬遜、雅虎等。現在請將注意力轉到雅虎。谷歌和雅虎都是入口網站，然而谷歌的市值幾乎是雅虎的九倍。很不可思議吧？可以肯定的是：谷歌一定是做了什麼正確的事情。

direct
(v.) 把…指向

portal
(n.) 入口

好用句型

Please direct your attention to...
請將注意力移到……

好用句

Now, please direct your attention to Yahoo.
現在請將注意力轉到雅虎。

範例 2

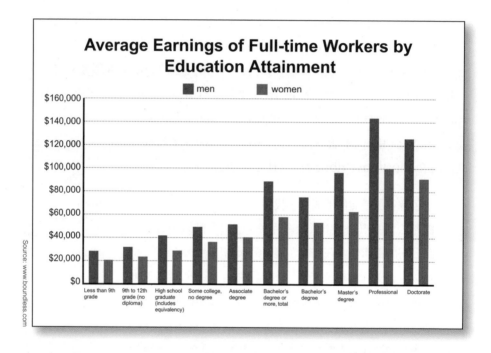

Step 1 To illustrate how women are under-represented in higher-status, higher-paying occupations, let's take a look at this bar chart. This shows the average earnings of full-time, year-round male and female workers by their education level. **Step 2** The X-axis represents different education backgrounds, with lower attainment towards the left and higher attainment towards the right, and the Y-axis is the average salary in US dollars. As the legend on the top

indicates, the blue bar represents male and the red female. `Step 3`
It is troubling to see women with the same level of education as men
earn less across the board. <u>Worse yet,</u> the disparity is even bigger
for women with higher education attainment. This huge gap clearly
shows that sexism does exist in the workplace, and it's time to do
something about it.

為了說明女性在高地位、高所得的職業中的比例是如何地
低，讓我們來看看這張條形圖。這是全職且整年工作的男性
和女性員工根據其教育程度所劃分的平均收入。X軸代表不
同的教育背景，向左代表較低教育程度，向右代表較高程
度，Y軸則是美元的平均工資。如上方的圖例所示，藍色條
形物代表男性、紅色（條形物）代表女性。令人苦惱的是，
教育程度相等的女性整體上都比男性賺得少。更糟的是，這
個差距在女性擁有更高的教育程度時更加明顯。此一巨大差
距清楚地顯示性別歧視確實存在於職場，而且是到了該改變
這個現狀的時候了。

across the board
全面地

disparity
(n.) 懸殊

好用句型

Worse yet,...
更糟的是，……

好用句

Worse yet, the disparity is even bigger for women with higher
education attainment.
更糟的是，這個差距在女性擁有更高的教育程度時更加明顯。

以下是一張條形圖的投影片以及其對應的講稿。請在講稿中標示 Step 1, Step 2, Step 3，代表解釋這張圖表內容的三個步驟。

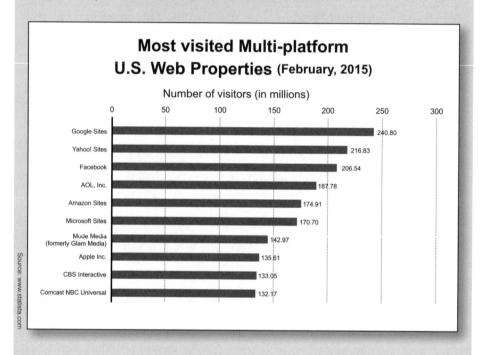

This bar chart shows the number of people visiting different multi-platform U.S. web properties. The information is courtesy of the Office of Trade and Industry. Before we go into the details, let me explain a couple of the terms here. The word "multi-platform" means people visiting websites from different connections such as mobile devices, desktops, laptops, etc. And "web property" means a collection of websites owned by one company. The web properties are listed on the left side of the screen, and the number of web visitors is in millions, and is shown right next to the bars. You can see that Google sites have the most visitors, with more than 240 million, more than Facebook, the most popular social network platform, and Amazon, one of the most popular e-commerce providers. So what are the popular Google online properties besides Google Search? Well, they are the online video platform YouTube, communication services such as Gmail and Hangouts, assorted online services such as Google Maps, Google Play, the app distribution platform, and so on. With these popular websites and services to suit web surfers' ever-changing needs and tastes, no wonder Google is deemed the Internet giant.

MP3 **58**

3 餅圖

餅圖 (pie chart) 通常以百分比的方式呈現，其目的是用來說明與比率有關的事物，例如市占率等。餅圖適用在不同事物的分類，視覺效果好，也清楚易懂，最能表現「部分 vs. 整體」的相對關係。

解說餅圖的內容時，順序通常從 12 點鐘的位置開始，按順時針方向 (clockwise direction) 說明，但若沒有固定的順序時，則可依事物比率的大小，通常從最大比率說到最小比率。此外，餅圖中若有「其他」(other/others) 一項，通常放在最後說明。當然，根據簡報目的及內容的不同，解說順序可以配合講者的需要做變更。以下是與餅圖相關的常見用語。

The red segment represents parents who have more than two children.
紅色部分代表有兩個以上孩子的家長。

Among popular Valentine's Day gift choices, chocolate takes up the largest piece of the pie.

在受歡迎的情人節禮物選項中，巧克力在餅圖上占了最大一塊。

Represented by the yellow wedge, vanilla is the nation's second-most-popular ice cream flavor.

香草由黃色楔形部分表示，它是我國第二最受歡迎的冰淇淋口味。

● wedge (n.) 楔形物　flavor (n.) 口味，味道

Toy-making only occupies a tiny portion, 6%, of the entire manufacturing industry.

玩具製造僅占整個製造業的一小部分，也就是 6%。

Among all the colored shirts at our store, pink is the least favorite color of shoppers who responded to our questionnaire.

根據購物者回應我們的問卷，在我們商店所有的彩色襯衫中，粉紅色是最不受歡迎的顏色。

● questionnaire (n.) 調查問卷

　　以下是兩個餅圖的範例，各包含一張投影片及其對應的講稿。同樣地，這裡所標示的 Step 1, Step 2, Step 3，即為解釋圖表內容的三個步驟。

Step 1
做整體介紹

● 說明圖表類型、主題及內容概要、資料來源等

Step 2
描述與解說

● 描述圖表概況、說明圖例並解說順序、描述並解釋圖表

Step 3
提出見解

◉ 說明發生原因、做出評析、預測未來

範例 1

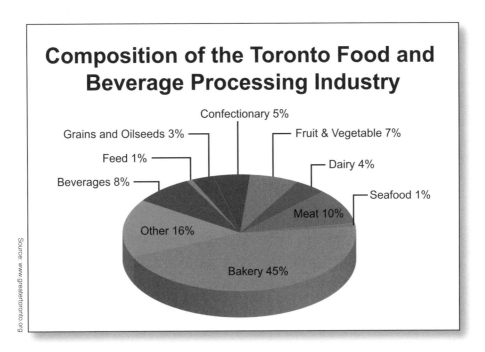

Composition of the Toronto Food and Beverage Processing Industry

Confectionary 5%

Grains and Oilseeds 3%

Fruit & Vegetable 7%

Feed 1%

Dairy 4%

Beverages 8%

Seafood 1%

Meat 10%

Other 16%

Bakery 45%

Source: www.greatertoronto.org

Step 1 Let's take a look at this industry profile pie chart. It shows the composition of the Toronto food and beverage processing industry by subsectors. This data was provided by the Ministry of Labor in 2014. **Step 2** As you all know, Toronto's food and beverage processing industry is one of the largest manufacturing sectors in Canada, and it consists of several subsectors. Among them, the bakery subsector is the biggest one, occupying almost half of the food and beverage processing industry. The second one is meat, occupying 10%, followed by beverages, 8%, and fruit and vegetables, 7%, and so on. **Step 3** The reason the bakery subsector is the biggest is that more than 70% of Canada's top-ranked bakery manufacturers are headquartered in Toronto. You may be surprised to find that seafood only occupies 1% of the processing industry, considering Toronto is such a metropolitan city and people here love seafood. The reason is because Toronto is an inland city and most of the nation's seafood is processed in cities that are adjacent to oceans.

讓我們看看這個產業概況的餅圖。它是由多倫多食品飲品加工業的分部門所組成。這項資料是 2014 年由勞工部所提供的。正如您所知,多倫多的食品飲品加工業是加拿大最大的製造業部門之一,而且它是由若干分部門所組成的。其中,糕餅業是最大的一個,幾乎占食品飲品加工業的一半。第二大的是肉品,占 10%,其次是飲品,占 8%,以及蔬果,占 7% 等。糕餅業是最大分部門的原因在於,加拿大排名最高的糕餅生產商中,有超過 70% 的總部都設在多倫多。考慮到多倫多是一個大都會,而且這裡的人們喜歡吃海鮮,您可能會驚訝地發現海鮮僅占加工行業的 1%。這是因為多倫多是個內陸城市,而且加拿大多數的海鮮加工是在鄰近海洋的城市裡進行。

bakery
(n.) 烘焙坊

headquarter
(v.) 將總部設在

metropolitan
(adj.) 大都市的

inland
(adj.) 內陸的

adjacent
(adj.) 鄰近的

範例 2

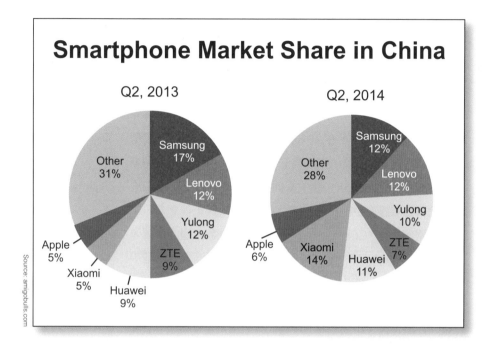

Source: amigobulls.com

Step 1 This is a pie chart showing the smartphone market share in China in the second quarter of 2013 and 2014. I obtained this data from an online survey institute called Cellphone Today. **Step 2** The different colored segments represent the different smartphone brands that are currently selling in China. <u>For the sake of comparison,</u> please focus your attention on only two brands: Samsung and Xiaomi. Let's take a look at the pie chart on your left. Here, in the second quarter of 2013, Xiaomi launched its latest high-end smartphone, gaining 5% of the market share, while Samsung had the largest market share at 17%. However, things were very different even just one year later. In the same quarter in 2014, Xiaomi had taken over the Chinese smartphone market share and outperformed Samsung, 14% versus 12%. **Step 3** Why? How did Xiaomi do it? Well, mostly because of its low price. You see, the quality of the two brands of phones are pretty much the same; however, Xiaomi's phones are only half the price. This is why Xiaomi is now China's biggest smartphone brand.

這是一張餅圖，顯示在 2013 與 2014 年第二季中國智慧型手機的市占率。我從一個名為 Cellphone Today 的線上調查機構得到了這份資料。圖中不同的扇形顏色代表目前在中國銷售的智慧型手機品牌。為了便於比較，請把注意力只集中在兩個品牌：三星和小米。讓我們看看在您左邊的餅圖。這裡，在 2013 年第二季，小米推出了最新的高端智慧型手機，取得了 5% 的市占率，而三星擁有 17% 的最大市占率。然而，情況在僅僅一年後便變得非常不同。在 2014 年同一季，小米攻占了中國智慧型手機的市占率，表現得比三星亮眼，為 14% 比 12%。為什麼呢？小米是如何做到的？其實最主要就是價格低廉。這兩個品牌手機的品質都差不多，然而，小米的手機卻只要一半價格。這就是為什麼小米目前是中國最大的智慧型手機品牌。

launch
(v.) 推出（產品）

high-end
(adj.) 高檔的

take over...
接收…

outperform
(v.)（表現等）
比…好

versus
(prep.) 與…相對
(= vs., v.)

好用句型

For the sake of comparison,...
為了便於比較，……

好用句

For the sake of comparison, **please focus your attention on only two** brands: Samsung and Xiaomi.

爲了便於比較，請把注意力只集中在兩個品牌：三星和小米。

 **Exercise** MP3 **59**

解答請見 ▶ p. 315

以下是一張餅圖的投影片及其對應的講稿。請在講稿中標示 Step 1, Step 2, Step 3，代表解釋這張圖表內容的三個步驟。

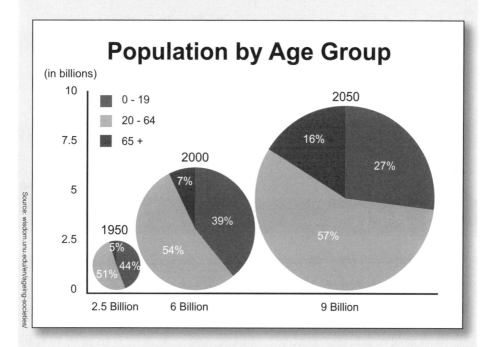

This chart shows the percentage of population by age group around the globe. The data is provided by the United Nations Secretariat. There are three pie charts here representing the world's population in the years 1950 and 2000, and the projected world population in the year 2050. The different colors show the different age groups. For example, blue represents people under the age of 19, and red represents people over 65 years old, as you can see from the legend on the upper left-hand corner. Let's take a look at the smallest pie chart on the left. In 1950, 44% of the world population was under the age of 19, and 5% were over 65. However, if you look at the pie chart on the right, you'll find that in 2050, it is projected that only 27% of the world population will be under 19, and 16% over 65. It is worrisome that as the world's total population is increasing, the percentage of young people is decreasing while the percentage of seniors is increasing. This shows that the world's population is aging, and it may have catastrophic consequences.

4 其他圖表

除了最常見的線圖、條形圖、餅圖，其他一些圖表在英語簡報中也常出現，而且各有各的使用時機與功能。

舉例來說，「表格」(table) 可以讓大量、繁雜的資訊藉由列或排 (row)、欄或行 (column) 的安排而顯得更有條理，例如時刻表、商品規格對照表等。「循環圖」(cycle diagram) 可以表現事物循環的過程，例如商品輸送流程、生命循環等。「流程圖」(process diagram) 可以表現事物的步驟過程，例如政策訂定流程、產品製作過程等。「金字塔圖」(pyramid diagram) 可以顯示具有階層 (hierarchy) 關係的資訊，而其不同大小的

分層也適合顯示與數量相關的概念，例如食物。「結構圖」(structure diagram) 可以表現不同事物從裡到外、從上到下、從左到右等的結構，適合用在事物的剖面圖、公司的組織圖等。

另外，欲製作出更美觀的簡報圖表，除了可以用 PowerPoint 本身附設的功能，還可以借助專業的商業軟體，如 SmartDraw 或 Visio。這類軟體可以幫助沒有高深繪圖知識及技術的講者快速且方便地製作具專業品質的各式圖表。

以下是五種圖表範例，各包含一張投影片及其對應的講稿。同樣地，這裡所標示的 Step 1, Step 2, Step 3，即為解釋圖表內容的三個步驟。

Step 1
做整體介紹

◉ 說明圖表類型、主題及內容概要、資料來源等

Step 2
描述與解說

◉ 描述圖表概況、說明圖例並解說順序、描述並解釋圖表

Step 3
提出見解

◉ 說明發生原因、做出評析、預測未來

A. 表格 (table)

Philips Airfryer vs. Tefal Actifry

	Philips Airfryer	Tefal Actifry
Adjustable Temperature	Yes	No
Auto Shut-Off	Yes	No
Operating Sound	Less noisy	Noisier
Taste & Texture of Food	Juicy & tender	Dry & tough
Average Customer Rating	4.7/5	3.5/5

Source: homekitchenfryer.com

Step 1 The table on this slide shows the comparison between our best-selling product Airfryer and our biggest competitor Actifry. **Step 2** On the left column are the four features for comparison plus the average customer rating. The middle column is our product, and the right column is Actifry. As you can easily see, we have the adjustable temperature and auto shut-off mechanisms while Actifry doesn't. Also, our operating sound is much lower than that of Actifry's. And we outperform on the thing our customers care about the most—the taste and texture of the food. The food made with our fryer is juicy and tender, while theirs is dry and tough. No wonder our customer rating is much higher than theirs. **Step 3** From this chart, we are proud to say that Airfryer is the best fryer on the market, and it will make your life better and a lot easier.

這張投影片上的表格顯示我們最暢銷的產品 Airfryer 與最大競爭對手 Actifry 比較的情況。左邊的欄位是四個供比較的產品特色項目，還有客戶的平均評分。中間的欄位是我們的產品，右邊則是 Actifry。您很容易就可看出，我們有可調節溫度和自動斷電機制，Actifry 卻沒有。還有，我們運轉的聲音也比 Actifry 小很多。而且我們在一項客戶最關心的事情上，也就是食物的味道和質感，表現得更好。由我們的產品所調理出來的食物多汁軟嫩，然而他們的則是又乾又硬。難怪我們的客戶評分比他們的高許多。從這張圖表我們可以很自豪地說，Airfryer 是市場上最佳的油炸機，它會讓您的生活變得更好，也更輕鬆多了。

adjustable
(adj.) 可調整的

shut-off
(n.) 終止

mechanism
(n.) 機制

outperform
(v.) 勝過

texture
(n.) 質地

B. 循環圖 (cycle diagram)

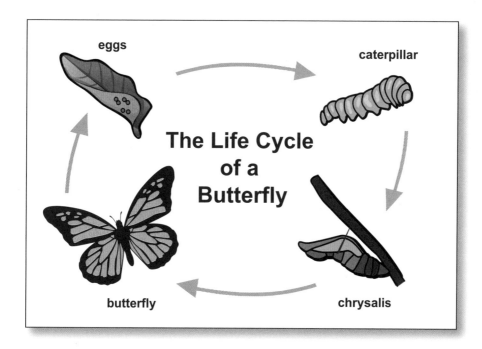

Step 1 This chart shows a life cycle of a butterfly. **Step 2** As you can see, a butterfly has four stages in its life cycle, and each stage has a different goal. I'll start from the upper left-hand corner and move clockwise as I describe this chart. In the first stage, a female butterfly lays eggs on a leaf. As you can see in the picture, eggs were laid very close together. About five days after the eggs are laid, a tiny worm-like creature hatches from each egg, and this takes us to the second stage—the caterpillar stage. A caterpillar is sometimes called a larva, and it is a long creature. The caterpillar starts to eat leaves and flowers once it has hatched. A caterpillar grows really fast, and this is because it eats a lot. And when the caterpillar is done growing, it moves into the third stage, in which it makes a chrysalis and starts to turn into a butterfly. This is the resting and changing stage, although it doesn't take a long time. In the last stage, the chrysalis opens and a butterfly comes out. Once the butterfly has rested, it will be ready to start flying. When it can fly, it will go look for food. Soon it will also find a mate. It will then lay eggs, and the life cycle will start all over again.

這張圖顯示出蝴蝶的生命週期。如您所見，蝴蝶在其生命週期中有四個階段，每個階段都有不同的目標。我會從左上角按順時針方向移動來描述這張圖。在第一階段，母蝴蝶在樹葉上產卵。正如您在圖上所見，卵產得非常接近。大約產卵五天後，一個小小的蠕蟲狀生物就會從卵裡孵化出來，進入第二階段——毛毛蟲。毛毛蟲有時也稱為幼蟲，是一個長形的生物。一旦毛毛蟲孵化後，便會開始吃樹葉和花朵。毛毛蟲長得很快，這是因為牠吃得很多。在毛毛蟲完全長成後，就會進入第三階段，也就是會造個蛹，開始變成一隻蝴蝶。

cycle
(n.) 週期，循環

caterpillar
(n.) 毛毛蟲

larva
(n.) 幼蟲

chrysalis
(n.) 蝶蛹

這是個休息與變化的階段，雖然這段時間並不長。在最後階段，蛹會打開，蝴蝶就出來了。一旦休息夠了，蝴蝶就會準備好開始飛行。當能飛時，蝴蝶就會去尋找食物，很快地也會找到一個交配伴侶，然後就會產卵，而生命週期將會從頭開始。

C. 流程圖 (process diagram)

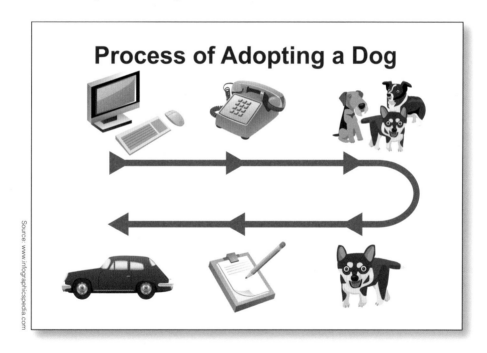

Source: www.infographicspedia.com

Step 1 If you are ready to add a new member to your family, please pay attention to this chart illustrating the process of adopting a dog.
Step 2 I'll move clockwise in explaining this process. The first step is to check online for shelter sites that advertise animals that are in

need of a good home. After that, you can contact the shelter or organization that is looking after the dogs. The next step is visit the shelter to spend time with the dogs. After the first visit, I advise you to visit the shelter several times so you and the dog you like can get to know each other better. After you've decided on which dog to adopt, you should do the paperwork to make the adoption formal. The last step is to take your new friend home by car.

Step 3 Congratulations! Now you have a best friend at home. And remember, once you adopt a dog, you're responsible for his or her well-being. So never abandon them. Also, spread the word: Adopt, Don't Buy.

如果您已準備好增添家中的新成員,請注意這張用來說明領養狗兒的流程圖。我會按順時針方向解釋此一流程。第一步是上網查看有刊登動物需要一個好家庭的收容所網站。在那之後,您可以聯繫收容所或照顧狗兒的組織。下一步是造訪收容所,花時間與狗兒相處。第一次造訪之後,我建議您多去幾次收容所,這樣一來您和您所喜歡的那隻狗便可以好好地了解對方。當您決定要領養哪隻狗後,便應該辦理文件,進行正式領養。最後一步便是開車接您的新朋友回家。恭喜您!現在您的家裡有一個最好的朋友了。而且要記住,一旦您領養了狗,便必須對牠的幸福負責。所以永遠不要拋棄牠們。此外,請宣傳:領養,而不要購買。	shelter (n.) 收容所 advertise (v.) 刊登 in need of... 需要… look after... 照顧… paperwork (n.) 文書作業 well-being (n.) 幸福

D. 金字塔圖 (pyramid diagram)

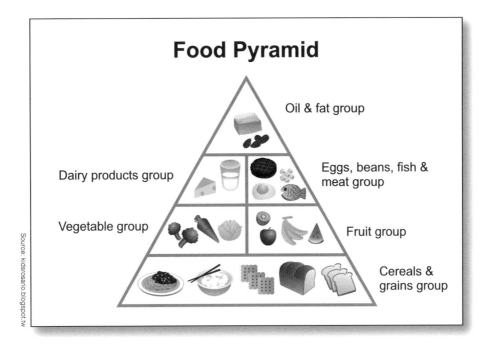

Source: kidsrosario.blogspot.tw

Step 1 Please look at this pyramid-shaped diagram. It shows the optimal number of servings to be eaten each day from each of the basic food groups in order to have a healthy diet. **Step 2** As you can see, the food pyramid is divided into four horizontal sections, and I will go from bottom to top in explaining this diagram. The bottom section is the largest section and it represents the cereals and grains group. It means you should eat 6 to 11 servings of bread, rice and pasta per day. The sections above are the vegetable group and the fruit group. It means that you should eat 5 to 8 servings of vegetables and fruits per day. The section above is the dairy products group and eggs, beans, fish, and meat group. You should consume 2 to 3 servings of food from each of the two groups. Finally, on the top is the oil and fat group. This is the smallest section, and that's why experts suggest that you only consume 1 serving a day. **Step 3** Therefore, to have a healthy diet, you should try to eat a variety of food every day at the right amount.

請看一看這張金字塔形圖。這張金字塔形圖代表為了獲取健康飲食，每天必須吃的每個基本食物群組的最佳份數。如您所見，食物金字塔被劃分成四個水平部分，我將從這張圖的底部到頂部依序解釋。底部是最大的部分，它代表穀物群組。這意味著您應該每天吃 6 到 11 份的麵包、米飯和麵食。它的上面是蔬果類組。這意味著您每天應該吃 5 到 8 份的蔬果。再上面的部分是乳製品群組和雞蛋、豆類、魚、肉群組，您應該從這兩個群組中分別吃 2 到 3 份的食物。最後，最上面的是油和脂肪群組；這個部分最小，這就是為什麼專家建議一天只吃 1 份。因此，要有健康的飲食，您應該試著每天適量地吃各式食物。

serving
(n.)（食物的）
一份

consume
(v.) 吃掉

E. 結構圖 (structure diagram)

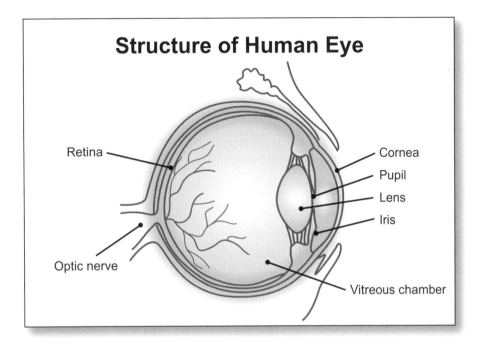

Step 1 To understand how light travels through human eyes, please take a look at this slide, the Structure of the Human Eye. **Step 2** This is a diagram of the cross section of the eye with the front of the eye on the right and the optic nerve on the left. I will go from the right, where the cornea lies, to the left, where the optic nerve is, to describe how exactly light travels. As you can see, the first eye structure to meet the exterior world is the cornea. When light enters a different medium, it is refracted, as in this case; the light will be refracted as it enters the cornea, where two-thirds of the refraction takes place. As the light continues on, it passes through the pupil and encounters a flexible structure, called the lens, where the rest of the refraction takes place. The lens is flexible so we can adjust it

according to how far away the object is. The light then goes through the vitreous chamber, which supports the shape of the eyeball. Finally, the light arrives at the retina, the structure that converts light into electrical impulses that are in turn transmitted into our brain for interpretation.

要了解光線如何穿越人的眼睛，請看這張「人眼構造」的投影片。這是眼睛的截面圖，眼睛的前面在圖的右邊，眼睛的視神經在左邊。我會從右邊，也就是角膜所在處，向左邊，也就是視神經所在處，來確切描述光線如何穿越。如您所見，眼睛接觸到外部世界的第一個結構是角膜。當光線進入不同的介質中時會產生折射，如同目前這種情況，當光線進入角膜時會發生三分之二的折射。隨著光線持續推移，它會穿過瞳孔，碰到一個有彈性的結構，叫作晶體，產生剩下的折射。因為晶體是有彈性的，所以我們可以根據物件有多遠來調整它。然後光線穿過用來支撐眼球形狀的玻璃體腔。最後，光線到達視網膜，視網膜會把光線轉換成電脈衝，電脈衝又被傳送到我們的大腦來進行解讀。

refract
(v.) 折射

vitreous
(adj.) 玻璃質的

chamber
(n.) 腔

retina
(n.) 視網膜

impulse
(n.) 刺激；脈衝

in turn
按順序，輪流

解答請見 ▶ p. 316

Exercise

本章在前面已經介紹過下面與圖表相關的英文說法,請你重新回想並寫下來。

1. X 軸 _____

2. Y 軸 _____

3. (表格的)欄,行 _____

4. (表格的)列,排 _____

5. 圖例 _____

6. 順時針方向 _____

7. 逆時針方向 _____

金字塔圖的使用時機

　　如本書前面所言，金字塔圖 (pyramid diagram) 有分層，且下面的分層大、上面的分層小，因此在使用這張圖表時有其特殊時機。第一，當講者想表現某事物有階層、順序關係時，便可以使用此圖。金字塔圖的階層可以由上往下，也可由下往上，但通常必須遵循一定的順序，不可跳躍（例如 Maslow's Hierarchy of Needs，見下圖及解釋）。第二，當講者想表現某事物有大小或數量之別（例如 p. 221 的範例所示），或者由廣泛的概念縮小到特定的概念時，便適合使用金字塔圖。

馬斯洛的人類需求層次理論

Self-actualization 自我實現

Esteem 尊重

Love/Belonging 愛與歸屬感

Safety needs 安全

Physiological needs 生理

Source: www.researchhistory.org

　　人類需求層次理論 (hierarchy of needs) 是美國著名心理學家馬斯洛 (Abraham Harold Maslow) 於 1943 年所提出。在此金字塔圖中，他將人類的需求以層次形式表現，由最下層的低階需求開始，逐漸向上發展到高級層次的需求，因此解釋這張圖時，必須遵循由下往上的順序。

在本章前面的單元中，我們提到了解釋圖表的三個步驟，以及如何清楚且有效地介紹與說明各類型圖表，在本單元中，我們則要提供更多簡報圖表的常用語句，包括描述圖表方位、解析特定圖表等，請好好學習！

1 描述方位

以下是描述方位的常用英文語句或說法，請在簡報時多加利用。

方位用語 MP3 **61**

on the left 在左邊	lower right(-hand) corner 右下角
to your left 在您（即聽眾）的左邊	at the top 在最上面
moving a little to your left 往您（即聽眾）的左邊移一點	at the bottom 在最下面
upper right(-hand) corner 右上角	the top row （表格）最上面那一列
the column on the extreme left-hand side 最左邊的那欄	
on the bottom row, third from the right （表格）最下面一列，右邊數來第三個	

on the left side of the picture,...

在照片的左邊，……

in the upper part of the picture,...

在照片的上方，……

in the foreground of the picture,...

在照片的前方，……

in the background of the picture,...

在照片的後方，……

I'll explain this diagram in a clockwise direction.

我會照順時針方向解釋這張圖表。

I'll move counterclockwise in naming the labels.

我會照逆時針方向說出這些東西的名稱。

　　以下是一個描述方位用語的範例，包含投影片及對應的講稿。紅字處是講稿中有關方位的用語。

Photoshop 軟體畫面 Adobe Systems Inc. 所有

範例

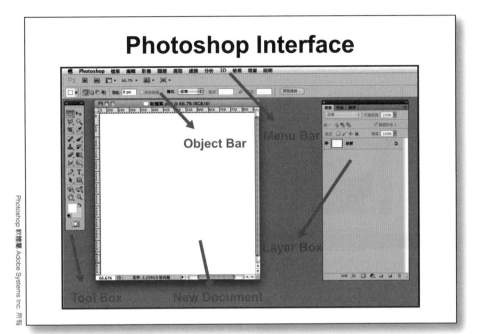

Let's take a look at this Photoshop interface from top to bottom, left to right. The top row is the Menu Bar and the one below is the Object Bar. The section on the left is the Tool Box, and the window next to the Tool Box is called a New Document. Last, the window on the right is the Layer Box, with different layers showing in the window.

讓我們從上到下、由左至右看看這個 Photoshop 的介面。最上面一行是功能選單,其下一行是物件選單。左側部分是工具列,在工具列旁邊的視窗叫作新增檔案。最後,右側視窗是圖層,不同的圖層會顯示在視窗內。

bar
(n.) 條形物

section
(n.) 部分

以下是一則關於「沙發客」(couch-surfer) 個人檔案的介紹，包含一張投影片及對應的講稿。請在講稿的空白處填入合適的方位用語。*

This slide shows a couch-surfer's profile. If you look at the (1) ＿＿＿＿＿＿＿＿＿＿, you will see the General Information section where a person's age, gender, nationality, occupation, birthday, etc. are displayed. Also, (2) ＿＿＿＿＿＿＿＿＿＿, you can see what language or languages the person speaks. (3) ＿＿＿＿＿＿＿＿＿＿, you can see more detailed information about the couch-surfer, including his or her personal description, how he or she wants to participate in couch-surfing, his or her experiences with couch-surfing, and so on.

---

* couch-surfer（沙發客）是指暫住在陌生人的家裡，並在沙發上過夜的旅遊者。目的除了節省住宿費，還有深入了解旅遊國家的在地生活，並與屋主分享生活經歷。

2 解析圖表

在簡報中，許多圖表都會需要用到與「上升」或「下降」相關的說法。以下便是關於這種現象或趨勢的例句，其中紅字處便是這類用語。

上升現象 / 趨勢

Greece's national debts rose at a double-digit rate.
希臘的國債以兩位數的速率增長。

● digit (n.) 數字

Our Africa sales edged up last year.
我們非洲地區的銷售在去年微升。

● edge up 緩慢上升

There was an increase in orders after last quarter.
訂單在上一季之後有所增加。

There was a rise in foreign investment of $15 million.
外國投資增加了 1,500 萬美元。

The number of endangered birds has grown 20% to 2,500.
瀕臨絕種的鳥類數量增加了 20%，達到 2,500 隻。

This branch showed only a single-digit rise in sales last year.
這家分行去年的銷售只有個位數的成長。

● branch (n.) 分行，分部

The house prices in Beijing skyrocketed over the last several years.
北京的房價在過去幾年急劇增長。

● skyrocket (v.)（物價等）猛漲

New toy sales soared to 250,000, and our profit hit \$2.2 million during the Christmas season.

在耶誕節期間，新玩具的銷售飆升到 25 萬個，而我們的利潤也達到 220 萬美元。

- soar (v.)（物價等）飛漲

下降現象／趨勢

The U.S. stock market dropped by nearly 300 points in 2015.

在 2015 年，美國股票市場下跌將近 300 點。

During this five year period, the oil prices plunged almost one third.

在這五年期間，石油價格大跌近三分之一。

- plunge (v.) 急降

Average household income slid from \$50,000 to \$38,000 from 2010 to 2015.

從 2010 年到 2015 年，家庭平均收入從 5 萬美元下滑到 3 萬 8 千美元。

- slide (v.) 下滑

The students' average test scores went down 12 points last school year.

學生的平均考試成績在上學年下跌 12 分。

Home stereo systems sales declined from the previous year to \$4 million.

家庭立體音響系統銷售從上一年下降到 400 萬美元。

This company's third-quarter net profit fell sharply due to declining panel prices.

這家公司第三季的淨利大幅下跌，原因是面板價格下降。

- net profit 淨利　due to... 由於⋯，因為⋯　panel (n.) 面板

Between second quarter and this quarter, the number of people hired was cut from 2,525 to 1,009.

在第二季和本季之間，僱用的人數從 2,525 人下降到 1,009 人。

達到最高點 / 最低點

BlackBerry sales reached a low point in 2011.

黑莓機在 2011 年銷售達到低點。

The company's losses hit rock bottom early this year.

這家公司的損失在今年年初觸底。

Luckily most of us sold the stock when it peaked.

很幸運地，我們大多數人在股票達到頂峰時賣出。　　　　● peak (v.) 達到最高峰

The Dow Jones reached an all-time high yesterday morning.

道瓊指數在昨天上午達到歷史新高。

Furniture sales reached a record high of 1.3 million units in 2016.

家具銷售在 2016 年達到破紀錄的 130 萬件。

In December, sales reached their lowest point, down 18% from June 2015.

12 月的銷售額達到最低點，較 2015 年六月下降了 18%。

The number of our client accounts reached an all-time low this quarter.

我們的客戶帳戶數目在本季達到空前低點。　　● all-time (adj.) 前所未有的，空前的

The experts are expecting the stock to reach its highest point in a matter of days.

專家預期股價會在數日之內達到最高點。　　　　　　● in a matter of days 數日之內

其他

It will take a long time for the market to rebound.

市場反彈需要花很長的時間。　　　　　　　　　　　● rebound (v.) 彈回

Taiwan's house prices show no sign of leveling out.

台灣的房價沒有趨向平穩的跡象。　　　● level out（上升或下跌後）保持平穩

The exchange rate remains constant with very little fluctuation.

匯率保持不變，幾乎沒有波動。　　　　　　　　● fluctuation (n.) 波動

The analyst thinks the market should bounce back in no time.

分析師認爲，市場應該在極短時間內會反彈。　　　　● bounce (v.) 彈回

Share values have leveled out after yesterday's steep drop.

股票價格在昨天急劇下跌後已趨於平穩。　　　　　● steep (adj.) 急劇的

House prices keep rising and falling, but they will eventually even out.

房價有起有落，但終究會穩定的。　　　● even out 變得平坦，變得穩定

Acer expects a strong turnaround in sales when its new laptop comes out in July.

宏碁預計其新的筆電在七月上市時，銷售會強勁反彈。

● turnaround (n.)（經濟等）突然好轉

My boss expects quarterly profits to stabilize at $1 million in the third quarter and continue to hold steady in the last quarter.

我的老闆預期第三季的季獲利會穩定在一百萬美元，然後在第四季度繼續維持穩定。

● hold (v.) 保持

3 讓簡報語言更生動

本章提供了許多有關上升／下降現象或趨勢的名詞或動詞，包括 rise（上升）、increase（增加）、decline（下降）、grow（成長）、drop（下跌）、fall（下跌）、go down（降低）等，如果你想強調這些字，便可以在它們的前面或後面加上形容詞或副詞，這樣會更生動。

A. 名詞

rise MP3 **64**

a rise 上升	a gradual rise 逐漸的上升
a significant rise 大幅的上升	a spectacular rise 驚人的上升
a modest rise 幅度不大的上升	a mild rise 溫和的上升

an increase 增加	a swift increase 迅速的增加
a sharp increase 突然的增加	an encouraging increase 令人鼓舞的增加
a substantial increase 大幅的增加	an exceptional increase 驚人的增加

decline

a decline 下降	a steady decline 穩步的下降
a significant decline 顯著的下降	a disappointing decline 令人失望的下降
a slight decline 些微的下降	an unexpected decline 無預警的下降

B. 動詞

grow

MP3 **65**

to grow 成長	to grow slightly 略有成長
to grow gradually 逐漸成長	to grow enormously 大幅成長

drop

to drop 下跌	to drop substantially 大幅下跌
to drop considerably 大幅下跌	to drop indefinitely 無限期下跌
to drop slightly 略有下跌	to drop unexpectedly 無預警下跌

fall

to fall 下跌	to fall modestly 小幅下跌
to fall substantially 大幅下跌	to fall gradually 逐漸下跌

go down

to go down 降低	to go down rapidly 迅速降低
to go down significantly 明顯降低	to go down steadily 穩步降低

將簡報內容具體化

　　你從本章中學會了介紹及說明圖表的方法，雖然圖表中的數字很實用，但要特別記住的是，簡報時別只顧著將各式各樣的數字一股腦地塞給聽眾，而是應該要將這些資料化成「具體」的東西，以方便聽眾理解這些數字代表的實際含意。

　　舉例來說，美國蘋果公司創辦人 Steve Jobs 當年在介紹公司某項產品的記憶體容量時，並沒有強調 30 GB，因為他知道大部分聽眾對於這個東西並沒有實際的概念，於是他選擇了「可以容納 7,500 首歌」、「25,000 張圖」、「75 小時長度的影片」這三個更具體的東西來代替 30 GB，讓聽眾更有感覺。這也是為什麼當他在介紹 iPod 時，並沒有詳述其規格（例如容量、長寬高、重量等），而是說它可以「容納 1,000 首歌」、「放在口袋中」(1,000 songs in your pocket)，如此一來，他不僅將冷冰冰的電子產品的功能具體化，也讓它與聽眾的生活產生連結，而這種具體化的數字對聽眾而言才是有意義的！

Chapter 7
轉換語的運用

Unit 1 轉換字詞與慣用句型

Unit 2 連結簡報各個部分

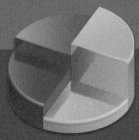

English Public Speaking
and Presentation

A good transition can save you time and energy, a bad one can cause you stress and even ruin your race.

—V. T., *Getting Ready for Triathlon*

一個好的轉換可節省你的時間和精力,一個壞的轉換則會造成壓力,甚至毀掉你的比賽。

——V.T.《準備鐵人三項比賽》

　　眾所周知,鐵人三項 (triathlon) 包含游泳、騎車、跑步三個項目,參賽者必須在完成一個項目後接著進行下一項,因此對選手的身體和心理皆是巨大考驗。要能從競爭激烈的賽事中獲勝,選手在三項運動彼此間的「轉換」(transition) 則十分重要!如同上面英文名句所述,好的轉換可以讓你「上天堂」(贏得比賽),反之則會讓你「下地獄」(輸掉賽事),不可不慎。將這個概念運用到簡報中,雖然「轉換語/連接語」(transition) 在整個簡報中不是那麼關鍵,卻常常扮演 icing on the cake(「蛋糕上的糖霜」,亦即錦上添花)的角色,適當地使用可以為你的簡報大大加分!在本章中,我們將介紹英文簡報中常常使用的轉換字詞及慣用句型,以及連結簡報各個部分的用語。

　　進行簡報時，講者的責任之一便是告知聽眾談話進行到何處。為什麼呢？因爲簡報的內容一般只有講者自己清楚，聽眾多爲被動接收訊息，因此好的講者會適時地利用轉換語或連接語，讓聽眾知道簡報目前的進度。

　　轉換語有許多形式，適當的轉換語可以提醒聽眾專心聆聽 (tune in and pay attention)。此外，轉換語也可以讓聽眾更容易了解整個簡報的脈絡流程。轉換語可以是單字、片語，甚至是句子；而它們出現的地方則可以是重點與重點之間、段落與段落之間、投影片與投影片之間，甚至是不同的概念、想法、項目、例子之間。

1 轉換字詞

　　在連接簡報每個重點之際，便是使用轉換字詞的好時機。你可以在句子中好好運用這些轉換字詞。

轉換字詞　🎧 MP3 **66**

First,... 首先，……	Another... 另一個……	Finally,... 最後，……
First of all,... 首先，……	Next,... 接著，……	Last of all,... 最後，……
Second,... 第二，……	Then,... 然後，……	In addition,... 此外，……

Moreover,... 此外，……	Proceeding on,... 繼續下去，……	In summary,... 總而言之，……
Furthermore,... 再者，……	Regarding... 關於……	For these reasons,... 由於這些理由，……
Consequently,... 結果，……	In particular,... 尤其，……	As a result,... 結果，……
Moving on,... 繼續下去，……	In brief,... 簡言之，……	Accordingly,... 因此，……
Last but not least,... 最後但同樣重要的是，……		With/In regards to... 關於……

以下提供一些與轉換字詞相關的好用例句。紅字處便是轉換字詞。

First, I would like to talk about things to look for when buying a car.
首先，我想要談談買車時要注意的事項。

Second, I want to elaborate on how the problem was finally solved by the government.
第二，我想要闡述政府最終如何解決這個問題。

Next, I want to stress the importance of positive thinking.
接著，我想要強調正向思考的重要性。

Then, comes the outcome of the latest mayoral election.
然後，（我要講的就是）市長選舉最新的結果。　　　● mayoral (adj.) 市長的

242

Last of all, let me underline the importance of product packaging.
最後，讓我強調產品包裝的重要性。　　　　　　● packaging (n.)（產品）包裝

Last but not least, let's not forget the legacy of the G20.
最後但同樣重要的，我們不要忘了 G20 的貢獻。　　● legacy (n.) 留給後人的東西

Furthermore, the shortage of clean water is another serious problem.
再者，缺乏乾淨的水是另一個嚴重的問題。

Consequently, the accident took more than 100 lives.
結果，這場意外奪走了超過一百條人命。

Moving on, let's focus on the issue of child labor.
繼續下去，讓我們專注在童工議題上。

Proceeding on, this graph concerns the price of petrol in Saudi Arabia.
繼續下去，這張圖表是關於沙烏地阿拉伯的汽油價格。
　　　　　　　　　　　　　　● concern (v.) 關於，涉及　petrol (n.) 汽油

With regards to the relationship between stress and work engagement, here are the findings.
關於壓力與工作參與度之間的關係，以下是研究結果。
　　　　　　　　　　　　● work engagement 工作參與，工作敬業

For these reasons, recycling can help with reducing pollution.
由於這些理由，資源回收可以減少汙染。　　　● recycling (n.) 回收利用

2　轉換慣用句型

　　進行簡報時，若要明確轉換前、後不同的話題，則可以用慣用句型來表達。講者使用這類慣用句型的目的是告訴聽眾「我（指講者自己）已經說完這部分的內容，接著要轉移到另一個話題。」慣用語通常包含前、後兩個部分，講者在使用時必須說明之前所講的東西為何，以及接著要講的東西為何。舉例來說，在 Now that I have talked about..., let me move on to... 的轉換慣用語中，Now that I have talked about... 的後面接的即是講者之前所講的東西，而 let me move on to... 的後面則是講者接著要說的東西。請看以下例子：

- Now that I have talked about my high school life, let me move on to (talk about) my college life.
  既然我已經說了我的高中生活，那麼讓我接下去講我的大學生活。

  　說明　講者之前所講的東西是 my high school life，而接著要講的東西則是 my college life。　　　　　　　　　　　● Now that... 既然……，由於……

　　以下是常見的轉換慣用句型，其中前面的「...」即是講者之前所講的東西，後面的「～」則是講者接著要講的東西。

轉換句型

 MP3 **67**

I will now leave ... and turn to ～
我現在要離開……，開始講～

Shifting to the next point of..., I'd like to touch on ～
換到下一個……重點，我想要簡述一下～

Having explained..., I will now detail ～
我已經解釋了……，現在則要詳述～

We've gone over..., let's turn now to ～
我們已經檢視了……，現在讓我們轉移到～

That does it for... Next, I'll outline ～
我說完……。接著，我會概述～

With the issue of ... in mind, I'd like to move to ～
知道了……的議題後，我想轉換到～

Let us shift the emphasis away from ... to ～
我們將重點從……轉換到～

So much for..., now I want to focus on ～
已經談了很多……，現在我想專注在～

While one issue remains..., another issue concerns ～
儘管這個議題仍舊……，但另一個議題是關於～

To recap, I have confirmed... Now I hope to discuss ～
重述要點，我已經確認……。現在我希望討論～

As I have discussed..., I would like to continue with ～
如同我已經討論的……，現在要繼續～

Now that I have finished talking about..., let me move on to ～
既然我已經說完……，那麼讓我接下來講～

If there are no more questions about..., I will proceed on to ～
若對於……沒有任何問題，我要繼續下去～

Thus far, I have noted... There are other concerns too, such as ～
到目前為止我已提到……。還有其他重要的事，例如～

　　以下是使用轉換慣用句型來表達的例句。紅字處即為轉換慣用句型。

I will now leave France and turn to Germany.
我現在要離開法國這個議題，開始講德國的議題。

Shifting to the next point of my presentation, I'd like to touch on the
subject of taxation.
換到下一個簡報重點，我想要簡述一下稅收的議題。

● shift (v.) 轉移　taxation (n.) 徵稅

Now that we all know the situation, let me provide some options for
you to consider.
既然我們都知道這個情況，那麼讓我提供一些選項供您考慮。

Having explained the objectives of the experiment, I will now detail the
procedure.
我已經解釋完這個實驗的目標，現在則要詳述實驗步驟。

So we've gone over all the options, let's turn now to the pros and cons of each one.

我們已經檢視了所有的選項，現在讓我們轉移到每個選項的利與弊。

● go over... 仔細檢查…

OK, that does it for the background information. Next, I'll outline the main points.

好，說完了背景資訊，接著我會概述主要重點。

● outline (v.) 概述

With the issue of work ethic in mind, I'd like to move to the next item on the agenda.

知道了職場倫理的議題，我想進行議程的下一個項目。

Let us now shift the emphasis away from the responsibility of teachers to the responsibility of parents.

現在讓我們將重點從老師的職責轉換到家長的職責。

Exercise

解答請見 ▶ p. 317

針對以下句子，請寫出講者之前所說的話及接著要說的話。紅字處是轉換慣用句型。

1. Now that we have explored Japan's economic situation, let us turn to its educational system.

講者之前所講的東西：＿＿＿＿＿＿＿＿＿＿＿＿＿＿＿

講者接著要講的東西：＿＿＿＿＿＿＿＿＿＿＿＿＿＿＿

2. So much for the problem; what about the solution?

　　講者之前所講的東西：＿＿＿＿＿＿＿＿＿＿＿＿＿＿＿＿＿＿＿

　　講者接著要講的東西：＿＿＿＿＿＿＿＿＿＿＿＿＿＿＿＿＿＿＿

3. That's it for the advantages. I'll move on now to the disadvantages.

　　講者之前所講的東西：＿＿＿＿＿＿＿＿＿＿＿＿＿＿＿＿＿＿＿

　　講者接著要講的東西：＿＿＿＿＿＿＿＿＿＿＿＿＿＿＿＿＿＿＿

4. We have spent a lot of time talking about the present. It's time now to discuss the future.

　　講者之前所講的東西：＿＿＿＿＿＿＿＿＿＿＿＿＿＿＿＿＿＿＿

　　講者接著要講的東西：＿＿＿＿＿＿＿＿＿＿＿＿＿＿＿＿＿＿＿

5. Now that we've looked at the development of the Korean computer game industry, we may now proceed to the discussion of Taiwan's.

　　講者之前所講的東西：＿＿＿＿＿＿＿＿＿＿＿＿＿＿＿＿＿＿＿

　　講者接著要講的東西：＿＿＿＿＿＿＿＿＿＿＿＿＿＿＿＿＿＿＿

6. That ends the background information on the product; I'll now turn to the technical specifications.

　　講者之前所講的東西：＿＿＿＿＿＿＿＿＿＿＿＿＿＿＿＿＿＿＿

　　講者接著要講的東西：＿＿＿＿＿＿＿＿＿＿＿＿＿＿＿＿＿＿＿

7. Reducing the amount of garbage produced daily is only one part of the solution. The other part is to ensure that citizens conserve natural resources.

講者之前所講的東西：＿＿＿＿＿＿＿＿＿＿＿＿＿＿＿＿＿＿＿

講者接著要講的東西：＿＿＿＿＿＿＿＿＿＿＿＿＿＿＿＿＿＿＿

Memo

　　轉換語 (transition) 另一個很大的功能便是「承上啓下」，亦即扮演串連簡報三大部分的角色。本書在 Chapter 1 裡提過，簡報基本上分成「開場」(opening)、「主體」(body) 及「結束」(closing)，因此從開場到主體或從主體到結束之際，你都可以善用轉換語，做好無縫接軌。

　　除了開場、主體及結束這三大部分的連結，若簡報的時間較長（例如 30 分鐘或更久）、簡報資料多且複雜，那你還可以善用「內部預覽」(internal preview) 與「內部摘要」(internal summary) 兩種轉換語來幫助聽眾記憶內容，並提醒聽眾簡報進行到何處。

 MP3 **68**

1 從開場到主體

So that concludes the introduction. Let me focus on the major part of my speech in the next 15 minutes.
我的開場部分就到此結束。讓我在接下來的 15 分鐘專注在演說的主要部分。

That's a brief introduction. I'll move on now to a more detailed description of the main points of my presentation.
以上是簡短的介紹。現在我會對簡報中的主要重點做更詳細的描述。

I hope you all have a basic understanding of our app. I'll now go into the more technical side of how it works and what users can do.

我希望您對我們的應用程式都已經有了基本的了解。我現在要進入更技術面的東西，說明此應用程式是如何運作，以及使用者可以怎麼使用。

● app (n.) 應用程式 (= application)

2　從主體到結束

I hope I've made my points clear. Now it's time to conclude.
我希望我已經將重點講清楚了。現在該是做結論的時候了。

If you're all happy with what you've heard so far, maybe we can end the meeting by taking a vote on what I've proposed?
如果您到目前為止聽得都還算滿意，或許我們可以對我所做的提議投票以結束會議？

So these are the new features of our blender. Let me end my presentation by summarizing these features briefly.
這些就是我們果汁機的新特色。讓我把這些特色做個摘要，來將簡報做個結束吧。

● feature (n.) 特色　blender (n.) 果汁機；（食物）攪拌器

3　內部預覽

　　在時間長、資料多且資料複雜的簡報中，內部預覽的目的是讓聽眾先知道講者接著要說什麼。要注意的是，一般而言，內部預覽只會出現在簡

報的「主體」部分，這是因為主體通常占簡報最主要的篇幅與長度，而且主體的每個主要重點通常也很長，這時講者便會在要講述的每個主要重點之前，先「預覽／預告」(preview) 一下即將要講述的內容，這也就是為什麼這種形式會稱為「內部預覽」(internal preview) 了。請看以下例子。

● In discussing how African Americans have been stereotyped in the media, in the next ten minutes, we'll look first at the origins of the problem, and second at its continuing impact today.
要討論非裔美籍人士在媒體所受的刻板印象，我們在接下來的十分鐘會先探討這個問題的起源，接著會探討這個刻板印象持續到今日的影響。

● stereotype (v.) 對⋯形成刻板的看法　origin (n.) 起源

由上面這段談話可以知道，講者在簡報主體中講到的一個主要重點是「非裔美籍人士在媒體所受的刻板印象」，由於這個主要重點要談十分鐘，時間較長，因此講者先利用這個句子預告此十分鐘的主要重點包含兩個次主題（或次要重點）：(1) 刻板印象問題的起源；(2) 刻板印象持續到今日的影響。接下來請看另一個例子。

● Now that we have seen how serious the problem of insomnia is, let's look at some solutions. In the next part of my talk, I will focus on three solutions—making sleep a priority, reducing caffeine intake, and doing yoga and meditation.
既然我們已經知道失眠這個問題的嚴重性，那麼讓我們來看看一些解決方法。在我接下來的談話中，我將會著重在三個解決方法——將睡眠擺在第一位、減少咖啡因的攝取、做瑜伽和靜坐。

● insomnia (n.) 失眠　priority (n.) 優先考慮的事　caffeine (n.) 咖啡因
intake (n.) 攝取（量）　meditation (n.) 靜坐

由上述談話可以知道，講者在簡報主體的前半段先談失眠這個問題 (problem)，接著在後半段要談解決失眠的方法 (solution)。因為後半段要講很久，所以講者先用這段話預告主要重點的三個次主題（或次要重點）：(1) 將睡眠擺在第一位；(2) 減少咖啡因的攝取；(3) 做瑜伽和靜坐。

要注意的是，這段談話的第一句使用了之前所提過的轉換慣用句型：Now that we have seen..., let's look at...。由此可知，不同的轉換句型、內部預覽及內部摘要，都可以一起出現在簡報中，達到相輔相成的效果！

4 內部摘要

和內部預覽很類似的是內部摘要，這種方式同樣使用在時間長、資料多且資料複雜的簡報中，不過目的並非在預覽或預告接下來要講述的內容，而是要「提醒聽眾再次回憶起所聽到的內容」。請看以下例子。

● I hope you all remember the three key sales points about our new yacht that I just talked about: style, performance, and price. Before I move on to the next topic, which is sales promotion activities, do you have any questions?
我希望各位都能記住剛剛所提我們新遊艇的三項賣點：樣式、性能、價格。在我繼續進行到下一個主題，也就是促銷活動之前，有任何問題嗎？

由上述談話可以知道，講者在簡報主體的某個部分花了許多時間提到公司新遊艇的賣點 (key sales points)，因此在此處利用內部摘要將三項賣點簡要地重述一次，然後接著要談下一個主題（或主要重點）：促銷活

動。接下來請看另一個例子。

● In short, my study showed that cultural instruction was considered beneficial by the immigrating students. It has also generated positive effects among their families. If there are no questions, I'll move on to the pedagogical implications of such instruction.

簡而言之，我的研究顯示移民學生認為文化教學對其有所幫助。文化教學對其家庭也有正面影響。如果沒有任何問題，我將繼續進行到文化教學的教學應用方面。

　　● positive (adj.) 正面的　pedagogical (adj.) 教學法的　implication (n.) 意涵，應用

　　由上述談話可知，講者在簡報主體中花了許多篇幅談到自己研究的發現，因此在進入到下一個主題，也就是在教學應用之前，花了點時間利用內部摘要將兩個主要的研究發現快速再說一遍。接著請看最後一個例子。

● To briefly summarize what I just said, the new products scheduled for next quarter will help us open up our overseas sales, rake in a total of $3 billion before tax, and most importantly, enable us to maintain our position as market leader. Now I'd like to move on to the next subject.

簡要總結一下我剛剛所說的內容：訂於下季要上市的新產品將會幫我們擴展海外市場，並賺進稅前共 30 億美元，以及最重要的是，讓我們能保持市場領導者的地位。現在我要進行到下一個主題。

　　● open up... 打開…，開發…　rake in... 大量賺進（金錢）

　　由上述談話可以知道，講者在簡報主體的某個部分花了許多時間談論公司下一季新產品對公司的助益，因此在此處利用內部摘要將此三點助益快速再說過一遍，然後準備進入下一個主題。

由本章可知，簡報中的轉換語相當有用處，它可以讓不同的重點、段落、投影片之間彼此連接。此外，轉換語不僅可以幫助聽眾知道講者接下來要講述的資訊，還有助於記住剛剛聽過的資訊，可說是好處多多，因此簡報時別忘了善加運用。

Chapter 8
其他簡報用語

Unit 1 與聽眾互動

Unit 2 處理各種情況

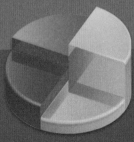

English Public Speaking
and Presentation

Fake it 'til you make it.

—Anonymous

裝久就成真。

——佚名

　　上面的引言為英文世界常見的　句話，多用來鼓勵沒有自信的人：在擁有真實的自信之前，應該先表現出有自信的樣子，並勉力而為，時間久了便會「習慣成自然」，真的成為有自信的人了。句子中的 fake（假裝）不只是裝給他人看，也要裝給自己看，意思是要發自內心感受到自信。在公眾演說上，你也可以運用這種增強自信的心理暗示，在真正做到有自信之前，先假裝自己可以這麼做，例如常想像自己在聽眾面前侃侃而談，並把握每次上臺的機會，相信久而久之便會成為一位熟練且成功的講者！

　　在前面幾章中，我們提到了許多讓簡報「內容」(content) 更豐富的方式與用語，在轉換到 Chapter 9，也就是簡報另一個重點，即「技巧」(delivery) 之前，讓我們再多學一些與聽眾互動及處理各種情況的實用英語簡報用語，讓整個簡報更臻於完美。

Unit 1 　與聽眾互動

簡報要成功，關鍵之一便是能將自己的想法順利傳達給對方，因此簡報中與聽眾的互動便很重要。若無法做到這一點，那麼再精彩的簡報內容也屬枉然。因此除了扎實的簡報內容外，簡報進行前後與聽眾互動、溝通的用語也要特別注意。以下是與聽眾互動的各式用語。

1　在簡報正式開始時閒聊

若你與聽眾是第一次見面，或者是第一次到簡報場所所在的城市或國家，則可以在簡報一開始時先花一點時間閒談，如此可以打破稍嫌緊張的氣氛，也可趁機了解聽眾屬性及當地風土人情，甚至將這些閒談取得的資訊順勢融入簡報當中。

請注意，閒談雖然隨性，但並非無所不談。一般而言，簡報場合適合閒聊的主題會因為聽眾的組成分子及其文化、政治，甚至其他因素而有所不同。若你清楚聽眾的屬性，便可以知道哪些議題可以談、哪些應避免。若不清楚聽眾屬性，則最安全的話題便是聊天氣、旅遊／旅途、文化等。不過請記得：若談到與文化相關的議題，應保持開放的心胸學習，若有與自己認知不同的地方，只可以比較，不可以批評！

聊天氣

Sure is freezing today!
今天真是冷斃了！

● freezing (adj.) 極冷的

What a beautiful morning!
今早的天氣眞好！

Couldn't have asked for a better day!
今天的天氣眞是太棒了！

So is it always this humid this time of year?
這個時節總是這麼潮濕嗎？

Is this normal weather for this time of year?
這種天氣在這個時節算是正常的嗎？

The weather sure changed quickly in the last few hours!
過去這幾個小時的天氣變化眞大！

聊旅遊 / 旅途

I landed last night, and the night view of the city was incredible.
我昨晚抵達，而這座城市的夜景眞是美麗極了。

This is my first time here, although I was in Houston for a trade show last year.
我是第一次到這裡，不過去年我有去休士頓參展。

I haven't been to Basel yet. What's it like?
我尚未去過巴塞爾。這座城市如何？

I arrived early this morning from Taipei, and actually I'm still feeling a little jet-lagged.

我今天一早才從台北抵達，確實還感到有點時差。　　● jet-lagged (adj.) 有時差的

聊文化

[jokingly] Someone offered me some snake wine last night, and I still have a hangover.

〔開玩笑地〕有人昨晚請我喝蛇酒，我到現在還在宿醉中。　　● hangover (n.) 宿醉

I tried the seafood pancakes, and they are totally different from what they sell in Korea.

我吃了海鮮餅，但是和韓國賣的完全不一樣。

I noticed that people here line up when waiting for the train. It's amazing.

我注意到這裡的人等車時會排隊，眞是了不起。

Although I don't understand the language, the TV programs here seem very interesting.

雖然我不懂這個語言，但是這裡的電視節目看起來很有趣。

 MP3 **73**

2　在簡報結束後私下交談

　　簡報結束後心情雖然輕鬆，但你最好不要連聲招呼都不打就快速離去。如果時間許可，建議你在簡報結束後留下來待個數分鐘，一方面可以與聽眾進一步交流，另一方面也可以讓在「問答時段」(Q&A session) 因

某些原因而沒有發問的聽眾私下向你請益。如果眞的有事情必須儘快離開，也應該委婉告知。

與聽眾進一步交流

You are a wonderful audience.
各位眞是很棒的聽眾。

. . . .

You guys have been great. Thank you so much.
各位眞的很棒。非常感謝。

. . . .

I'm looking forward to working with you again.
我期待還有機會與您共事。

. . . .

Please keep in touch.
請保持聯絡。

. . . .

表示有事須離開

I'm afraid I have to be on my way.
我可能要先行離開。

. . . .

My flight is in three hours, so I need to be excused.
我三小時後要搭飛機，所以必須離開。

. . . .

I only have half an hour before my next appointment.
我離下一個約之間只有半小時。

. . . .

Excuse me for a moment. I really need to take this call.
抱歉，請等一下。我必須接這個電話。

. . . .

MP3 **74**

3 簡報時與聽眾互動

　　簡報進行中，常常可能會因為某個理由而必須向聽眾解釋，這些情況包含話題的轉變、離題，或因為時間限制、準備資料缺乏、花在同一個議題太久、議題對聽眾過於艱深而必須限制簡報討論的範圍等。這些狀況很難一時之間用英語向聽眾解釋，因此你平日就應該熟悉這些用語或說法，以免臨場支吾其詞。

向聽眾解釋

As I said before,...
就如同我之前所說的，……

As I said in the introduction,...
就如同我在開頭介紹時所說的，……

As I mentioned earlier,...
就如同我之前所提到的，……

As I said in the previous part,...
就如同我在前個部分所說的，……

As we've already seen,...
就如同我們所見，……

遇到離題時

I'd like to get off track for a moment.
我想離題一下。

● get off track 離題

Let me sidetrack the discussion for a few minutes.
讓我離題幾分鐘。

● sidetrack (v.) 使轉換話題

Let's get back to the topic now.
我們現在回到正題吧。

I'm sorry for getting sidetracked.
很抱歉，我離題了。

想要進行下一個主題

Let's turn to the next topic.
我們進行下一個主題吧。

I'd like to talk about another issue.
我想談談另一個議題。

May I proceed to the next topic?
我可以進行下一個主題了嗎？

Is it OK if we continue with the next subject?
我們能否繼續下一個主題呢？

Why don't we go to the next item on the agenda?
我們何不來進行議程的下一個項目呢？

Next on the agenda is product development. Let's get to it.
議程的下一個議題是產品研發。我們來討論吧。

Before we close, we need to get back to the delivery issue.
在結束前我們必須再回到交貨這個議題上。

I think we should skip the pricing issue and jump to delivery schedule.
我想我們應該跳過定價這個議題，直接討論交貨時程。

若議題較艱深或複雜時

I'll explain this chart in more detail in the next section.
我會在下一個部分更詳細地解釋這張圖表。

Before we go any further, I think it's best to give you some background information.
在我們進一步討論之前，我想最好給您一些背景資訊。

Don't worry; I'll go into further detail on this issue towards the end of the presentation.
別擔心，我會在接近簡報結束時進一步詳述這個議題。

This issue is too complicated to be examined in detail here.
這個議題太複雜了，不適合在這裡詳細檢視。

This theory is quite complicated, so I won't discuss the details today.
這個理論蠻複雜的，因此我今天並不會討論細節。

Let me expand on this issue again later when I talk about...
等會當我談到……時，我會再充分說明這個議題。

基於時間限制

As time is limited, I will limit/shorten the discussion to five minutes.
因為時間有限，我會將討論限制／縮短成五分鐘。

....

Due to time constraints, I'll leave out the details and jump over to the next section.
由於時間限制，我就不講細節，而是跳到下一個部分。　　　● constraint (n.) 限制

....

Given the time available to me today, I won't be able to go into greater detail on this issue.
就我今天有的時間，我沒辦法對這個議題講得太詳細。

....

This issue is interesting, but it is not our present concern.
這個議題很有趣，但並不是我們現在要關心的事。　　　● concern (n.) 關心的事

....

Unit 2　處理各種情況

做簡報時，不管講者再如何演練或準備，臨場可能還是會碰到一些小狀況。一旦遇到突發狀況，除了默不作聲或向聽眾道歉，講者其實還可以有其他選擇，例如向聽眾解釋、請求他人協助等。以下是做簡報時，常會使用到的各種情況用語或說法。

 MP3 **75**

1　遇到設備問題

I'm afraid the computer froze up.
我想電腦當機了。

● freeze up 卡住

Looks like I have to restart the computer.
看來我得重新開機。

The speakers are not working.
擴音器壞了。

● speaker (n.) 擴音器，喇叭

There's something wrong with the microphone.
麥克風有問題。

I don't think the wireless pointer is working.
我想無線簡報器壞了。

● wireless pointer 無線簡報器

真人重點示範影片 11
YouTube 搜尋作者和書名

267

I'm sorry about the technical problems.
不好意思，技術問題。

Could someone please help me with this?
有人可以幫我弄一下這個嗎？

I apologize for the technical problems. Sorry for the inconvenience.
抱歉，技術問題。造成不便請見諒。

Sorry for the delay. It will take a few minutes to fix the projector.
不好意思耽誤時間。需要幾分鐘的時間來修理投影機。

 MP3 **76**

2　處理場地相關問題

Can someone dim the lights?
有人可以幫忙把燈關暗一點嗎？　　　　　　　　　　　• dim (v.) 使變暗

Please turn off/on the lights.
請關／開燈。

Please shut the door.
請關門。

Please close the drapes/blinds.
請拉下窗簾。　　　　• drapes (n.) 窗簾　blinds (n.) 窗簾，百葉窗

Could you all move to the front of the room?
可以請大家都移到場地前面嗎？

There are still plenty of seats available in the front.
前面還有很多空位。

Can you all hear me clearly? Speak up if you can't.
大家都聽得清楚嗎？如果不行，請大聲說一下。

Can you hear me (if I speak) without the microphone?
（如果我演講時）不用麥克風，大家都聽得到嗎？

🎧 MP3 **77**

3 將講義或簡報檔案發給聽眾

There are some handouts on that table. Please take one of each.
那個桌上有些講義。請每種拿一份。

Here's a set of handouts that I'd like you to browse through.
這是一份講義，我希望您從頭開始翻閱一下。　　　　　● browse (v.) 瀏覽

Please fill in the suggestion sheets that have just been passed out.
請填一下我剛剛發下去的建議表。　　　　　● pass out... 分發…

I hope everyone has a copy of the handout. Please raise your hand if
you don't (have one).
我希望每個人都有一份講義。如果您沒有（講義），請舉手。

The handouts I'm passing out have all the supplemental information you'll need.
我現在發下去的講義包含您所需要的所有補充資料。　　● supplemental (adj.) 補充的

All the slides in my presentation today are in the handout.
我今天簡報中所有的投影片都在講義中。

If you leave your e-mail address with me, I'll send the PowerPoint file to you.
如果您留電子郵件給我，我會將 PowerPoint 檔案寄給您。

Don't worry about taking notes. I'll give you the slides in a handout at the end of the presentation.
不用記筆記。我在簡報的最後會給大家一份投影片的講義。

Don't bother copying the information on the slides. I'll e-mail the PowerPoint file to all of you.
不用記投影片的資訊。我會用電子郵件將 PowerPoint 檔案寄給大家。

 MP3 **78**

4　提議更改時程

Why don't we skip the next section?
我們跳過下一個部分好了。

Maybe we could take that issue up at another meeting?
或許我們可以再另外開會討論那個議題？　　● take up... 繼續…

I think I need another 10 minutes to finish my presentation.
我想我還需要十分鐘才能完成簡報。

I know you're busy, but let me try to wrap up my report in 10 minutes.
我知道各位都很忙，但請給我十分鐘讓我完成報告。

We're supposed to finish at 3:30, but can we go for 15 minutes longer?
我們本來預計 3 點 30 分結束，但是可以再延長 15 分鐘嗎？

●be supposed to V. 應當…

Do you think it's a good idea to extend this workshop so that we can finish all the activities?
各位認爲是否可以延長工作坊的時間，以便完成所有活動呢？

🎧 MP3 **79**

5　提議中場休息

Why don't we take a break for a few minutes?
我們休息幾分鐘如何？

I think we should take a short break.
我們應該稍微休息一下。

Does anyone need a coffee break? I do.
有誰需要休息一下，喝點咖啡的？我自己需要。

Let's meet again in 10 minutes.
我們十分鐘後再開始。

We'll restart our meeting at one o'clock sharp.
我們一點整重新開會。   ● sharp (adv.)（…點）整

Is everyone ready to resume the meeting?
大家準備好重新開會了嗎？   ● resume (v.) 重新開始

 MP3 **80**

6　請求聽眾參與活動

Please stand up and form a big circle.
請站起來圍成一個大圓圈。

Why don't you get into groups of three?
請各位三個人一組。

I'd like you to form groups of four to work on the activity sheet.
請各位四個人一組，一起做活動單。   ● work on... 從事於…，進行…

Please discuss this issue with the person (sitting) next to you.
請和（坐在）您隔壁的人討論這個議題。

延伸
學習

增加與聽眾的互動

進行簡報時，除了講者一個人唱獨腳戲外，還可以邀請聽眾一起參與活動，例如請聽眾彼此分享想法或故事，或者在產品演示 (product demonstration) 時邀請聽眾上台體驗等。這樣一方面可以增加「講者與聽眾」及「聽眾與聽眾」之間的互動，還可以增加簡報的變化性與趣味性。

除了與聽眾進行實體的互動外，也可以在簡報語言中「刻意」將聽眾包含進去，利用 you 或 we 這兩個代名詞，直接對聽眾說話，讓聽眾有參與感。以下是幾個將聽眾包含進去的說法。紅字處便是將聽眾包含進去的字詞。

Like most of us, I have to battle an expanding waistline.
和大多數的人一樣，我也必須和一直增加的腰圍奮戰。

I'm sure you'll agree that we must make more sales in Asia next year.
我相信各位都會同意，我們明年必須在亞洲市場上提高銷售量。

I think you all realize that what he said may not necessarily be true.
我相信各位都意識到，他所說的不盡然是真的。

I believe you all understand the basics of the theory.
我相信各位都了解這個理論的基礎。

As most of you in this room are probably aware, Manila has a lot of traffic problems.

這個會場裡大多數的人大概都很清楚，馬尼拉的交通問題真的很嚴重。

I can see that some of you know what I'm talking about.

我看得出各位當中有些人知道我在說什麼。

Chapter 9
簡報技巧演練

English Public Speaking
and Presentation

Having something to say is not enough. You must also know how to say it.

—Stephen Lucas, *The Art of Public Speaking*

有東西要説還不夠，你必須知道要怎麼説。

——史蒂芬・盧卡斯《公眾演説的藝術》

　　我在本書的作者序中提到，雖然簡報的「內容」(content) 很重要，但是做簡報的「技巧」(delivery) 也同樣重要，有時甚至更重要，因為講者就算有最豐富的內容，若簡報技巧薄弱，導致聽眾呼呼大睡或藉機離席，那麼再好的內容也是枉然。這就是為什麼知道要「說什麼」(what) 還不夠，你還必須知道要「怎麼說」(how)。本書最後一章的重點便是要教你怎麼說，也就是簡報的技巧。

簡報前的準備

　　一場成功的簡報取決於很多因素，但好的演說家都會同意，「反覆地演練」是成功的不二法門。當然，演練並非指機械式地重複或背誦講稿，而是有建設性地在每一次演練時讓簡報更臻於完美。

　　若要讓簡報成功，你必須有效地與聽眾溝通。溝通 (communication) 分成「語言溝通」(verbal communication) 與「非語言溝通」(non-verbal communication)；也就是說，進行簡報演練時有兩個重點，一是語言技巧的演練，另一個是肢體語言的演練，本章最後兩個單元會詳述兩者。在此之前，身為一個講者，你必須為即將到來的簡報做周全的準備。

　　簡報前需要做哪些準備呢？以下為四個重點。

- **Q** 反覆練習，直到滿意為止
- **Q** 準備適當的備忘稿或小抄
- **Q** 預設現場突發狀況與解決方案
- **Q** 提早抵達會場

1 反覆練習，直到滿意為止

英諺云 Practice makes perfect.，的確，「熟能生巧」，因此在你做正式簡報前，必須完全了解自己製作的簡報內容及每張投影片的順序。若你愈熟悉簡報內容、準備愈充分，臨場時便愈不容易緊張。此外，請記得本書之前所提示的：愈短的簡報，愈需要長時間的準備，因為你必須在短時間內將所有內容精簡地傳達給聽眾，而這需要縝密的思慮和計算。

在這裡要提醒的是：期望將整個簡報內容一字不差地背下來並不切實際，也會帶給自己莫大的壓力，因此建議你，若能記住講稿內容的70%～80% 便已經足夠，至於其他的講稿內容，若臨場用字遣詞與演練時不同，也無須在意。

不過根據我實務上所觀察到的，講者通常最容易在簡報一開始時感到緊張，因此若你能大致背下簡報前一～二分鐘的每句話，甚至記住說話時相對應的姿態及手勢，那麼便可以適度減少緊張。換句話說，簡報稿不需完全背誦，只要反覆演練到自己覺得滿意即可，但若希望可以減少臨場緊張感，則建議確實背下簡報一～二分鐘的講稿。

最後，演練時記得保持正常語速，並在該強調之處就加以強調，亦即將每次的演練都當作是正式演說。請注意：所謂正常語速還是會隨聽眾人數多寡而稍有不同。一般而言，聽眾人數愈多時，簡報說話速度要愈慢；反之，聽眾少時，說話速度則可快一些。

2 準備適當的備忘稿或小抄

要如何完全記住所製作的簡報內容及每張投影片的順序呢？很簡單，你可以善用 PowerPoint 或其他簡報軟體。現今新版的簡報軟體通常都會有可供講者看到「下一張」投影片的功能（例如 PowerPoint 新設計的「簡報者檢視畫面」），這些功能可以讓講者在自己的電腦螢幕上看到目前以及下一張投影片的內容，甚至連「備忘稿」都可以看到（放心，聽眾在投影機的螢幕上只能看到目前的投影片，看不到其他內容），因此可以大大減少你忘記或出錯的恐懼感。此外，你也可以利用傳統的方式，在列印時選擇「備忘稿」或「講義」，這些都可以在簡報時給予你適時的提示。

不管如何，要產生紙本的備忘稿，首先你必須在製作 PowerPoint 檔案時先在每張投影片下方鍵入實際的講稿，然後列印時選擇「備忘稿」，如此每個投影片便可以產生一張上方有投影片、下方有講稿的備忘稿（請見下頁圖片紅框處）。也就是說，如果你製作了 20 張投影片，便會產生 20 張備忘稿。另一方面，若列印時選擇「講義」，所列印出來的資料，除了可以當成聽眾實際拿到的講義，還可以用來提醒自己每張投影片的順序。有了這些輔助資料，你便不需要將整個簡報內容背下來。

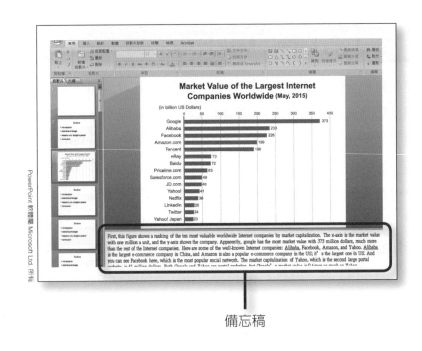

備忘稿

PowerPoint 軟體畫面 Microsoft Ltd 所有

不過根據許多講者的實務經驗，利用「備忘稿」輔助記憶並不見得適合每個人，因為除了麥克風和無線簡報器，如果還要再騰出一隻手一頁一頁翻動備忘稿，是一件很麻煩的事，因此建議你實際演練後再自行決定。

其實簡報的小抄 (reminder) 形式眾多，有些講者習慣將所有講稿印出來，如此便不需要如備忘稿般隨投影片每頁翻動，有些講者則是在多次演練後，只將自己講稿中容易遺忘的部分寫在小卡紙上，供簡報時使用，如此一來便不需攜帶整份講稿。還有些講者會試圖記住大部分的講稿，並事先安排好連接簡報每個主要重點的「記憶點」，只在紙上記下這些記憶點及少許提示資料，這樣便能避免頻繁看稿，讓簡報更流暢地進行。至於哪種方式適合你，還需要你實際演練後再做決定。

3　預設現場突發狀況與解決方案

科技再發達,不能保證永不出錯,同樣地,任何一種視覺材料都有可能臨場出狀況,因此簡報前便要設想可能的突發狀況,以及對應的備案。尤其當簡報以英文進行,必須用英文向聽眾解釋或請他人幫忙,因此事先熟練相關用語有其必要。相關內容可參考本書的 Chapter 8。

要減少狀況發生時的不知所措,便要在事前盡可能掌握相關資訊,例如詢問主辦單位演講場地大小、座位是否可移動、燈光是否可控制、是否備有麥克風,以及是否有網路、電腦、音效等。這些事先取得的資訊都可以幫助你減少突發狀況,因此千萬不要因為不好意思而疏於詢問。

此外,建議你將簡報所需要用到的影片、音樂檔案、播放軟體、網頁等都先存放在隨身碟,而不要臨場才用網路下載,因為就算主辦單位有提供網路,也很難確保當天不會剛好有問題或狀況。至於其他細節,例如若你需要特殊的字體檔案等,也必須自行備妥,不然如果主辦單位提供的電腦沒有你要的軟體,便會造成不便。

4　提早抵達會場

簡報當天建議比預定時間提早半小時抵達會場,抵達後可以先熟悉環境,並確認設備,做聲音大小或燈光等最後的調整,這樣可以幫你緩和緊張的情緒。此外,你也可以先與早到的聽眾閒聊,打破彼此陌生的關係,並了解聽眾對簡報的相關需求。

Memo

Unit **2** 語言技巧演練

　　「語言溝通」顧名思義著重在講者的語言技巧，演練時應注意以下五個部分。

> Q 講者的聲音 (speaker's voice)
> Q 聲音的變化 (vocal varieties)
> Q 暫停的運用 (pause)
> Q 發音與清晰度 (pronunciation & articulation)
> Q 方言及其他語言的使用 (dialect & other languages)

1 講者的聲音

　　一般人說話時通常不太會注意自己的聲音品質，認為只要對方聽得到、聽得懂就可以了，但是在簡報當中，身為講者的你必須特別注意說話時的音量 (volume)、音調 (pitch) 及速度 (rate)。為什麼呢？原因在於音量太小聽眾聽不清楚，太大又讓人覺得痛苦；音調太高會讓聽眾覺得刺耳，太低聲音又容易模糊；速度過快容易讓人感到緊張，太慢又容易讓人昏睡。由此可知，保持自己說話時音量、音調、速度的適中 (moderation)十分重要。

2　聲音的變化

前面一段雖然提到聲音適中的重要性，但如果你整場簡報的音量、音調和速度都沒有變化，那便會像唸經一般，很快就會讓聽眾進入夢鄉！由此可知，在聲音適中的同時，還必須保持音量、音調和速度的變化，例如在「強調」重要的概念時，就必須像本書 Chapter 4 中「延伸學習」(p. 124) 所介紹的將這些字的「音量加大、音調提高、速度放慢」；反之，在沒有特別強調的地方，便可將音量縮小、音調降低，並加快速度。如此一來，你的聲音才會有抑揚頓挫及韻律感，才能表達不同情緒，也才能吸引聽眾的注意力。

俗諺云 Variety is the spice of life.（變化是生活的調劑品。）同樣地，我們也可以說 Vocal variety is the spice of a speech.（聲音的變化是演說的調劑品。）因此簡報時，你的聲音必須適中但有變化，如此才能讓聲音更豐富，讓簡報更吸引人！

Exercise　🎧 MP3 **82**　　　　　　　　　　　　　　　　解答請見 ▶ p. 319

以下是美國總統歐巴馬 (Barack Obama) 於第一次就職演說時所說的三段話。請朗讀這三段文字，並根據語意想想哪些字詞可能會特別強調。記得強調時必須將這些字詞的音量加大、音調提高並放慢速度。另外，這裡也提供就職演說的影片（請掃描下一頁的 QR Code），每題最後標示其在影片中所出現的時間。

1. Today I say to you that the challenges we face are real. They are serious and they are many. They will not be met easily or in a short span of time. But know this, America—they will be met. (36:52)

2. On this day, we gather because we have chosen hope over fear, unity of purpose over conflict and discord. (37:13)

3. The question we ask today is not whether our government is too big or too small, but whether it works—whether it helps families find jobs at a decent wage, care they can afford, a retirement that is dignified. Where the answer is yes, we intend to move forward. Where the answer is no, programs will end. (41:54)

美國總統歐巴馬 2009 年就職演說

 MP3 **83**

3　暫停的運用

「暫停」(pause) 指的是在簡報中間的停頓，目的是為了引起聽眾注意並強調重點。一般來說，講者在句子與句子中間都會稍做暫停，但這類的暫停通常非常簡短，因此並非此處所說的暫停。此處的暫停，指的是長度較長且「刻意」的停頓，例如，在簡報開始前，講者多半會刻意安靜幾秒（即暫停幾秒），待聽眾注意力集中後才開始演說。此外，當講者在陳述一連串的資訊時，也必須在每個字串間暫停。舉例來說，當你說下面這句話時，你會在標有「‧」的地方稍微暫停。

● People around the world consider Chinese, ‧ German, ‧ Greek, ‧ and Russian to be the hardest languages to learn.
世界各地的人都認為中文、德文、希臘文及俄文是最難學的語言。

同樣地，當你說下面這句話時，你會在標有「‧」的地方稍微暫停。

- On Mother's Day I usually give my mom flowers and presents, ·
  take her to restaurants, · and help her with housework.
  母親節當天我通常會送我媽花和禮物、帶她上餐館,並幫她做家事。

最重要的是,每次要提到主要重點前都要暫停得稍久些,以便增加主要重點的分量。例如在以下的簡報主體中,提到每個主要重點前,都應該暫停得久一點(標有「·」處)。

- So that concludes the introduction. Now let me focus on the major
  part of my speech. · First, I'd like to talk about what can be done
  for our nation's troubled economy by the local governments... ·
  After knowing what local governments can do to help improve
  the nation's economy, I'd like to offer ideas for growth in different
  industries... · Finally, allow me to propose changes that need to be
  implemented at the highest level...
  我的開場部分就到此處。現在讓我專注在演說的主要部分。首先,我想談談地方政府對國家問題重重的經濟該如何做……。知道了地方政府可以怎麼做來促進國家經濟,我想提供刺激不同產業成長的想法……。最後,讓我提出政府高層應該要做的改變方法……

暫停的運用在簡報中很重要,其作用類似繪畫技巧中的「留白」,若善加運用,不僅能強調簡報中的重點,還能增加簡報的力道。你或許會問:「爲什麼?」,那是因爲聽眾通常會對「無聲」的時刻更敏感。想想看,如果你一邊做家事一邊聽廣播,而廣播忽然沒有任何聲音,這時你應該會好奇地朝收音機看一眼吧?同樣的道理,如果你在簡報中暫停,甚至停頓久一點,這時反而會吸引聽眾的注意力。當然,這並不是說你需要長時間的暫停,而是比前面提到的句子與句子中間的暫停再長一點點即可。

最後要注意的是，暫停指的並非所謂的 filler（亦即說話時夾帶的一些沒意義的聲音或短語）。一般人說話時不自覺出現的 um, uh, hmm，或是 well, you know, like, anyway, okay 等口頭禪，都可算是 filler。用太多這類字眼會讓聽眾覺得講者很緊張或準備不充分，因此都要盡量避免。如果你不清楚自己在簡報中是否會出現 filler，最簡單的方式便是自行錄影，然後加以改進。

 MP3 **84**　　　　　　　　　　　　　　　　　　　　　解答請見 ▶ p. 320

以下是美國總統甘迺迪 (John F. Kennedy) 於就職演說時所說的三段話。請根據語意在需要暫停的地方稍做停頓。另外，這裡也提供就職演說的影片（請掃描 QR Code），每題最後標示其在影片中所出現的時間。

1. Let every nation know, whether it wishes us well or ill, that we shall pay any price, bear any burden, meet any hardship, support any friend, oppose any foe, to assure the survival and the success of liberty. (03:40)

2. Let both sides seek to invoke the wonders of science instead of its terrors. Together let us explore the stars, conquer the deserts, eradicate disease, tap the ocean depths, and encourage the arts and commerce. (10:00)

3. And so my fellow Americans: ask not what your country can do for you; ask what you can do for your country. (13:56)

美國總統甘迺迪 1961 年就職演說

4 發音與清晰度

用英語做簡報時，發音與清晰度很重要，因為這關乎聽眾是否能聽懂簡報內容，然而，因為英語並非你的母語，因此除非特別離譜，不然聽眾多半不會特別在意或要求。

有些講者用英語簡報時很在意自己的「口音」(accent)，認為若無法講出標準 (standard) 或無口音 (accent-less) 英語，便會被認為英語不道地，其實英語口音眾多，千萬不要因為口音而喪失自信，也不需要因自己的口音向聽眾道歉。如果你真的擔心自己濃重的口音會造成聽眾困擾，便可以在簡報一開始時先告知聽眾，並請聽眾在有疑慮時隨時向你確認，但仍不須為此道歉。關於這方面的用語可參考本書 Chapter 3 中的「延伸學習：英語非母語時」(p. 72)。

要注意的是，英文中有些字若發音不正確，的確會造成聽者的誤解，而母音相較於子音更容易造成誤解。以下提供數個常常造成誤解的母音，並以兩個為一組的方式進行比較，請仔細聆聽 MP3 來分辨清楚。

(1) [i] 與 [ɪ]

🎧 MP3 **85**

feet / fit	heat / hit	beat / bit
seat / sit	peel / pill	deep / dip
deed / did	leak / lick	lead / lid
leek / lick	meal / mill	feel / fill
steal / still	piece / piss	scene /sin

(2) [ɪ] 與 [ɛ]

 MP3 **86**

bill / bell	fill / fell	lift / left
sit / set	tin / ten	bit / bet
did / dead	will / well	pin / pen
miss / mess	disk / desk	spill / spell
hill / hell	bitter / better	listen / lesson

(3) [e] 與 [ɛ]

 MP3 **87**

sail / sell	taste / test	wait / wet
bail / bell	gate / get	fail / fell
bait / bet	late / let	raid / red
waste / west	tail / tell	mate / met
dates / debts	rake / wreck	paper / pepper

(4) [ɛ] 與 [æ]

 MP3 **88**

bed / bad	head / had	leg / lag
said / sad	pen / pan	set / sat
send / sand	ten / tan	dead / dad
men / man	Beth / bath	lend / land
vest / vast	left / laughed	pedal / paddle

(5) [e] 與 [æ] MP3 **89**

fate / fat	paid / pad	gape / gap
lake / lack	bake / back	tape / tap
made / mad	Kate / cat	cape / cap
hate / hat	rate / rat	rape / rap
pale / pal	grace / grass	snake / snack

(6) [ʌ] 與 [ɑ] MP3 **90**

hut / hot	nut / not	mud / mod
putt / pot	duck / dock	luck / lock
cut / cot	gut / got	fug / fog
cup / cop	fund / fond	muck / mock
hug / hog	color / collar	stuck / stock

(7) [ɔ] 與 [o] MP3 **91**

saw / sew	raw / row	called / cold
law / low	cost / coast	mall / mole
ball / bowl	bald / bold	Paul / pole
saw / so	pause / pose	hall / hole
caught / coat	bought / boat	tossed / toast

5 方言及其他語言的使用

一般用英語做簡報時，應該盡量避免使用其他方言或語言（例如法語、波蘭語等），若一定要用到方言或其他語言，則必須解釋。以下為兩個好用的句型。

解釋方言或其他語言句型　 MP3 **92**

〈... + 方言或其他語言 + ; that is ... in English.〉

〈... + 方言或其他語言 + , which means...〉

He said to her, "Tu es belle;" that is "You're beautiful" in English.
他對她說 Tu es belle，英文的意思就是「你很美麗」。

One of our best-selling foods is Pierogies, which means Polish dumplings.
我們賣得最好的食物之一是 Pierogies，亦即波蘭餃子。

另一個要注意的是，在簡報中應避免說髒話及帶有歧視性、會導致聽眾不悅的語言，就算是開玩笑也應盡量避免。此外，簡報與聊天不同，除非是在講者與聽眾十分熟識的場合，不然就算講者希望營造輕鬆愉悅的氣氛，也盡量不要使用十分口語或隨性的字眼，例如 gonna（即 going to）、wanna（即 want to）、cuz（即 because）、gotta（即 got to）、outta（即 out of）等。當然，現在有些專家認為，演說是「日常生活會話的延伸」，也就是說，簡報語言及方式不應該太正式僵硬，而是應該更隨性輕鬆、更接近與聽眾對話，這個觀點見仁見智，聰明的你可以自行決定。

Memo

語言溝通雖很重要，「非語言溝通」(non-verbal communication) 有時可能更重要，因為你的一舉一動都可能讓他人對你產生不同的觀感，甚至影響到他人對你的評價。這也是為什麼要評斷一個簡報是否成功，根據的不只是內容，還有講者的表達方式，包括肢體語言等。

一般而言，非語言溝通通常包含下列五項。

- **Q** 眼神接觸 (eye contact)
- **Q** 手勢 (gesture)
- **Q** 姿態 (posture)
- **Q** 儀容 (personal appearance)
- **Q** 身體移動 (bodily movement)

1 眼神接觸

眼神接觸是簡報時非常重要的非語言溝通方式。注視聽眾不只可以讓聽眾感到受尊重，也可以讓你知道聽眾的反應，例如是否理解簡報內容、是否感到無聊等。如果你看到有聽眾點頭或做筆記，通常也會受到鼓舞。

真人重點示範影片 12
YouTube 搜尋作者和書名

有人認為，簡報時聽眾的注意力會放在投影片上面，因此就算講者悶著頭唸稿，聽眾也不會知道。這其實是錯誤的；簡報時不能只看講稿，或只注視投影片，或只盯著「三板」（即地板、天花板、黑／白板），而是應該時時注視聽眾，讓聽眾感受到你的誠意與熱情。

　　你一開始注視聽眾時，可先環視室內，找到一、兩位友善的聽眾，先將視線鎖定在他們身上，這樣可減輕自身的緊張。請記得，一開始避免望向冷漠或氣勢嚇人的聽眾，最好等到自己較放鬆時再看他們。此外，眼神接觸時，最好一次望向一位聽眾，眼神交會時可停留數秒，但不宜過長，也不要整場簡報只鎖定一位聽眾，或只注視第一排或最後一排的聽眾，不然會令這些聽眾不安。還有，開始訓練自己時，若你真的不敢與聽眾做眼神接觸，可以試著看他們的頭頂或下巴，由於聽眾通常無法分辨你視線停留的確切位置，因此還是會認為你與他們有眼神接觸。

　　與聽眾視線接觸時，不管場地大小，都可以將簡報場地分成左、中、右三個大區塊（請見下頁圖片），一次注視一個區塊的某位聽眾數秒，然後移到下一個區塊的某位聽眾，以此類推，如此便可以確保眼神照顧到全場，也可以避免眼神快速飄移，令聽眾覺得你不夠誠懇。

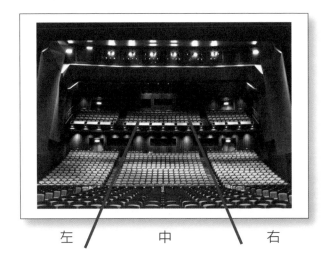

左　　　　中　　　　右

2　手勢

不同的手勢會帶給聽眾不同的感受。善用手勢可以增加簡報的分量，也可讓聽眾感染到你的情緒。使用手勢時必須注意以下幾點：

- 手勢適中即可，過多的手勢反而容易使聽眾分心。
- 手勢沒有固定的動作或形式，但必須有變化，不要從頭到尾都用同一個手勢。
- 若要知道自己的手勢是否得宜，最好的方式是請身旁的人觀看並給予你建議。此外也可錄影觀看自己的手勢，或對著鏡子反覆練習。
- 若不習慣講話時做手勢也無妨，這時只要讓手臂自然放鬆，垂放於身體兩側即可。

要注意的是，在一般認知裡，若講者在簡報時用手指著聽眾，通常表示講者想要向聽眾展現力量，或者是在責罵人，因此使用此手勢時必須格

外小心。此外，如果講者雙手交叉抱胸，會讓聽眾覺得其防禦心過重，無法包容或接納他人想法。若講者在簡報時雙手緊握並絞動，會讓聽眾覺得講者正處於緊張狀態。最後，若講者快速變化各種手勢，則會讓聽眾感受到講者不安的情緒。因此除非必要，上述這些手勢都應該盡量避免。

3 姿態

　　姿態可以顯示一個人的自信及所擁有的精力與精神。姿態與手勢不同，一般人以為演說只要手勢運用得宜即可，但姿態也很重要，因為這是聽眾第一眼會注意到你的地方，也因此，從你步入簡報會場的那一秒鐘開始，便要時刻提醒自己維持好的姿態。簡報時要有好的姿態，請記住以下三個要訣：身體站直 (stand still)、肩膀向後 (shoulders back)、抬頭挺胸 (head held high)（見下圖左側示範）。

Good Posture　　**Bad Posture**

　　除此之外，現今做簡報的趨勢也強調講者應採取「開放姿態」(open posture)，亦即講者將雙腳分開站立、胸膛挺出、雙臂張開、手掌向上、手指分開（見下圖左側示範）。這種姿態通常被認為帶有友善且正面的態度，請多加利用！

Open Posture　　**Closed Posture**

　　簡報時，不管你手上有沒有拿著講稿或其他東西，請記得以下幾點：不要將手插腰或插在口袋，不要將手放在臀部，也不要將手在背後交叉。此外，雙臂交疊在胸前、坐在椅子上、將身體倚靠在講桌旁等，也都是不良的姿態，都應該盡量避免。

4　儀容

　　好的儀容及表情可以讓簡報加分。雖然相貌和身材無法改變，但你可以藉由適當的打扮及合宜的衣著來改變自己的外表，包括梳理頭髮、刮鬍子（男性）、化淡妝（女性）等。

　　簡報時除非有特別理由，否則應該穿著正式服裝，千萬不要奇裝異服，或穿過於鮮豔花俏的衣服，不然除了顯得不專業，也會分散聽眾的注意力。下圖爲簡報時的標準穿著。

5　身體移動

　　簡報時，你應該要面向聽眾，不要只顧著看投影片的內容而將背部朝向聽眾。此外，如果可以使用無線簡報器及無線麥克風，便可以不受限於

講桌，適時地移動身體。移動時注意不要擋到前排的聽眾，也不要太過頻繁或快速踱步。你可以接近聽眾，但不要太靠近，不然會帶給聽眾一股壓迫感。

Exercise

解答請見 ▶ p. 321

進行簡報時，講者的哪些肢體動作可能會讓聽眾分心？請寫下來。

_____

_____

_____

_____

_____

_____

_____

_____

　　本章詳述了各種簡報技巧及演練方式，請你多多演練。本書的附錄附有「簡報評量表」(p. 329)，可以提供你在演練時自我評量，或者請親朋好友幫忙評量。想達到成功的簡報沒有捷徑，唯有多加練習，才能讓簡報臻至完美。讓我們一起加油！

延伸學習

不看講稿便可做簡報

　　進行簡報時,雖然看講稿是件很正常的事,但是仍有許多講者希望自己在簡報時看起來既自然又不費力,甚至完全可以不看講稿。要達到這個目標,除了多加練習外,沒有其他方法。除此之外,也可以嘗試利用下列五個步驟,一步一步訓練自己做到簡報時不看講稿的境界。

Step 1 ⊙ 將講稿逐字逐句打在簡報檔個別投影片的「備忘稿」中。

Step 2 ⊙ 將「備忘稿」中特別重要的地方「標註」(highlight) 起來,演練時將這些標註起來的字句當作是提醒自己的「記憶點」,忘記時可以瞄一下這些記憶點。

Step 3 ⊙ 幾次演練後,將講稿中其他沒有標註的字句都刪掉,只保留「關鍵字」(keyword) 作為提醒。

Step 4 ⊙ 重新檢視已製作好的投影片,確保每張投影片上有特定的字句或圖示來提醒自己講稿的內容。即每張投影片的內容都必須對應一個或多個提示的記憶點。如此一來,當你一看到投影片時便可馬上想到此記憶點,即可繼續講下去。

Step 5 ⊙ 嘗試不看任何備忘稿或講稿,只使用簡報檔案的投影片當作提示,完成簡報。

Answers
解答篇

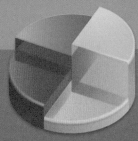

English Public Speaking
and Presentation

下面收錄本書所有 Exercise 的參考答案，並標註 Exercise 所在的頁碼，方便你查找和對照。

Chapter 2 │ 簡報檔案的製作

Exercise (p. 25)

1. ○ tasty food　食物美味

   ○ cheap　便宜

   ○ cozy　舒適

   ○ playroom for kids　有小孩遊戲間

   ○ authentic Thai food　泰式料理很道地

   ○ discounts for families　提供家庭優惠

   ○ relaxed atmosphere　氣氛輕鬆

   ○ nice background music　背景音樂好聽

   ○ clean environment　環境乾淨

   ○ special utensils for kids　有給孩童用的特製餐具

   ○ friendly waiters　服務生很友善

   ○ booths　有包廂

   ○ long tables for groups　有給一群人坐的長桌

   ○ pet friendly　可帶寵物

   ○ sanitary　很衛生

2. ○ friendly people　人們友善

   ○ night markets　有夜市

   ○ roadside stands　有路邊攤

- MRT—clean, priority seats 捷運——很乾淨且有博愛座
- buses—frequent, convenient 公車——班次密集且很便利
- cultural activities 有藝文活動
- bike lanes 有自行車道
- night clubs 有夜店
- nightlife 有夜生活
- exhibitions 有展覽
- shopping 可購物
- exotic cuisines 有異國美食
- convenience stores 有便利商店
- 24-hour bookstore 有 24 小時書店
- Taipei 101 有台北 101

Exercise (p. 27)

1.

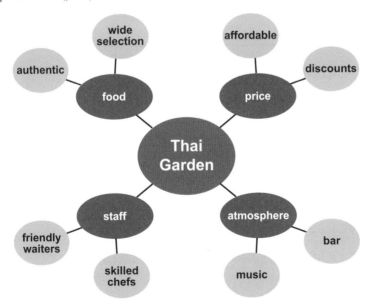

2.

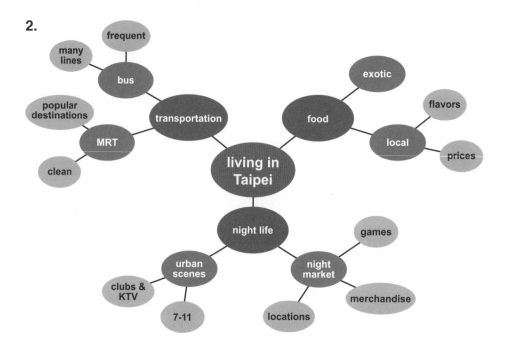

𝕰xercise (p. 29)

1.

主要重點 1：Delicious food 食物美味

　　次要重點 1：Authentic Thai cuisine 泰式料理很道地

　　次要重點 2：Wide selection of dishes and desserts
　　　　　　　　料理及甜點的選擇眾多

主要重點 2：Reasonable price 價格合理

　　次要重點 1：Affordable for everyone 人人皆可負擔

　　次要重點 2：Discounts for parties of four or more
　　　　　　　　四人以上同行有優惠

主要重點 3：Well-trained staff 員工訓練有素

 次要重點 1：Friendly waiters 服務生很友善

 次要重點 2：Skilled chefs 廚師的手藝佳

主要重點 4：Pleasant atmosphere 氣氛愉悅

 次要重點 1：Light music 音樂很輕柔

 次要重點 2：Open-air bar 有露天吧檯

2.

主要重點 1：Quality public transportation 有高品質的大眾運輸

 次要重點 1：MRT 捷運

  次次要重點 1：Lines serving popular tourist destinations
    有熱門旅遊景點的路線

  次次要重點 2：Clean, safe, and orderly
    乾淨、安全且有秩序

 次要重點 2：Buses 公車

  次次要重點 1：Many lines spanning the entire city
    整個城市遍布許多路線

  次次要重點 2：Frequent services and stops
    班次頻繁且站點多

主要重點 2：Delicious food 食物美味

 次要重點 1：Exotic cuisines 異國食物

次次要重點：Diverse cuisines from different countries and regions

有來自不同國家及地區的多樣化料理

次要重點 2：Local delicacies　在地美食

次次要重點 1：Unique flavors　口味獨特

次次要重點 2：Reasonable prices　價格合理

主要重點 3：Colorful nightlife　夜生活多采多姿

次要重點 1：Urban scenes　都會活動

次次要重點 1：Night clubs, live music, KTVs

有夜店、現場表演及 KTV

次次要重點 2：Convenience stores, 24-hour bookstore

有便利商店及 24 小時書店

次要重點 2：Night markets　夜市

次次要重點 1：Several locations　有多個地點

次次要重點 2：Wide variety of merchandise　商品具多樣性

次次要重點 3：Fun games　有好玩的遊戲

𝕰xercise (p. 31)

1. Thai Garden: It's All About Taste

泰花園餐廳：品味 / 味道決定一切

說明　這是一個很有創意的簡報題目，原因是 taste 這個字帶有兩個含意，一個是「品味」，另一個是「味道」，用來形容餐廳時兩個含意都有。

2. There is No Place like Taipei

沒有一個地方像台北一樣

<blockquote>
說明　這個簡報題目改編自諺語 There is no place like home.（金窩銀窩，不如自己的狗窩。），這裡把 Taipei（台北）類比為 home（家），可說是相當具有創意的簡報題目。
</blockquote>

Exercise (p. 50)

這裡提供 (a) 和 (b) 兩張好用的投影片，(a) 和 (b) 的四個字詞串都是以原形動詞開始，格式工整，兩者的差別在於 (b) 比 (a) 更簡潔。

(a)

Suggestions for PowerPoint Presentation Slides

- Use headings to show the main points of the slide
- Follow formal typing rules
- Pay attention to the layout
- Use animation to make your presentation livelier

(b)

Suggestions for PowerPoint Presentation Slides

- Use headings

- Follow formal typing rules

- Pay attention to the layout

- Use animation

Exercise (p. 55)

每份講稿都提供 (a) 和 (b) 兩張好用的投影片，差別在於 (a) 包含較多的資訊且較完整，(b) 則較簡潔。

1. (a)

Five-Course Menu

- **1st Course: Soup**
  - Tomato Basil Soup
  - Clam Chowder

- **2nd Course: Appetizer**
  - Goat Cheese Risotto Balls
  - Pork Potstickers

- **3rd Course: Salad**
  - Caesar Salad
  - Fruit Salad

- **4th Course: Entrée**
  - Smoked Salmon
  - Roasted Chicken Breast
  - Grilled Rib Eye Steak

- **5th Course: Dessert**
  - Bread Pudding
  - Chocolate Torte

(b)

Five-Course Menu

- **1st Course: Soup**

- **2nd Course: Appetizer**

- **3rd Course: Salad**

- **4th Course: Entrée**

- **5th Course: Dessert**

2. (a)

Basic Wine Tasting Procedure

- **Pour wine**
  - Hold glass by stem
  - Pour enough for a few sips

- **Observe wine**
  - View against white background or light
  - Tilt glass away

- **Swirl wine**
  - Let wine breathe

- **Sniff wine**
  - Insert nose into glass and breathe deeply
  - Repeat several times

- **Sip wine**
  - Chew or roll over tongue

- **Swallow wine**

(b)

Basic Wine Tasting Procedure

- **Pour**
- **Observe**
- **Swirl**
- **Sniff**
- **Sip**
- **Swallow**

𝕰xercise (p. 90)

Here is an overview of my presentation. First, I'll start off by introducing what orienteering is, including its history and origins, as well as its game rules. Next, I'll talk about the equipment needed for participating in such an activity, including the map, the sheet and card, and the compass. After that, I'll provide you with some tips when participating in orienteering. And the last part is my conclusion.

這個是我的簡報概要。首先，我會從介紹何謂定向越野運動開始，包括它的歷史和起源，以及遊戲規則。接著我會談到參與此類活動所需的設備，包括地圖、表卡及羅盤。在那之後，我會提供您一些參加定向越野運動的祕訣。最後一部分是我的結論。　　◦ orienteering (n.) 定向越野運動　compass (n.) 羅盤，指南針

Chapter 4 | 簡報主體用語

𝕰xercise (p. 105)

1. (a) growing awareness of women's rights
愈來愈多對女性權利的體認

(b) better education and jobs for women
女性有更好的教育及就業機會

(c) society's changing view on marriage
社會對婚姻的觀念改變

2. (a) A traditional hand-written letter gives a personal touch and adds value to the letter. If you want to say thank you to someone, there is no more personal way to do so than to send a letter.
傳統的手寫信件具有個人特色，並可增添信件的價值。如果您想對一個人說謝謝，沒有比寄一封信更個人的方法了。　　◦ touch (n.) 風格，手法

(b) Information in a registered letter is usually safe. On the other hand, an e-mail can be hacked and the confidential information can be easily leaked out.

掛號信件中的資訊通常很安全。反之，電子郵件會被駭客攻擊，機密資訊也容易被洩漏。　　　　　　　　　　● hack (v.) 非法侵入　confidential (adj.) 機密的

(c) A well-written letter makes an impression that no e-mail can replicate. A personally addressed letter is far more likely to be opened and its contents carefully examined.

一封寫得好的信所帶給人的印象，是沒有任何一封電子郵件可以取代的。一封署名給某人的信更有可能讓對方打開並仔細閱讀內容。

● replicate (v.) 複製

Chapter 6 ｜ 介紹並說明圖表

ℰxercise (p. 198)　　　　　　　　　　　　　　　　　 MP3 **55**

1. **Step 1** To understand more about the various search engines, please take a look at the statistics shown on this slide. The statistics are from comScore, Inc. This line chart illustrates the market share of different search engines in the United States as measured by search queries. **Step 2** The X-axis shows the quarterly timeline, from 2008 to 2015, and the Y-axis shows the percentage of search queries using each search engine. On the top of the chart, you can see the legend, with the blue line representing Google sites, black Microsoft sites, gray Yahoo, red Ask, and green AOL. **Step 3** As can be seen, it is obvious that Google has been the dominant search engine since 2008. It holds the

majority of the market share, with more than 60% of the market most of the time and leaving the remaining four players far behind. Also, another interesting trend to observe is that although Yahoo used to be the second largest search engine, it has been surpassed by Microsoft since October 2011. No matter what, both companies have a lot of catchingup to do in comparison with their biggest rival, Google.

如果要更加了解各種不同的搜尋引擎，請看這張投影片上所顯示的統計數據。這些統計數據來自於 comScore, Inc.。這張線圖顯示出將美國各個不同搜尋引擎進行搜索查詢後，所測量出來的市占率。X 軸顯示從 2008 年到 2015 年每季的時間軸，Y 軸顯示每個搜尋引擎的搜索查詢百分比。在圖表上方可以看到圖例，藍色代表谷歌網站，黑色代表微軟網站，灰色代表雅虎，紅色代表 Ask，綠色代表 AOL。如您所見，很顯然谷歌自 2008 年以來一直是最主要的搜尋引擎。它占了大部分的市場，大部分時間都在 60% 以上，將其餘四個遠遠甩在後面。此外，另一個有趣的趨勢觀察是，雖然雅虎曾經是第二大搜尋引擎，但自 2011 年十月開始就被微軟追趕過去。無論如何，與他們最大的競爭對手谷歌相比，這兩家公司都必須努力追趕。

> ● statistics (n.) 統計數據，統計資料　timeline (n.) 時間軸　dominant (adj.) 主要的
> surpass (v.) 超過　catchingup (n.) 趕上，追上　in comparison with... 與…比較

2. 編號順序： (5) → (3) → (1) → (4) → (7) → (6) → (2)

This slide shows the relationship between gender and suicide behavior in Finland. The horizontal-axis shows the year, and the vertical-axis indicates the suicide rate. The blue line represents males while the orange represents females. As you can see clearly, the male suicide rate is usually two times higher than the female rate, over the years 1971 to 2004. There are two reasons for the gap. The first is that men usually experience higher levels of stress when trying to fulfill traditional gender roles such as being "emotionally tough" and being the "breadwinner" of the family. The second reason is that men usually take more dramatic measures than women when it comes to suicide. In other words, while women tend to show higher rates of non-fatal suicidal behavior, men have a much higher rate of completed suicides.

這張投影片顯示出芬蘭的性別和自殺行為之間的關係。橫軸顯示年分，縱軸顯示自殺率。藍線代表男性，橘線則代表女性。您可以清楚地看到，男性在 1971 年到 2004 年之間的自殺率通常都要比女性高出兩倍。這個差距有兩個原因。第一是因為男性通常要去滿足傳統的性別角色，例如「情感上要堅強」與「養家活口」，因而承受程度較高的壓力。第二是因為男性通常會採取比女性更激烈的手段來自殺。換句話說，雖然女性傾向出現較高的非致命性自殺行為，男性的自殺完成率卻要高出許多。

> ● fulfill (v.) 滿足（期望） breadwinner (n.) 養家活口的人 dramatic (adj.) 激烈的 measures (n.) 手段 when it comes to... 當提到… fatal (adj.) 致命的

Exercise (p. 206) 🎧 MP3 **57**

Step 1 This bar chart shows the number of people visiting different multi-platform U.S. web properties. The information is courtesy of the Office of Trade and Industry. **Step 2** Before we go into the details, let me explain a couple of the terms here. The word "multi-platform" means people visiting websites from different connections such as mobile devices, desktops, laptops, etc. And "web property" means a collection of websites owned by one company. The web properties are listed on the left side of the screen, and the number of web visitors is in millions, and is shown right next to the bars. You can see that Google sites have the most visitors, with more than 240 million, more than Facebook, the most popular social network platform, and Amazon, one of the most popular e-commerce providers. **Step 3** So what are the popular Google online properties besides Google Search? Well, they are the online video platform YouTube, communication services such as Gmail and Hangouts, assorted online services such as Google Maps, Google Play, the app distribution platform, and so on. With these popular websites and services to suit web surfers' ever-changing needs and tastes, no wonder Google is deemed the Internet giant.

這張條形圖顯示出人們造訪不同的多平臺美國網域資產的數目。這項資訊是由貿易及產業辦公室所提供的。在我們進入細節前，讓我先解釋幾個術語。「多平臺」一詞是指人們從行動裝置、桌上型電腦、筆記型電腦等不同的連接點造訪網站。「網域資產」是指由同一家公司所擁有的一堆網站。網域資產公司列在左邊的螢幕上，而緊鄰條形物旁邊的是以百萬計數的網站造訪人數。您可以看到谷歌網域資產擁有最多訪客，超過 2 億 4,000 萬人，比最受歡迎的社交網路平臺臉書更多，也比最受歡迎的電子商務供應商之一亞馬遜更多。那麼除了谷歌搜尋外，最受歡迎的谷歌網域資產還有什麼？嗯，有線上影音平臺 YouTube，有如 Gmail 及 Hangouts 等的通訊服務，有如谷歌地圖、谷歌商店、應用程式分配平臺等的多樣化線上服務。有了這些受歡迎的網站和服務來滿足網友不斷變化的需求與口味，難怪谷歌被視為網際網路巨頭。

● a couple of... 幾個…，兩三個…　device (n.) 裝置　e-commerce (n.) 電子商務
assorted (adj.) 各式各樣的

Exercise (p. 213)　　　　　　🎧 MP3 **59**

Step 1 This chart shows the percentage of population by age group around the globe. The data is provided by the United Nations Secretariat.

Step 2 There are three pie charts here representing the world's population in the years 1950 and 2000, and the projected world population in the year 2050. The different colors show the different age groups. For example, blue represents people under the age of 19, and red represents people over 65 years old, as you can see from the legend on the upper left-hand corner. Let's take a look at the smallest pie chart on the left. In 1950,

44% of the world population was under the age 19, and 5% were over 65. However, if you look at the pie chart on the right, you'll find that in 2050, it is projected that only 27% of the world population will be under 19, and 16% over 65. **Step 3** It is worrisome that as the world's total population is increasing, the percentage of young people is decreasing while the percentage of seniors is increasing. This shows that the world's population is aging, and it may have catastrophic consequences.

這張圖表顯示出全球各地人口按年齡所占的百分比。這些資料是由聯合國祕書處所提供的。這裡有三張餅圖，代表 1950 年和 2000 年實際的世界人口，以及 2050 年所預估的世界人口。不同的顏色顯示不同的年齡組。例如藍色是 19 歲以下的人，紅色是超過 65 歲，就如您從左上角的圖例所看到的那樣。讓我們看看在左邊最小的餅圖。在 1950 年，有 44% 的世界人口是低於 19 歲、有 5% 超過 65 歲。然而，看到右邊的餅圖後，您就會發現到了 2050 年，世界人口預計只有 27% 在 19 歲以下、16% 超過 65 歲。令人擔憂的是，隨著世界人口總數持續增加，年輕人的比例正在減少，而老年人的比例卻在增加中。這顯示出世界人口正在老化，而這可能導致災難性的後果。

• project (v.) 推算，預計

Exercise (p. 225)

1. X 軸：(the) X-axis 或 horizontal axis

2. Y 軸：(the) Y-axis 或 vertical axis

3.（表格的）欄，行：(a) column

4.（表格的）列，排：(a) row

5. 圖例：legend 或 key

6. 順時針方向：(a) clockwise direction 或 move clockwise

7. 逆時針方向：(a) counterclockwise direction 或 move counterclockwise

ℰxercise (p. 230)　　　　　　　　　　　　🎧 MP3 **62**

This slide shows a couch-surfer's profile. If you look at the (1) <u>upper left-hand corner/upper left corner/upper left/upper left-hand side/upper left side</u>, you will see the General Information section where a person's age, gender, nationality, occupation, birthday, etc. are displayed. Also, (2) <u>on the bottom left/on the lower left-hand side/on the lower left side</u>, you can see what language or languages the person speaks. (3) <u>Moving to the right/Moving to your right/To your right/On the right</u>, you can see more detailed information about the couch-surfer, including his or her personal description, how he or she wants to participate in couch-surfing, his or her experiences with couch-surfing, and so on.

這張投影片顯示出一名沙發客的個人檔案。請看左上角，您會在「一般資訊」部分看到一個人的年齡、性別、國籍、職業、生日等全都顯示在這裡。此外，在左下方，您可以看到這個人說何種語言。向右移動／在右邊／在您的右邊，您可以看到關於這名沙發客更詳細的資訊，包括個人描述、想以何種方式參加沙發衝浪活動、參加經驗等。

Chapter 7 | 轉換語的運用

ℰxercise (p. 247)

1. Now that we have explored Japan's economic situation, let us turn to its educational system.

   既然我們已經探討了日本的經濟情況，現在讓我們轉移到它的教育制度上。

   講者之前所講的東西：<u>Japan's economic situation</u>

   講者接著要講的東西：<u>Japan's educational system</u>

2. So much for the problem; what about the solution?

對於問題本身（我們）已經談了很多，來談談解決方案如何？

講者之前所講的東西：the problem

講者接著要講的東西：the solution

3. That's it for the advantages. I'll move on now to the disadvantages.

這些就是優點。我接下去要談的是缺點。

講者之前所講的東西：the advantages

講者接著要講的東西：the disadvantages

4. We have spent a lot of time talking about the present. It's time now to discuss the future.

我們已經花了許多時間談論目前的狀況。現在該是討論未來的時候了。

講者之前所講的東西：the present

講者接著要講的東西：the future

5. Now that we've looked at the development of the Korean computer game industry, we may now proceed to the discussion of Taiwan's.

既然我們已經談論過韓國電玩產業的發展，現在可以接下去討論台灣電玩產業的發展了。　　　　　　　　　　　　　　　●proceed to...（朝特定方向）前進…

講者之前所講的東西：the development of the Korean computer game industry

講者接著要講的東西：the development of Taiwan's computer game industry

6. That ends the background information on the product; I'll now turn to the technical specifications.

結束這項產品的背景資訊介紹後，我現在要轉而介紹技術規格。

◦ specifications (n.) 規格，標準

講者之前所講的東西：<u>the background information on the product</u>

講者接著要講的東西：<u>the technical specifications of the product</u>

7. Reducing the amount of garbage produced daily is only one part of the solution. The other part is to ensure that citizens conserve natural resources.

減少每日垃圾量只是解決方案的一部分。另外一部分是要確保市民都能節約天然資源。　　　　　　　　　　　　　　　　◦ conserve (v.) 節約，保存

講者之前所講的東西：<u>reduce the amount of garbage produced daily</u>

講者接著要講的東西：<u>ensure that citizens conserve natural resources</u>

Chapter 9 | 簡報技巧演練

Exercise (p. 284)　　　　　　　　　　　　　　　　 MP3 **82**

紅字處是根據語意會特別強調的地方。請仔細聆聽 MP3，並跟著模仿與練習。

1. Today I say to you that the challenges we face are real. They are serious and they are many. They will not be met easily or in a short span of time. But know this, America—they will be met.

今天我要告訴各位，我們所面臨的挑戰是真實的，這些挑戰非常嚴峻，而且不在少數。它們不是可以輕易或在短時間內解決。但是我們美國必須明白，這些挑戰將會被解決的。

2. On this day, we gather because we have chosen hope over fear, unity of purpose over conflict and discord.

今天我們聚在一起，乃是因為我們選擇希望而非恐懼，並選擇用團結來戰勝衝突與分歧。

3. The question we ask today is not whether our government is too big or too small, but whether it works—whether it helps families find jobs at a decent wage, care they can afford, a retirement that is dignified. Where the answer is yes, we intend to move forward. Where the answer is no, programs will end.

我們今天所問的問題並非我們的政府組織是否太大或太小，而是它是否行得通——是否能幫助一般家庭找到薪水不錯的工作、獲得支付得起的健保費用，並過著有尊嚴的退休生活。如果答案是肯定的，我們就繼續進行。如果答案是否定的，那計畫就會停止。

Exercise (p. 287) MP3 **84**

標示「·」處會稍做暫停，而紅字處則是會特別強調的字詞。請仔細聆聽MP3，並跟著模仿與練習。

1. Let every nation know, whether it wishes us well or ill, that we shall pay any price, · bear any burden, · meet any hardship, · support any friend, · oppose any foe, to assure the survival and the success of liberty.

讓每一個國家知道，無論他們對我們抱持著善意還是敵意，我們將付出所有代價、擔負所有責任、面對所有困難、支持所有朋友、對抗所有敵人，以確保自由的存在與實現。

2. Let both sides seek to invoke the wonders of science instead of its terrors. Together，let us explore the stars，conquer the deserts，eradicate disease，tap the ocean depths，and encourage the arts and commerce.

讓雙方都謀求激發科學的神奇力量，而不是科學的恐怖因素。讓我們一起探索星球、征服沙漠、消除疾病、開發海洋深處，並鼓勵藝術及商業活動。

3. And so my fellow Americans：ask not what your country can do for you；ask what you can do for your country.

我的美國同胞們：不要問你的國家能為你做什麼；要問你能為你的國家做什麼。

Exercise (p. 299)
以下這些肢體動作都有可能會使聽眾分心，因此進行簡報時，應該盡量避免出現這些動作。

- 肢體動作過多或動作變化過於頻繁
- 身體一直動來動去，例如前後搖晃、上下移動等
- 手伸進口袋把玩零錢，甚至發出聲音
- 一直聳肩或點頭
- 一直眨眼睛
- 一直看上面或看下面，就是不看聽眾
- 一邊講話一邊用手碰觸臉上部位，例如鼻子、嘴巴等

Appendix
附錄

簡報檔案完整範例

簡報評量表

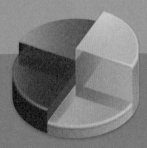

English Public Speaking
and Presentation

簡報檔案完整範例

1

Optimizing the Application Life Cycle to Minimize Risk

Galaxy Software Services
Brian Lin
Sales Representative
Brian.Lin@gss.com.tw
9/10/2016

2

Overview

- **Programs and Benefits**
  - Development & Integration
  - Automated Software Quality
  - Production Readiness
  - Availability Management
- **Global Presence & Technical Support**
- **Market Share**
- **Our Customers**
- **Conclusion**

Galaxy Software Services

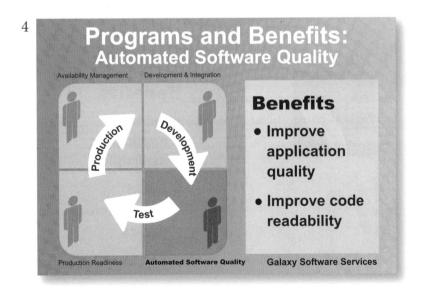

5

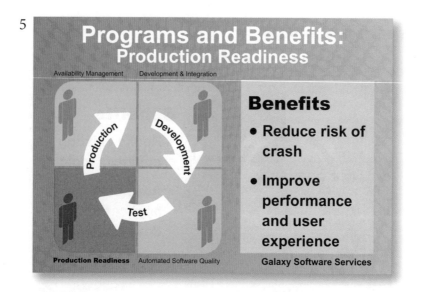

6

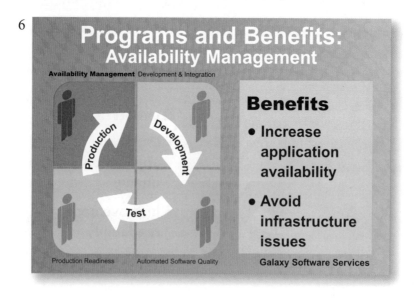

7

8

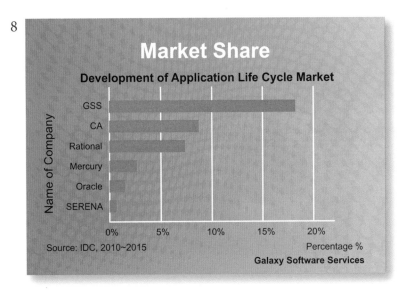

9

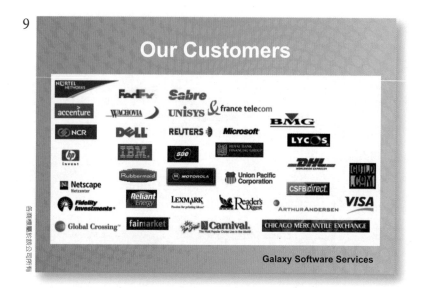

10

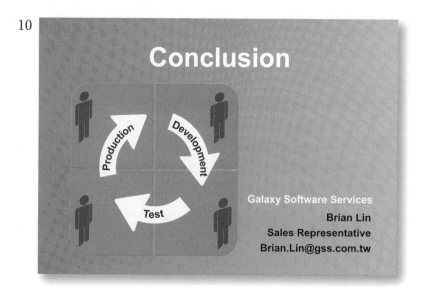

簡報評量表

簡報的兩大要素是「內容」(content) 和「技巧」(delivery)，因此評量表的設計也是針對這兩者的各個細項來做評量。

在進行正式簡報前的演練時，可以先觀看自己的簡報錄影檔案後再勾選自己確實有做到或完成的選項。如果是請他人幫忙，則可以事先將此評量表交給對方，並告知對方你簡報預先設定的聽眾背景、須達成的目標等，請對方在你做簡報時注意是否有順利達成。當然，如果你可以在正式簡報完後請聽眾幫你填寫此評量表，那是再好不過了。

簡報評量表

請勾選講者有做到或完成的項目。

1. 內容 (content)

A. 開場 (opening)
- ☐ 講者的自我介紹合宜
- ☐ 講者的引言 (hook) 能引起聽眾的興趣
- ☐ 講者有說明簡報的目的與主題
- ☐ 講者有說明簡報的架構與流程
- ☐ 講者有提供足夠的背景資訊給聽眾
- ☐ 講者在開場的最後有可順利連接到主體 (body) 的轉換語 (transition)

B. 主體 (body)
- ☐ 講者有說明主體的結構（包含主要重點）

□ 講者有適切地說明每個主要重點

□ 講者有提供足夠的例子與理由來支持主要重點

□ 講者所提供的例子與理由適切且合乎邏輯

□ 講者有說明引用資料的出處

□ 講者有介紹並說明每張圖表的重點

□ 講者在主體中都有可以順利連接到下一個主要重點的轉換語

C. 結束 (closing)

□ 講者有陳述結論及摘要

□ 講者有重複強調主要重點

□ 簡報的問答時段 (Q&A session) 進行順利

□ 講者有盡力回答聽眾的提問

□ 講者有向聽眾致謝並道別

D. 其他 (others)

□ 講者有適時使用轉換語串連整個簡報

□ 講者有舉出明確易懂的例子與理由來幫助聽眾理解簡報內容

□ 講者有使用不同的視覺材料（如圖片、動畫、影片等）來增
　加簡報的生動性

□ 講者有照顧到不同聽眾（視覺型、聽覺型及動覺型）的需求

□ 講者使用的圖表合宜

□ 簡報每張圖表都有合適的標題

□ 簡報投影片的設計簡單明瞭

□ 簡報投影片的安排符合邏輯

□ 簡報投影片的拼字正確

2. 技巧 (delivery)

☐ 講者有足夠的演練與準備

☐ 講者的簡報流暢

☐ 講者說話的音量 (volume)、音調 (pitch) 及速度 (rate) 合宜

☐ 講者有根據簡報內容將聲音做變化

☐ 講者的暫停 (pause) 運用合宜

☐ 講者的發音與清晰度佳

☐ 講者的語言使用合宜

☐ 講者與聽眾有眼神接觸

☐ 講者做簡報時肢體動作（含手勢、姿態、身體移動等）合宜

☐ 講者與聽眾的互動良好

☐ 講者能順利處理簡報進行中的突發狀況

Memo

Memo

Classified Ad

看照片說英語：自問自答學好英文口語

作者：黃玟君、Michael McMaster

定價：400 元

MP3

精選 70 張涵蓋各式情境的彩色照片，搭配「3 步驟英文口語訓練」及「5W1H 自問自答法」，來幫助讀者提升英文口語能力。讀者可藉由獨創的三個口語訓練步驟，逐步提升實力，並運用 5W1H 自問自答法，擴展說話內容。所附 MP3，全英語錄音，特別適合用來自我訓練一問一答。

黃玟君教你一次學好英語發音和聽力

作者：黃玟君

定價：380 元

MP3

作者根據自己學英文的心得，以及在國立台科大教授英語多年的經驗，深知台灣讀者聽力無法突破的關鍵因素在於「發音沒學好」。因此從最基本的音標，到進階的連音、削弱音、語調等循序講解。筆調輕鬆幽默，並提供大量、多變化的練習題。讀者可從實際練習中，增進整體的英語聽說能力。

英語聽力大翻轉：6 技巧突破英聽困境

作者：黃玟君

繪者：白吐司與兔子

定價：380 元

MP3

聽力的提升需要有計畫的訓練，在本書中，作者整理出邊聽邊畫圖、畫表格、做筆記等六大聽力技巧，並設計出豐富的練習題，結合眼耳手口四種感官，搭配「聽出關鍵字」訓練，幫助學習者逐步精熟英語聽力，並能在任何英聽測驗中獲取高分。

和英文系學生一起上英語聽說課

作者：黃玟君

定價：280 元

2CD

作者於國立台科大教授英語多年，首次公開英文系學生的課堂訓練方式「懶人聽說法」，幫助讀者從基礎的發音和語調練習起，對於外國人日常使用的「連音」、「削弱音」及「彈舌音」，提供易懂易記的口訣以達到事半功倍的效果。用對方法，英文也能比本科系學生還要好！

Classified Ad

上班族 60 秒簡報英文

作者：David Thayne

定價：220 元

MP3

將用英文做簡報的慣用語句，依職場的使用情境做分類，挑選簡單易說，且使用頻率最高的英文句子。此外，也提供豐富且經常使用的替換句，職場人士可依實際情況靈活運用。

看場合說英語：正式╳非正式的 10 種說法

作者：白安竹 (Andrew E. Bennett)

定價：350 元

MP3

作者白安竹以 20 多年的英語教學經驗，深切體認到英語學習者常欠缺看場合或對象，適當運用英語的能力，因此整理出 50 種溝通目的，各列出 10 個代表句型，依不同正式程度排列，並從中挑選出五個較重要句型做介紹，同時提供相關例句。

提升英語溝通能力，95% 的場合都能靈活應對

作者：濱田伊織

定價：350 元

MP3

本書分成「和他人對話時的基本句型」、「以成熟態度回應對方的句型」、「站在對方立場發言的句型」等三大部分，涵蓋感謝、道歉、請求、提議、拒絕、讚美、插話等場合及情境，收錄與主題相關的英文句型，並提供解說及豐富的應用語句。

商務英文書信寫作

作者：有元美津世

定價：350 元

從推銷產品、寄送人事信函，到草擬合約、處理智慧財產權糾紛，各種職場領域所需的英文書信祕訣，本書提供即查即用、簡潔切要的中英對照範例，教你一次就把商務英文書信寫完、寫對、寫好！

國家圖書館出版品預行編目 (CIP) 資料

英語簡報演說技巧 / 黃玟君作 . -- 初版 . -- 臺北市：眾文圖書 , 2016.10
面；公分
ISBN 978-957-532-483-4（平裝附光碟片）1. 英語　2. 簡報　3. 讀本
805.18　　　　　　　　　　　　　　　　　　　　　　　　　　105014103

OE025

英語簡報演說技巧

定價 450 元
2016 年 10 月 初版 1 刷

作者	黃玟君
英文校閱	Neesha Wolf
責任編輯	黃琬婷
主編	陳瑠琍
副主編	黃炯睿
資深編輯	黃琬婷
美術設計	嚴國綸
行銷企劃	李皖萍・王碧貞
發行人	黃建和
發行所	眾文圖書股份有限公司
	台北市 10088 羅斯福路三段 100 號
	12 樓之 2
網路書店	www.jwbooks.com.tw
電話	02-2311-8168
傳真	02-2311-9683
郵政劃撥	01048805

ISBN 978-957-532-483-4
Printed in Taiwan

The Traditional Chinese edition copyright © 2016 by
Jong Wen Books Co., Ltd. All rights reserved. No part of
this publication may be reproduced, stored in a retrieval
system, or transmitted in any form or by any means,
electronic, mechanical, photocopying, recording, or
otherwise, without the prior written permission of the
publisher.

本書任何部分之文字及圖片，非經本公司書面同意，
不得以任何形式抄襲、節錄或翻印。本書如有缺頁、
破損或裝訂錯誤，請寄回下列地址更換：新北市
23145 新店區寶橋路 235 巷 6 弄 2 號 4 樓。